THE]

To Mel.

For giving me the guts to try something new.

THE EYE THIEF
A DI Erica Swift Thriller
Book One

• • • •

M K Farrar

• • • •

Warwick House Press

THIS IS A WORK OF FICTION. Similarities to real people, places, or events are entirely coincidental.

THE EYE THIEF

First edition, May 15th 2020
Copyright @2020 M K Farrar
Published by Warwick House Press
ISBN: 9798645637323
Written by M K Farrar

Chapter One

Her heels clip-clopped on the pavement, painfully loud in the otherwise quiet night.

Though it was the early hours, it was never truly silent in London. There was always a distant drone of traffic, or the wail of an emergency vehicle, or a car alarm going off. Right now, however, the tap of her impractical shoes was the only sound she focused on, echoing around the empty street, bouncing off her eardrums.

Becca reached across her body and gripped the strap of the handbag on her shoulder. She wished she'd taken Phil Dentry up on his offer of accompanying her off the night bus, but she hadn't wanted him to think there would be something more than a simple 'thanks' waiting for him after he'd walked her home. She hadn't missed the way he'd been buying her drinks all evening, even when she'd told him she was fine, or how he'd always seemed to end up standing or sitting beside her, no matter which bar they'd gone to.

She'd felt comfortable enough on her own when she'd jumped off the bus on the main road, but now she'd turned into the estate, heading for the terraced house she shared with two other students who hadn't been out with her that night, she'd grown painfully aware of how late it was and that she was a woman, alone. She did her best to push away her vulnerability; Becca prided herself on being independent and tough.

One of the streetlights flickered, and she glanced up, her stomach clenching with anxiety. She hoped it wasn't going to go out, plunging her into darkness. The moon was a faint, white semi-circle in the night sky, not enough to guide her way. No stars were visible—the light pollution from the city had done a good job of hiding them.

The stuttering lamp came on fully again, and she allowed herself to breathe.

She was always nervous walking this section of her route home. On her left was the Tower Hamlets Cemetery Park—one of seven Victorian cemeteries in London. It was a much-needed green space in the middle of this part of the city, but, filled with ancient headstones, it took on a different feel at night. On the other side, where she was walking, there was only a tall wall which led onto the back of a set of garages that served some of the other houses on the estate. That no one overlooked this part of the road only added to her sense of defencelessness.

Becca's attention went back to the cemetery. Black, wrought-iron railings divided her from the darkness beyond, thick brambles coiling through the metal. An empty cider can was caught in the thickets, the middle crushed, and heavy with orange rust. It wasn't a welcoming sight—not that she had any intention of entering the cemetery. She was sticking to the well-lit streets. But still, the knowledge of what the place contained was enough to send shivers crawling down her back.

Movement up ahead caught her attention, and Becca jerked back and sucked in a breath.

Shit.

On the same side as the cemetery railings, a person staggered out onto the street. From the size and shape, she assumed it was a man, but from this distance and the way they held themselves, it was impossible to know for sure. The figure was bent almost double, arms stretched out in front of them. Their stance reminded her of a zombie television series her flatmates liked to watch but that she couldn't stand. Why on earth would someone find watching dead people eating others entertaining?

The person took a couple of steps closer.

Yes, it was definitely a man. The breadth of his shoulders and the way he walked, legs slightly spread, as though riding a horse, was definitely male. Was he a drunk? A homeless man? Both? Where had he come from?

Becca hoped he didn't notice her. Once more, she found herself regretting not inviting Phil back. Surely, spending the night with him would have been better than ending up raped and murdered on the way home.

She hesitated, the tap of her heels against the pavement slowing with her, a ticking of a clock with its battery running out. The man was ahead of her, and even though he was on the opposite side of the street, it meant she would have to pass him to get home. There was little chance he wouldn't see her.

The man took a step, and one of his legs went out from under him. He stumbled to one side before righting himself again.

Becca startled.

It'll be fine. He's too drunk to pay me any attention.

Even if he did, he'd probably just shout something inappropriate at her. Looking at the state he was in, if he tried to come after her, she could easily run. She'd kick off her heels and leg it all the way if she had to, trying not to think about the possibility of standing in dog shit or on a piece of glass. Any of that would be better than being raped or even killed.

Her house wasn't far away. Two more streets. Five minutes, if she really hurried. She didn't want to die five minutes from home. Not that it was really her home. She'd only been there six months, and the student house was a far cry from where she'd grown up in Cheltenham. Her parents had never been terribly happy about her moving to this part of London, but she'd wanted to experience city life, warts and all, and Bow wasn't far from her university on Mile End Road.

For the first time, she wondered if they might have been right.

Cautiously, keeping her gaze fixed on the man, priming herself for a change in his body language that would tell her to run, she kept going. Every footstep brought her that little bit closer to his position, but she still hoped she would simply be able to walk by without him acknowledging her.

He stretched out a hand in her direction, and she knew she'd been noticed.

"Help me."

Something about his tone made her stop. There was a slight slur to his words, but not in the way she'd expect from someone who was drunk. And it was more than that. It was desperation and terror and pain.

How did she get all that from only two words? Two syllables, even.

"Please..." His words were punctuated by a sob. "I don't know where I am. It's so dark." He gave another whimper.

Becca glanced at the streetlight and then the pale moon. It was night, but it wasn't completely dark. He must be seriously wasted.

Somehow, that didn't sit right with her. Drunk people didn't act this way. They stumbled around and might not know where they were, but this man wasn't giving off that kind of body language. Drugs, then? There was some nasty shit on the streets right now. Some of it was even legal. It wasn't something Becca was ever interested in. She'd tried a couple of puffs on a joint at a party once and had ended up feeling sick, so she'd been more than happy sticking to wine or the occasional gin and tonic from then on.

No, not drunk. But something was wrong. Something was very, very wrong. She felt it right down to the marrow of her bones. Her mouth had run dry, her heart hammering so hard she was sure he must be able to hear it.

This man needed help.

It's all a trick! Go home.

Yes, it probably was. Just a trick. A way of making her let down her guard, and then when she got close enough, he'd probably spring into action and attack. He'd take her by surprise to knock her down and use his greater bodyweight to pin her to the ground. Then, if she was lucky, he'd rape her and steal her handbag, but if she was unlucky, he'd strangle her once he'd done what he wanted.

All these thoughts went through her head, yet she found herself taking a step closer. She ducked slightly, trying to see the man's face, wanting to get a better look at him so she could figure out what was wrong, but the way he was hunched over, his hands held out in front of him, made it impossible.

Her blood raced through her veins. Every part of her screamed *run!* but she found she couldn't.

She had her phone in her bag. The bag was tiny—only big enough to fit her purse, phone, keys, and a couple of emergency items of makeup—and Becca unzipped the top without taking her eyes off the man hunched over on the other side of the street. She delved inside and quickly located her phone. She had an emergency call already set up, so all it would take was a swipe of a screen, should he try anything, and then the police would be here to help.

Unless he kills me before they get here.

Despite her initial instincts, the man didn't seem threatening. Quite the opposite. She really did think he needed assistance.

She took a cautious step in his direction.

He stumbled into the beam of the streetlight overhead, a circle of illumination around his feet. Something darkened the front of his shirt and his hands.

Jesus Christ. Was that blood?

She found her voice. "Are...are you okay?"

His head snapped up. "Who's there? Please, you've got to help me." He reached both hands in her direction.

Becca sucked in a breath, widening her eyes in horror. Her phone dropped from her fingers, hitting the pavement, the screen shattering. She didn't even care, her gaze fixed on the young man in front of her.

She opened her mouth and screamed.

Chapter Two

The phone rang, and DI Erica Swift took her eyes off the road for a second to glance at the name displayed on the screen embedded in the car dashboard. She was on an early that day and had only left home less than half an hour ago. At least it being June meant it was already light. She hated heading in to work during the winter when it was dark and cold and still very much felt like the middle of the night.

Her husband's name, Christopher, was displayed on screen.

Her stomach sank.

Using the hands-free, she answered the call. "Everything okay?"

Chris's voice came through the speaker, filling the interior of the car. "You have to come home, Erica. He's not good. He doesn't know where he is, and he doesn't recognise either me or Poppy. He's shouting and saying some horrible things. He woke Poppy up, and she's terrified."

Her heart twisted for her family, picturing their four-year-old daughter upset and frightened of one of the people she should love most in the world.

"Can you put him on the phone?" She thought again. "Or put the phone on speaker so he can hear me."

The sigh was evident in her husband's voice. "Okay, but I really don't think it's going to help. We can't keep going like this."

"I know, Chris. I'm so sorry you're having to deal with him."

"It's not your fault. It is what it is."

Erica's dad, Frank, had been suffering with dementia for several years now. It broke her heart. He wasn't even seventy yet, and though he appeared well enough from the outside, his brain was a mess. He'd been a respected DCI in the Met, where she was now a DI, until his failing memory had forced an early retirement. Over the past few years, he'd got progressively worse, until it was no longer safe for him to live alone. Unable to face him going into a home, she'd moved her dad in with them a couple of weeks ago.

It hadn't been going well. The move had disorientated him more than normal, and since he'd moved in, none of them had got any sleep. Her dad wandered the house all night, searching for her mother, Yvonne, who'd died over ten years ago. He came in and out of their bedroom multiple times a night, waking them all up, asking where Yvonne was.

"Have you called Natasha?" Erica asked, referring to her older sister.

"I tried, but she didn't answer. I can't say I blame her. It's still painfully early."

She exhaled a steady breath. "Plus, she probably has her hands full with the kids."

"I've got my hands full, too," he protested. "I'm trying to take care of Poppy and your dad, and I've still got work to do myself." He dropped his voice a level. "Honestly, it's a fucking nightmare."

Something in her chest tightened. "I know. I'm so sorry." She found herself blinking back tears. This simply wasn't manageable. "It was wrong of me putting this on you."

His tone softened. "Hey, we're a team, and I'll always do whatever I can to support you, even taking care of your dad, but I'm shattered, and I'm struggling to hold it together."

The weight of responsibility sometimes felt so heavy it was hard to breathe. Chris was a good man, and she was expecting far too much from him. But they'd been out of options. Her sister, Natasha, had a three-bedroom house and was struggling for space already with five of them living there. She simply didn't have room for their dad to move in as well. Erica and Christopher only had one child, which meant they at least had a room free for Frank. Until recently, it had been Chris's office, but they'd converted it back into a bedroom—yet another sacrifice he'd made for her—so Chris was now working in the corner of the living room, his laptop and stacks of paper in among Poppy's toys and half-drunk cups of tea. He'd joked that it wasn't really much different to the mess he'd normally have worked amongst in his office, but she knew he was just trying to make light of a horrible situation. She loved him even more for that.

"Here, I'm putting you on speaker now," Chris said.

The tone of the call changed as her voice was sent out into her house.

"Dad?" She deliberately spoke louder but did her best not to shout. She needed to stay calm. "It's Erica, your daughter. Everything is okay. You're at my house right now, do you remember? You're staying with us for a little while."

Muffled voices sounded in the background, and then Chris came back on the line. "He doesn't want to talk. He says he's going back to bed."

"Oh, okay. I guess that's good."

"Yeah, for the moment, anyway. Sorry to have bothered you about all of this. I know you're busy."

She pressed her lips together, holding back her emotions, and shook her head. "No, it's fine. This isn't really your responsibility. I'll pop back and make sure everything is okay."

"Thanks, love. See you soon."

Ending the call, she let out a sigh, her shoulders sagging. She gripped the steering wheel with both hands, exhaustion washing over her. Even after twelve years working for the Met, she wasn't sure she'd ever get used to such early starts. She'd spent the previous shift visiting with a victim of domestic violence. The boyfriend had been arrested after shouting and sounds of things breaking had been reported by one of the neighbours. The victim had been found with a black eye, among other noticeable bruises, but she was now saying she didn't want to press any charges and that it had all been her fault, that she'd pushed him too hard and he'd only retaliated. Erica had seen cases like these often enough and always found them incredibly frustrating. The men in question rarely changed, no matter how many promises they made, and the woman found the beatings getting increasingly more violent until eventually she'd be forced to run, or else the worst happened and Erica ended up working on a murder case.

If a big case came in, she'd sometimes have only a matter of a few hours' sleep a night. She could function, but it wasn't easy.

Erica signalled to turn the car around and head home. She'd pop in for ten minutes to show her face and make sure

Christopher knew he wasn't having to do this all by himself, even if it must feel that way at times.

The phone rang again, and she assumed it would be Chris to tell her that her father had taken a turn for the worse, but instead her boss's name, DCI Gibbs, was displayed on screen.

She answered the call. "Swift speaking."

Gibbs's gruff voice came over the speaker. "I hope you're heading in. You're needed in Bow."

She sat up straighter. "What's happened?"

"There's been a stabbing."

"Damn it. Not another one." No one had been able to ignore the recent rise in knife crime. "What's the location?"

He gave her an address in Bow, not far from where she was.

Erica nodded, though he couldn't see her. "I'm on my way."

She ended the call then glanced back down at the phone. There was no way she'd be able to nip home now. Gibbs didn't like her personal life mixing with work, and they already had a terse professional relationship. Her husband wasn't going to be happy, but what could she do? Besides, Chris had said Frank had gone back to bed. Hopefully, he'd stay there.

• • • •

ERICA PARKED HER CAR a short distance from the crime scene, not far from where an Incident Response Vehicle blocked the road. The area was already busy with uniformed police, who'd cordoned off the crime scene, though she hadn't yet spotted SOCO. She must have beat them here.

She reached into the back of her car and grabbed her suit jacket—one that matched with her straight-legged grey trousers—then swung open the door and climbed out.

She experienced an inkling of guilt, hoping things had settled down at home. Chris was incredibly understanding, but it wasn't easy for him. She'd sent him a quick text when she'd stopped the car, but he hadn't responded yet. Hopefully, he'd managed to get everyone back to bed for an hour.

Several heads turned her way as she approached. She didn't recognise either of the police constables who must have been part of the Response Team from that borough, and she reached for her ID to ensure access to the scene.

She spotted the back of DS Shawn Turner's head, his tight black curls buzzed military short. He was easily recognisable by the shape of his left ear, misshapen and bulbous from being punched one too many times when he'd been a teenager growing up. Shawn had come from a rough background, as many young, black men in this part of London did, but, instead of following the path of many of his peers and going into a life of gangs and crime, he'd taken the opposite route and had joined the Met a couple of years out of school. She'd been working with Shawn as both her sergeant and shift partner for the past eighteen months, since their special Violent Crime Task Force had been put together in response to the rising issue of knife crime on London's streets. He was a few years her junior, but he was a good detective.

He turned to face her, a cup of takeaway coffee in each hand.

Erica nodded to one of the cups. "I hope one of those is for me."

He handed her one. "Black, two sugars."

"Thanks." She took a sip, needing the caffeine. "What have we got?"

"Male, twenty-three years old, found at approximately three-fifteen a.m. by nineteen-year-old Rebecca Bird. She's waiting back at the station in the interview room. The victim is in hospital in a critical condition. This isn't just a simple stabbing, though."

He'd piqued her interest. "In what way?"

Shawn paused as though for dramatic effect. "The victim was found with both his eyes gouged out."

She arched her brow. "Both eyes?"

"Yeah, and he was wandering the street in the middle of the night. Apparently, he didn't seem to know where he was or what had happened. He also didn't seem to be in a huge amount of pain when he was found, so I expect some kind of drugs were involved, possibly a sedative."

"Hopefully, he'll be able to answer some questions for us at the hospital. How come we're here and not there?"

"He needed to go into surgery to have his wounds cleaned up, so there didn't seem much point in us being dispatched straight there when we wouldn't be able to do anything for a few hours yet. He had a uniformed officer ride along in the ambulance with him in case he was conscious enough to say anything."

She put her hand to her mouth as what he'd told her sank in. "Someone gouged out his eyes. Jesus fucking Christ."

Shawn pulled a face. "Yeah, it's pretty bad."

"Any other injuries?"

"Not sure yet. There weren't any defensive injuries that were immediately obvious, but he was whisked out of here by the paramedics."

She twisted her lips, thinking. "So, it's possible he did this to himself?"

"It's a possibility," he agreed.

"What about the young woman who found him? Rebecca Bird?"

"She's okay. Shaken up by what she saw, understandably, but seems pretty level-headed. She was on her way home after a night out."

Finding someone in that condition would be traumatic for a young woman. "That must have been one hell of a shock for her. Anyone else with her?"

"No, she was alone."

Erica couldn't help imagining her daughter as a nineteen-year-old student. She hoped Poppy would never find herself walking home alone at three in the morning. There were too many dangers on the streets these days, and Erica got to see them every single day.

She took a moment to assess their surroundings. On one side of the street was a wall which backed onto some garages, and on the other was the cemetery park.

"Where did the victim come from?" she asked, thinking out loud. "The cemetery?"

Shawn turned and surveyed the area, his hands on his hips. "He might have figured it was a fun place to get wasted and then reacted badly to whatever he took and used a knife to pluck out his eyes. Too many young men are carrying knives these days, we all know that, and the park is open at night, so it's more than possible."

A spatter of dark droplets marked the pavement. Erica's line of sight followed them towards the gate leading into the cemetery. But other than a few more drops, there was nothing to suggest the victim had stumbled from the cemetery having recently had his eyes stabbed out.

She looked around at the uniformed police. "Where's SOCO?" she asked, referring to the Scenes of Crime Officer. "Shouldn't they be here by now?"

"They're on their way."

She nodded. "Good. And who's coordinating the scene?"

"Sergeant Reynolds. She's on her way over."

Erica glanced over to see the female sergeant striding towards them. Erica had met Diana Reynolds on a number of occasions and had always got on with her. She had a stern, no bullshit attitude about her that Erica appreciated.

"DI Swift," Reynolds greeted as she approached.

She didn't address Shaun, which made Erica think they'd already spoken.

"Messy business," she said, huffing air out through her nose. "Damn knives. It's like some kind of trend with the younger generation."

"This one seems a bit different, though," Erica said.

Reynolds nodded. "Yes, it's more methodical, for sure. Not sure I've come across a case quite like this before."

"Where are you up to?"

"I've dispatched a team of officers to look for more witnesses or possible victims," Reynolds said.

Even though it had been the middle of the night, someone might have seen something—the headlights of a car pulling over right before the victim was found, perhaps. If they had some idea what time the victim was left here, or which direction they'd come from, they'd be able to check security cameras around the area.

Shawn glanced back over at the wrought-iron railings. "What about the cemetery? We need to get a search team onto it, see if we can find the location where this might have originally happened."

"The officers are checking the cemetery as well," Reynolds said, "though we might need to intensify the search there, depending on the witness statement and that of the victim once we're able to get one. But the cemetery is a big place. It covers thirty acres."

Erica jerked her chin towards the far end of the street, where the brick wall gave way to terraced houses. "One of the neighbours might have seen something, too. He might have even come from inside one of the houses."

Reynolds glanced towards the house. "Yes, I've got two officers going house to house."

Erica nodded. "I'll get a couple of my DCs to do house-to-house as well, follow up on anything they might find."

"What are your thoughts on the lack of blood?" Reynolds asked her. "Do you think this happened somewhere else?"

"Yes, I do. And if it happened somewhere else, how the hell did the victim get here? You think he could navigate London's streets completely blind?"

"Any sign of the knife that was used?"

Reynold shook her head. "Not yet, but the officers combing the cemetery might find something."

"We'll know more once SOCO have had the chance to go over the scene," Erica said.

"Sergeant?" one of the uniformed officers called.

Reynolds glanced over her shoulder and jerked her chin to show she'd heard, and then turned back to Swift and Turner. "Excuse me."

Swift threw her a smile. "Of course."

She and Turner remained silent until Reynolds was a distance away then turned back to each other.

"If the incident didn't happen here, where did it happen?" Erica mused out loud.

"He could have done it some distance from here," Shawn suggested, "and by the time the witness found him, he'd already started to clot."

"Some distance would mean he'd done what we thought he wouldn't be capable of, and navigated London while completely blind."

Shawn shrugged. "Some drugs make people do crazy things."

A year or so ago, a man had almost bled to death cutting himself because he'd been trying to dig out worms he'd believed were wriggling around under his skin. It was perfectly feasible that something similar had happened here.

"Yeah, I think we've already ascertained that. But for him to have gouged out his own eyes and then wandered through the cemetery, blind, bleeding for long enough for it to have almost stopped by itself, on a Friday night, and no one else saw him?" She cocked both her eyebrows, waiting for his answer.

Shawn nodded in agreement, understanding where she was heading. "So, someone did this to him somewhere else, and then dumped him off in the cemetery?"

"Or he *did* do it to himself, but whoever he was with was so freaked out that they dumped him instead of taking him to hospital."

He exhaled a long breath. "Jesus, with friends like that, eh?"

"Either way, it means someone is out there who knows more than we do. I'll go to the hospital and hope the victim isn't unconscious too much longer."

Several marked vans pulled up, signalling the arrival of SOCO.

"About time," Erica commented.

Her phone buzzed, and she quickly checked her messages. It was from Chris.

Don't worry. Everything's calmed down here now. See you later.

She breathed a sigh of relief. At least that was one thing she could put off worrying about. The current setup wasn't working, and though having her dad living with them might be easing her own guilty conscience, it wasn't fair on the rest of her family either. She hated the idea, but they were going to have to rethink the situation.

Chapter Three: Eighteen Years Earlier

His brother's voice was a hissed, urgent whisper.
"Hide! She's coming!"

Nicholas was supposed to be taking care of his younger brother, but so often, it ended up that Danny was the one taking care of him. At eight and seven respectively, there was only eighteen months between them—hardly enough for anyone to notice there was any age difference at all, but looks-wise, they were opposites. Their mother never talked about who their father had been, but Nicholas assumed from their appearances that they hadn't been the same man.

"Where are you, you little shits?"

Her voice was too loud, slurring on the word 'shit', so it sounded as though it was no longer spelled with a 't', and both boys jumped as a thud signalled her stumbling into the hallway wall.

"Come on." Danny grabbed his hand and yanked him towards the set of bunk beds they shared. "Hide."

Nicholas glanced towards the dark space underneath the bottom bunk, which was his bed. He'd never admit it to his brother, but in the night, that gap between the bottom of his bunk and the floor was a source of nightmares. If he got up during the night to use the toilet, he'd dive from the square of light from the landing, across the room, to land on his mattress. He could never walk it, certain that something would reach out from under the bed and grab at his ankles.

But during the day, the only monster they had to fear was that of their very real parent, and the spot became a place of safety.

If she came into the room and didn't immediately see them, there was a good chance she'd just think they were somewhere else and would lose interest. Their mother's ability to forget things when she'd been drinking was borderline impressive. She'd stagger into a room to do or get something, fail to remember what it was a moment later, and pass out on a bed or a sofa, or sometimes even on the floor. He'd witnessed her literally in the middle of doing something—more often than not, getting herself another drink, but sometimes she'd suddenly decide to be a good mum and make them something to eat—and pass out cold. She'd fall backwards, as though she was playing one of those 'trust' games where people stood with their arms linked behind you and encouraged you to fall into them. Except there was no one around to catch their mother, and Nicholas had seen enough to know better than to try.

Danny was on his stomach, pulling himself under the bed, his legs and feet vanishing. Nicholas dived after him, commando crawling in his wake.

The swish of the bedroom door opening—the bottom of the door against the threadbare carpet—came from behind him. It was followed by heavy footfalls and a slurred exclamation.

Nicholas was painfully aware that he wasn't yet fully hidden. The lower half of his body still stuck out from beneath the bed, and no matter how drunk she was, there was little chance of her not noticing him.

Ice-cold hands wrapped around his bare ankles—his trousers had been too short for him for a couple of years now, but there was never any money around to buy him new ones—and tightened their grip.

He'd always feared the monsters under his bed reaching out and pulling him under, but instead it was the monster outside of his bed, dragging him out.

Danny's eyes widened in the shadows, and his little brother reached for him, as though he thought he could haul Nicholas back under with him. But Nicholas knew all that would happen was Danny would slide out with him. He didn't want that to happen. Maybe she would forget about his brother if she could take out her drunken rage and spite on him. He tucked his hands into his body, not giving Danny anything to get hold of, and their mother yanked him the rest of the way out from under the bed.

"Where the fuck do you think you're going?" she slurred, hoisting him to his feet. "Think you can hide from me, you little shit?"

Nicholas clamped his lips together and did his best not to look at her. When she was in this kind of mood, she took everything badly. Even catching her eye would be taken as him being defiant or rude, and he would end up with a slap as a reward. He'd never be able to win an argument with her either. It was impossible to reason with her. All he could hope for was that she'd either lose steam or decide she needed more alcohol and would leave him alone to go and find her next drink.

Stay where you are, Danny, he willed. *Don't come out here.*

She had him by both shoulders and gave him a shake, his head rocking back and forth. "Don't you want to spend time with your poor mum, eh? You want to leave me, just like everyone else."

He couldn't help himself; he shook his head.

"No?" she blurted, sending a wave of stale alcohol over him, strong enough that he turned his face to try to avoid it. "Was that a no? The only reason you would never leave me is because no one else would want you. Look at the state of you. I can hardly believe I gave birth to you. What the fuck went wrong? Must be your goddamned father's genes. Useless piece of crap, he was."

Nicholas did his best not to cry.

She released one of his shoulders and gripped his face, her thumb digging into one side of his jaw, her fingers into the other. She gave him another shake.

"Face only a mother could love." She barked cold laughter. "Do you know that saying?"

Still in her grip, he did his best to shake his head again. His eyes brimmed with hot tears.

"Well, *you're* so ugly, not even your mother could love you!"

He tried not to let her words hurt, did his best to create a crust around his heart to prevent them from penetrating. He knew he was ugly. His mother had told him practically every day for as long as he could remember.

Each year that had gone by, his deformity had grown worse. He spent hours staring at himself in the mirror, watching, over the passing of time, as his lower eyelids dropped and hung, exposing the pale flesh, with miniscule red blood vessels threading through. The same thing had happened to the corners of his mouth, drawing down so that even when he tried to smile—which happened so rarely, he couldn't remember the last time—he looked as though he was trying to twist his face into some kind of grotesque expression. His nose was a misshapen lump of flesh, squashed to the middle of his face like an afterthought, a piece of clay someone had left over when they were creating him.

Shame. That was the overriding emotion that swallowed his childhood. He was embarrassed about absolutely everything. His appearance, the clothes he wore, how dirty he was, the lunches he brought to school. He could never let anyone else in the house, knowing what they would find.

A woman from Social Services had come around a few times when they'd been younger. Their mother had turned up drunk to pick them up from school one too many times, and the school had raised concerns. It made things better for a short while, at least. Their mother, even if she hadn't stopped drinking, had curtailed it enough to make sure she wasn't completely out of it around school pick-up time. It meant she held it together enough to actually make them dinner, instead of them having to rifle around in the cupboards for whatever might be available.

It never lasted, though. He'd never understood completely how it worked, but after a while, the woman from the social must have signed them off again, deciding everything was okay, and so things slipped back to how it had been before.

The seconds ticked into minutes. What did she want from him? Sometimes, he thought she wanted him to retaliate, to scream at her about what a terrible mother she was and how he wished he had a different parent. He did think all those things, but he knew giving in to what she wanted would only make it worse. She wanted to have someone to lash out at. Sometimes, she brought men home, and they hung around for a while, but then *they* became the ones she lashed out at, and of course, they fought back, not knowing any better. It wasn't that the men were particularly bad people—they only existed in Nicholas's periphery for a while and barely ever had anything to do with the two boys—but he knew they would never stay around. They'd soon be at the receiving end of his mother's vehemence and decide it was easier to bail.

Her hand fell from his face, and she swayed, her eyelids heavy, her chin dropping. The anger had burned itself out, as it often did, and left her drunk and exhausted. She staggered to one side, and without saying another word, turned and stumbled her way to the bedroom door.

Nicholas stayed rooted to the spot, not wanting to say or do anything that would bring her back again. The slightest thing could set her off, and he'd had more than enough of her for one evening. He prayed Danny would stay in position as well. Their mother hadn't even asked where her younger son was. Maybe she knew. Danny never received the kind of hatred from her that Nicholas did. Danny was cute and blond, and the complete opposite to Nicholas. Whatever strange genetics had caused his mishappened features hadn't affected his sibling. Not that Nicholas would ever wish it on Danny. He loved his brother.

He waited until her bedroom door slammed shut, then allowed himself to breathe.

Danny must have heard it as well, as he dragged himself out from under the bed.

"You okay?" he asked Nicholas.

Nicholas nodded. "Yeah. I'm okay."

It was no different from what he'd experienced almost every night of his life.

Suddenly sick with the realisation that this was what his existence was like, and that he'd have years of it before he'd be able to escape, Nicholas climbed into the bottom bunk.

"Aren't you going to put on your pyjamas?" Danny asked, already taking off his school stuff and changing them for a set of Spiderman nightclothes he'd got as a Christmas present a few years ago. Nicholas suspected the pjs were a knock-off version, and not the real branded thing, but Danny loved them. Like with their school clothes, they were inches too short on him now, the hems grazing his shins and the sleeves ending at his forearms, but he still wore them every night.

"I'll do it later." Nicholas tugged the bedcovers over himself, getting a whiff of body odour. He didn't know when the sheets had last been washed, but it was probably months ago.

The bunk bed creaked and groaned as Danny hauled himself up onto it, not even bothering to use the little wooden ladder. One day, the whole contraption would probably collapse on top of him.

They lay in silence for a moment, Nicholas staring up at the wooden slats and the stained bottom of Danny's mattress. Neither of them had turned out the light before they'd got into bed, but that was okay. Sometimes it felt safer to sleep with it on.

Movement came from above, and then Danny's upside-down face and shoulders appeared, hanging off the top bunk.

"She doesn't mean it," Danny said. "It's only because she's drunk."

He was trying to make Nicholas feel better, perhaps experiencing guilt of his own that Nicholas was almost always the one on the receiving end of their mother's vitriol, but Danny's words didn't mean anything. It *was* the drink talking, but Nicholas thought the drink and their mother were one and the same. She didn't exist without it.

Nicholas turned to face the wall, pulling the dirty bedcovers up over his shoulders. "Go to sleep, Danny."

Chapter Four

Erica had always hated hospitals. She didn't imagine there were too many people who actually liked them. No one came here for a nice day out, did they? What with the exorbitant parking charges and the terrible food, it wasn't a place people went to willingly. There was something about the smell of them, too, the tang of disinfectant mixed with underlying sickness. Any time she found herself on a hospital ward, no matter the reason, she was always paranoid she was going to come down with some horrific vomiting bug. She knew it wasn't typical for people in her job to feel that way, and she was often the recipient of plenty of ribbing from her colleagues about her squeamishness to germs. She could handle as much blood or guts as anyone threw at her, but mention the word 'norovirus' and she'd be running for the hills.

She paused at one of the alcohol stations at the entrance to the ward and applied the cold gel liberally and rubbed it into her skin. Yet another thing that was unpleasant about this place, but at least it might prevent her from becoming ill. She tried not to think about all the germs lingering in the air, the ones she might be sucking into her lungs right at this very moment. She wasn't normally obsessive about things like that, but hospitals brought it out in her.

A burly woman in her mid-forties, with a formidable shelf of a chest, sat behind the reception desk for the Intensive Care Unit. From her uniform, Erica assumed she was a nurse, and the woman lifted her head to greet her.

Erica flashed her ID. "You had a young man brought in during the early hours. Injuries to his eyes."

"Yes, of course." The nurse rose to her feet. "I'm Jeanne. I'm one of the ICU Staff Nurses. He's not awake, though, I'm afraid, so I'm not sure how much use seeing him is going to be. You're not going to be able to ask him any questions."

"I don't have an ID on him yet, so it would be good to try to find out who he is. There might be clues in his appearance that could give me an idea."

"This way."

Erica clocked the nurse's name badge and made a mental note of her surname—Hay.

Jeanne led her down a corridor. They passed doors marked ICU, and large glass windows allowing a view onto the patients' beds on the other side, with privacy curtains that could be drawn. Most of these patients appeared to either be unconscious or sleeping, however, so Erica doubted they'd care too much about their lack of privacy.

The nurse stopped outside one of the rooms. "Here we are." She opened the door and showed Erica through.

A man lay in a hospital bed, surrounded by beeping machines. It was hard to get a good look at his face. White bandages were wrapped around his eyes and the back of his head, so only his nose, mouth, and crown of his head were visible.

A uniformed police officer sat on a plastic chair beside the bed, and he got up as they entered.

"DI Swift," Erica introduced herself.

He ducked his head in a nod. "PC Buckley. He's not shown any sign of waking up yet."

She jerked her chin towards the door she'd just entered through. "Can I ask you a few questions outside?"

"Of course."

"We won't be a minute," she told Jeanne. "If you could see if there is a doctor available to speak with, I'd appreciate it."

"I'll page one now."

They left the nurse walking around the bed, checking the drip that fed into his arm, and stepped into the corridor.

Erica turned to face Buckley. "You rode with the victim in the ambulance, is that right?"

"Yes, I did. He was still conscious then, but he wasn't making much sense. Can't say I blame him. He must have been terrified."

"What was the exact time you reached the hospital?"

He took a small notepad from his pocket and checked. "Twenty-five past four this morning."

"Who was the attending doctor?" she asked.

"Dr Sharma. He's a registrar here, but I believe a consultant was the doctor who took him into surgery, a Ms Arora."

"Good, thank you. Hopefully, one of those two will be free to speak to me." She glanced back at the hospital room door. "Any luck with an I.D.?"

"Not yet. He wasn't printed at the scene. The paramedics wanted to get him straight to hospital."

"And he had no identification on him at all when he was found? Not even a mobile phone?"

Buckley shook his head. "No, nothing."

"Could he be homeless?" she wondered out loud.

"Possibly, though the clothes he was wearing were fairly new, and he had an expensive pair of trainers." Buckley shrugged. "I'm not saying that means he wasn't homeless, but shoes like that would most likely have been stolen off his feet while he was sleeping if he was on the streets."

"But who comes out these days without so much as a phone or a set of keys on them?"

"You think he might have been robbed?" The officer frowned as he thought for a moment. "Maybe he saw the thief and that's why he stabbed him in the eyes? He was trying to protect his identity?"

Erica didn't buy that theory. "We need to find out who he is. It might give us a clue as to who did this to him. I'll keep an eye on missing persons reports. Someone must be missing a boyfriend or son, or even a work colleague who hasn't shown up."

"Today's Saturday," he pointed out. "He might not be working."

"Plenty of people still work Saturdays." She gestured either side of her. "We are."

He offered her a rueful smile. "That's true."

Movement came from farther down the corridor, and a female doctor, a sharp suit beneath her white coat, approached.

"DI Swift?" the woman asked. "I'm Ms Arora, the consultant who operated on our patient. I got a page that you were here to speak to me."

Erica nodded and extended her hand to shake the doctor's. "Yes. Thank you for coming so quickly."

"Not at all. Shall we go in?"

Ms Arora gestured to the hospital room, and they all stepped back inside. The nurse smiled at them as they entered.

"How's he doing?" the consultant asked Jeanne.

"No change yet," she replied.

"That's probably to be expected."

"How long do you think it's going to be before he wakes up?" Erica asked.

"Hopefully, only a matter of hours, but it might be longer. He was taken into surgery when he arrived and sedated so we could clean up his injuries."

"But he *will* wake up?" she asked.

Ms Arora gave Erica a tight smile. "We certainly hope so, but it's hard to tell how he'll react to what's happened. He might go into shock, which could lead to cardiac arrest. With no medical history, I'm afraid your guess is almost as good as mine at this point."

"I'd better do my job and find out who he is, then." Erica studied the victim, as though hoping to read his identity on his skin. "White male, early twenties, brown hair." Her gaze flicked down the length of his body. "Approximately five feet eleven. Tattoos on his neck." She looked to the consultant. "I'm going to need a comprehensive list of his injuries, including the exact measurements of the injuries to his eyes, or what's left of them. I'd also like to order a toxicology screening, if that hasn't been done already."

Arora nodded. "Of course. I'll make sure all the reports are sent over to you. One thing I should mention, though, is that while I was working on him I noticed this."

The consultant pulled the hospital gown away from the victim's neck, and Erica leaned in.

On the side of his neck, about one inch down from his earlobe and the same distance across from his hairline, was a red mark circled in bruising.

"A puncture wound?" Erica hazarded a guess.

"Looks like it to me."

The puncture wound might not be related to the case. If he was an intravenous drug user, he might have injected himself. The neck was the most common injection site after the arms. Nevertheless, she made a note of it.

Erica turned back to Buckley. "Were samples taken from under his nails?"

"Yes, the samples were sent to the lab, together with the clothes he was wearing when he was brought in."

"Good. There's not much I can do until he wakes up and I can question him. In your professional opinion, Ms Arora, is there any chance he did this to himself?"

The consultant pressed her lips together. "I doubt it. He might have gouged out one of his eyes, but both? Once he'd done one, I doubt he'd have had it in him to manage the second. There are also no nicks around the eye socket where I'd expect someone who might be on drugs or shaking from shock would have caught their skin while they located their eye socket with the tip of the blade. There are also these."

Arora stepped closer to the bed and lifted the sheet covering the side of the victim's body. She nodded down at his wrist where an abrasion circled the skin.

Erica leaned forward to check. "Could be from a watch or something." She checked the other arm. The red ring around his wrist was almost identical. "But then how many people wear two watches?"

The consultant moved to the bottom of the bed and removed the sheets from his feet. Two red rings circled his ankles.

"Those look like ligature marks to me," Erica said. "He's been tied up. Someone must have cut him loose, or he managed to escape himself."

"You can rule out the possibility of him doing this to himself, then?" Arora confirmed.

Erica nodded. "Yes, I'd say so."

The idea of there being someone out there who would do this to another person was even more horrifying than the idea of him gouging his own eyes out while high on some cocktail of hard drugs.

The consultant's pager vibrated, and she checked it and threw Erica an apologetic smile. "Sorry, I'm needed elsewhere."

"No problem. Thank you for your help."

The doctor gave them a nod and slipped out of the room.

"I need to go down to the station and interview the woman who found him," she told Buckley. "If he dies, this becomes a murder investigation, and right now, we haven't got the slightest idea who did this to him. I'm going to send someone over with an INK device so you can print our man here and see if he's on our system. I want the results right away, if you get a match."

The INK—Identity Not Known—device was a great piece of kit, and Erica kicked herself for not having brought one with her in the first place. It was a portable device that securely communicated with the Biometric Services Gateway which searched the Criminal Records Office for any matches. It might have saved them some time.

Buckley nodded. "No problem."

She thanked Jeanne Hay for her help and left the hospital—though not without using more hand sanitiser—and went back to the car. The drive to the station wasn't far, but London traffic was always slow. Sometimes she thought she'd move quicker if they walked.

Her stomach growled, reminding her she'd not had any breakfast yet. The coffee Shawn had presented her with had been the only thing she'd consumed so far that morning.

She'd speak with the key witness first and see if they could get any leads via her, and then she'd deal with her stomach.

Chapter Five

Erica opened the door to the interview room.

A young woman sat at the table, her hands on the surface, her fingers interlinked. She was pale, dark bruises under eyes that had lifted at the opening of the door.

"Rebecca Bird?" Erica asked with a smile. She knew the young woman's name but found asking was a way of making her more comfortable instead of launching right in by announcing herself. People were more open when you were friendly towards them. Not that she thought this girl had anything to hide.

The witness pressed her lips into a thin line. "It's Becca. Everyone calls me Becca."

"Okay, Becca. I'm DI Swift. I'd like to ask you a few questions about last night, if that's all right."

Becca glanced down at her hands. "Of course."

"This room is fitted with video and audio equipment, so the interview will be recorded, okay?"

The young woman nodded.

"I'm sorry to have kept you waiting," Erica continued, slipping into the plastic chair across the table from Becca. "I'd like to be able to tell you this will be quick so you can go home and get some rest, but I'm afraid we will most likely be here awhile. Can I get you anything to eat or drink—a coffee or some breakfast?"

Erica was aware that the witness had been up all night.

"No, thanks." Her voice was small. "I'd rather just get this over and done with. I'm pretty shattered."

"I'm sure you are."

"I doubt I'll get much sleep even after I get home, though," she continued. "Not after seeing...that." She chewed on her lower lip, nibbling at a piece of dried skin. "Is...is the man all right?"

"He's alive," Erica said carefully. "But the doctors are keeping him sedated."

Becca let out a long sigh and put her face in her hands, pressing the balls into her eye sockets. "You think someone did this to him? I mean, he wouldn't have done it to himself, right? Unless he was on drugs. I thought he might have been, at first. Could he have taken some kind of hallucinatory drug and dug out his own eyes?"

"We're keeping all lines of enquiry open for the moment."

The witness gave her head a slight shake. "Sorry, you're supposed to be asking me questions, aren't you? Not the other way around."

"That's okay. I understand you must have a lot of concerns about what happened last night. We have support for you if you feel you need it."

"No, I'll be fine. I just feel awful for that poor man. Can you imagine waking up in a hospital and discovering that someone stole your eyes?"

Someone stole your eyes... Was that really what happened? Or was this simply a horrible accident, or, like Rebecca had suggested, that he'd done this to himself while high? But the marks on his wrists and ankles suggested otherwise, as did the puncture wound. There was the possibility he'd got the marks some other way, of course.

Erica checked the folder of notes. "You're a student at the university?"

She nodded. "That's right. Second year."

"What are you studying?"

"English with Art History."

Erica smiled. "Sounds interesting."

The girl returned the smile, relaxing for the first time. "It is. I love it."

"That's good." She took a breath. "Okay, can you run me through your day leading up to finding the victim. How did it start?"

"Just like most days. I got up, went to my lectures, and at lunch some of the other students suggested going into the city later that evening for some drinks, so I did."

"Did you travel into the city on your own?"

"No, there were a few of us."

"And where did you go?"

Becca reeled off a number of different bars and clubs. They'd clearly had a bit of a pub crawl.

"Then what happened on your way home," Erica asked.

"I caught the bus from Holborn just after two a.m."

"Were you alone?"

Becca shook her head. "No, I got on with another student, Philip Dentry. He didn't get off with me, though."

Erica made a note of the name. She'd get one of her DCs to go and have a chat with the other student and make sure their recollection of times and events matched up.

"It says here you got off the night bus on Mile End Road at approximately three a.m.," Erica continued.

"Yes, that's right. I have to walk down the road adjacent to the cemetery to get to my house. It's always kind of creepy, but even in my imagination, I never thought I'd see…that."

She stared down at her hands again and blinked rapidly several times, as though trying to wash the image from her eyeballs.

"And was there anyone else around that you can remember? Any cars parked nearby that caught your attention?"

She shook her head. "No, nothing like that. If I'd seen anyone else, I'd have called for help or something."

"You did call for help, though." Erica checked her notes. "You called us at three twenty-three a.m."

"Yes, I meant that I'd have called for help before I'd seen his face." She gave a shrug. "I didn't know what it was about him, but I could tell something wasn't right. It was a feeling, you know? At first, I thought he might be drunk, but he wasn't—or at least I didn't think he was." She glanced up at Erica for confirmation of her suspicions.

"We're not sure about his blood alcohol level yet," she said. "We're waiting on the toxicology screening to come back." She motioned with her hand. "You were saying about when you first saw him."

Becca stared back down at her fingers. "That's right. He was reaching out in front of him, not quite keeping his balance, and then he stepped under the streetlight. But his head was still down at that point, so I couldn't really see much, but then I asked him if he was all right, and he looked up. When I saw his face, I dropped my phone, and then he collapsed, and I didn't know what else to do. I didn't feel like I could leave him there to go and get help, not when he was so badly hurt. I remember screaming and then picking up my phone again. The screen was cracked, but it was still working, thank God, and that's when I phoned the police."

"And what about the direction he came from? You were walking from Mile End Road, is that right?"

"Yes," she confirmed.

"And the victim was on the side of the cemetery, coming towards you."

"He wasn't really coming towards me, not at first, anyway."

"Do you think he came from out of the cemetery?"

Becca nodded. "That was my first thought. They leave the place open at night, and though there's a park warden, I don't think it's covered twenty-four hours."

Erica made another note to make sure someone went to speak to the warden.

A knock came at the interview room door.

"Yes?" she called.

The door opened, and Shawn stepped in. "I just wanted to let you know that I'm back from the scene."

"Great, thanks. I'll join you to debrief Gibbs when I'm done here."

Shawn nodded. "I won't go far." He backed out of the room again and closed the door behind him.

Erica turned back to Becca and went over everything she'd said, asking the same questions, only phrasing them slightly differently, making sure her story matched up the second time around. She paused mid-way through to make the witness another offer of coffee, but once more the young woman declined.

After another hour, they were finally done.

"I think that's everything for now, but we may need to speak to you again at some point." Erica slid her card across the table. "Call if you think of anything else."

Becca nodded. "I will."

"Great. I'll get one of my DCs to give you a lift home. I won't be long."

Erica rose from her seat and left the room in search of Shawn. She found him in the office.

"How did it go?" he asked.

"Okay, but she's understandably exhausted. Can you see if Rudd is free and get her to drop Miss Bird home? After she's done that, she can go and have a chat with the park warden, since she'll already be in the area, see if the warden has seen or come across anything unusual. Actually, tell her to take Howard with her as well."

The two DCs were part of her Violent Crime team. DC Jon Howard was new and a little cocky for her liking, considering his lack of experience, but DC Hannah Rudd knew how to hold her own and wouldn't take any crap from her colleague. Rudd was educated, with no family yet. An ambitious young woman, she put herself out there, even for the jobs no one else wanted to do. She reminded Erica of how she'd been when she'd first joined the Met, before the reality of the job had taken its toll.

Shawn nodded. "Will do."

Her phone buzzed in her pocket, and she took it out and checked the screen. It was a message from Chris.

Really need you home. Your dad is going nuts again. Sorry.

"Shit."

Shawn cocked an eyebrow. "Everything all right?"

"Not really. My dad isn't doing so well."

"He's living with you now, isn't he?"

Shawn knew a little of what her family had been going through over the past few months. She tried to keep her work and personal life separate, but when you worked so closely with someone, it was hard to keep them completely apart.

"Yeah, but it's not been going great. He seems even more confused than ever, and he's wandering around the house at night, keeping everyone awake." She gave a wry smile. "Tempers are a little frayed, and one thing a dementia sufferer needs is other peoples' patience. Unfortunately, when no one has had any sleep, that's the one thing that's in short supply."

"Don't worry. You go and take care of your family. I'll find Rudd and Howard and get them to deal with Miss Bird and the park warden, then I'll check the missing persons reports, see if anything has come in that we might be able to link back to the victim."

"Thanks, Turner. Hopefully, I won't be too long. Keep me posted, yeah?"

"Of course."

Chapter Six

The moment she stepped out of her car and onto the driveway, she winced at the commotion coming from the house. God only knew what the neighbours must think about all the sudden shouting.

Erica pushed her key into the lock and opened the door. "Only me!" She tried to sound bright, though the knot in her stomach belied her true emotions. She already missed the days where she'd come home only feeling guilty about not spending enough time with her husband and daughter. It had felt like a big deal back then, and something she agonised over, even though she was the main breadwinner, and she doubted she'd be feeling this way if she was a man, but now it seemed like small fry compared with what was happening now.

How had it only been a couple of weeks? Admittedly, worries about her dad had been going on for a lot longer, but it had been easier to distance herself from the reality of how bad he'd got when he hadn't been living with them. Prior to now, she'd dropped in to visit him at home when she'd got the chance, the shorter visits not allowing her to get a full insight into how he really was. She'd exchanged phone calls with her sister, Natasha, both mentioning how worried they were about him, but neither of them really wanting to voice their concerns fully. It was as though saying it out loud would make it real, and they both wanted to pretend for a little longer.

Frank had been on medication to slow the onset of the dementia for years now, but it was no longer working. Neighbours had reported finding him lost and disorientated in a part of the city he'd lived his whole life, unable to even remember why he'd left the house in the first place.

It broke her heart to see him this way. She'd always looked up to him and admired him massively, her big, strong, authoritative father. She'd been so proud of him as a child, that her dad was an important detective. He had been the whole reason she'd followed him into this profession.

Now he wasn't even safe living alone.

Her husband's familiar voice called out. "In here."

Thank God Poppy was at school already. She'd only started that year and was one of the youngest in her class, with her birthday in the summer. But she seemed happy there and had made plenty of friends, many of whom had come up from the pre-school with her. It meant they had a few hours without her in the house, so they could focus on Frank for a while.

She dropped her handbag in the entrance hall and followed Chris's voice into the living room.

The two men sat on opposite sides of the room—her dad in the easy chair they'd brought from his house in the hope of making him feel more at home, and her husband perched on the edge of the sofa. His hands were clasped between his knees, hunched over, his head down, though he looked up at her as she walked in. Frank was leaning back in his chair, his elbow on the armrest, his finger pressed to his lips. His legs were crossed, the top foot jiggling up and down. Tension radiated from the pair of them.

"How are you, Dad?" she asked. "Everything okay?"

"No, it's not. That man over there"—he pointed at Chris—"won't let me go to my meeting. I'm going to be very late, and I'm not happy about it. People are waiting for me. I don't know who he thinks he is."

She was relieved he at least seemed to recognise her today. "That's my husband, Christopher. You've met him before." She shot Chris a tight smile, and he forced one back but exhaled air through his nose. "And your meeting got cancelled today, so there's no need to worry."

She patted her dad's knee.

He frowned at her. "Did it? Why?"

Erica thought quickly. "No one else could make it either."

Frank huffed out a breath. "Well, I wish someone had phoned me directly to let me know."

"I'm sure they tried, Dad. Maybe you were just busy."

"Hmm. Maybe."

She needed to change the subject. "How about I make everyone a nice cup of tea."

"Thank you, sweetheart. I could do with one." He took her hand and squeezed it. "You're a good girl."

She found herself blinking back tears. "Thanks, Dad. I'll go and make that tea. Chris, think you can give me a hand?"

"Yeah, of course."

Her husband got to his feet and followed her into the kitchen. Erica picked up the kettle and filled it from the tap.

"This isn't going to get any easier," he said from behind her.

She flicked the kettle on and turned to face him. "I know."

"I'm sorry. I feel like I'm letting you down."

"And I feel like I'm letting *him* down. Like I'm giving up on him, and I'm handing him over to become someone else's problem."

"It's not like that. There's a reason people have been trained to do this. He needs specialist care, people who know what they're doing. Not us. You're a detective, and a mother, and wife. You can't expect to be his carer as well."

Erica fought a rise of resentment. Chris was fighting for her attention as well, and she knew his words, though meant kindly, also contained a jibe about how she wasn't being his wife while both of them had to take care of her father. He had a point, but that didn't stop the flash of anger. It wasn't as though this was her fault.

She took a breath. "I know that. I'll make some calls, okay? And then I'll talk to him."

"It can wait until after your birthday," Chris said.

She shook her head. "No, that's fine. You know I don't care about that, anyway."

Her birthday was in a few days, but she didn't celebrate it anymore. That day had been ruined, and when the anniversary arrived, she simply wanted to get through it.

"Okay," Chris relented. "Thank you."

The kettle finished boiling, and she moved to make the tea, but Chris stepped forward.

"I've got that."

She let him add teabags to the mugs and pour in the boiling-hot water. Remembering she hadn't eaten yet that morning, she opened the bread bin and fished out a loaf to make some toast. It was hardly a balanced meal, but it was quick and easy and would do for the moment.

"Did Poppy go into school all right?" she asked, suddenly missing her daughter.

It wasn't easy, not being around. She felt as though Poppy missed out on playdates and birthday invitations because Erica wasn't one of those mums who was always gossiping at the school gates. The school mums all seemed to have their little gangs, arranging to go out or do things with the children, and both Erica and Poppy were noticeably absent from the invitations. She wasn't sure if it was simply because she wasn't around enough to be a part of things, or if they found her job as a detective a little intimidating, or maybe it was because she wasn't all over social media or up with the latest trends, but she definitely felt on the outside. Not that it bothered her at all, but she hated to think it might affect Poppy.

"She was fine. Maybe a bit clingier than normal, but I think it was just because she was tired."

"It must be scary for her when Dad goes off on one like that."

Chris gave a small laugh and handed her the cup of tea. "It's scary for me. I was a bit worried he was going to take a swing at me. I didn't want to have to explain why I got beaten up by a seventy-year-old man."

"He's not seventy yet," she said with a rueful smile.

Her toast popped, and she set about buttering it and slathering it in Marmite.

Chris wrinkled his nose at her breakfast. "You know I hate that stuff."

She took a big bite. "Good thing you're not the one eating it, then."

He wrapped his arm around her waist and nuzzled her neck, and she couldn't help but smile. She was lucky to have him. She'd met Chris when she was twenty-five and he was thirty, at a funeral of one of the force's support staff, who had also happened to be the mother of one of Chris's old school friends. Their eyes had met across the coffin being lowered into the ground, and they'd sought each other out at the wake over a plate of mini sausage rolls. It perhaps wasn't the most romantic of meetings, but it had worked for them. They were married and had bought a house by the time she was twenty-seven. Only a year or so later, she'd discovered she was pregnant with Poppy, and that was that.

Her phone buzzed.

"Just leave it." The reproach in Chris's tone was clear.

"I can't. There's a case that needs some extra attention."

She checked her phone. It was a message from Shawn.

The INK device gave us an ID on the victim, and the toxicology screen came back.

"Sorry," she told him, "but I have to go. I'll make some calls about Dad today, okay?" She raised her voice. "Bye, Dad. See you later."

His grunt of a response came from the living room.

With a piece of toast clamped between her teeth, she left the house.

Chapter Seven: Eleven Years Earlier

A hand hit Nicholas around the back of the head. It wasn't too hard—only a playful tap, really—but it was enough that he jumped.

"Come on, dickhead," Danny declared. "What are you looking at?"

Nicholas had been staring at a young mother picking up one of the smaller kids from school. The boy must have been a year seven who'd only recently started at secondary, and was clearly embarrassed at his mum turning up at the gates, his cheeks burning pink as she swept him into a hug and kissed the top of his head. An ache in the middle of Nicholas's chest had made it hard for him to breathe. Was it possible to mourn something you'd never really had? If you never had it, was it even able to have lost it?

Nicholas peered guiltily around at his brother standing behind him, feeling as though he'd been caught doing something he shouldn't. At fourteen years old now, Danny was still his little brother. Only Danny had shot up over the past twelve months and was now several inches taller than Nicholas. They couldn't have looked less like brothers if they'd tried. Where Nicholas's already ugly face now sported a crop of hideous red spots that crusted over with a yellow head, Danny's skin was still clear. Despite his fair colouring, Danny also somehow managed to appear tanned and healthy, even through the winter months.

Danny was able to walk through school with his head held high, laughing and joking with his mates. The girls stood together and whispered things about him behind their hands, but not in the same way they did with Nicholas. When they talked about Nicholas, it was with wrinkled noses and smirks of disdain, but they flicked their hair when Danny passed by and pouted their pretty lips and fluttered eyelashes thick with mascara. On the odd occasion, one of them did try to talk to Nicholas, but it was only ever so they could ask him something about Danny.

Nicholas didn't really care. He wasn't interested in girls. He didn't try to kid himself that he was the type of person people could fall in love with—not looking how he did. Even his own mother told him constantly about how hard it was to love a boy like him. If his mum couldn't love him, how could he expect anyone else to?

Danny loved him, though. His younger brother didn't seem to see what everyone else did—he didn't see the twisted nose, or the droopy lower eyelids, or the way the corners of his mouth pulled down instead of up.

Nicholas kept his head down and his face hidden by a hood, as much as possible. At school, though, he got told off by the teachers if he wore the hood of his jacket up. Instead, he'd let his hair grow longer, so he could walk with a stoop, letting his jaw-length hair fall over his face. It wasn't much of a disguise, and of course, everyone knew the horror that was hidden beneath it, but it helped.

"Nothing," he told his brother. "Just waiting for you, that's all."

"Well, I'm here now, so let's go. I don't want to stay in this shithole any longer than we have to."

The school was an uninspiring concrete block, surrounded by six feet high railings. An equally grey playground offered the children somewhere to play, but the space was most often dominated by boys and football. A square of grass at the top of the slope, which backed onto one of the buildings, was a non-officially dedicated spot for the girls to hang out, and the boys took great delight in attempting to boot the football as hard as they could into the groups of girls, hoping in equal measure to both hurt them and gain their attention.

Nicholas had been waiting outside the school gates for Danny. It was stupid, but Nicholas didn't like to walk home alone. It was less about the walking part and more to do with the state their mother would be in by the time they got there. At the weekends, she'd make some effort to be normal, for the first few hours of the day, at least, but when they were both at school and she was awake earlier and they weren't around, she started drinking earlier, too.

Things had got easier the older the boys had grown. Their mother no longer needed to accompany them to and from school, so there was no one to notice what kind of state she was in. Nicholas helped himself to money from her purse—on those rare occasions she hadn't already drunk it away—and bought food for him and Danny. He was always careful to hide the food from her, though, knowing she'd binge on it herself and leave nothing for her sons.

"Yeah," Nicholas agreed. "I fucking hate school."

Danny nodded, as though Nicholas had said something enlightening. "Total waste of time."

While Nicholas didn't really hate school, he didn't mind it either. It had its good points. He liked the work. There was some stuff he was good at—like maths—where he seemed to know the answer while everyone else struggled. Other subjects, like English and art, didn't come so easily to him. The subjects he was good at, he found the teachers treated him with a little less disdain. He'd never go as far as saying they liked him—even the adults knew there was something wrong with him, something that made him stand out from all the other kids, and not in a good way—but they tolerated him.

He was envious of those students who, even after a shit day at school, got to go home to a normal family. Nicholas felt unsafe, no matter where he was. At school, he had to brace himself for the bullying—which would have been far worse had he not been Danny's brother—and then at home he had to deal with his mum. The only time he really felt like he could breathe was when it was just him and Danny. He could be himself then. He didn't need to hide. But Danny was getting older, and every day, he grew that much farther from Nicholas. He had his own friends, who he'd spend time with after school sometimes, leaving Nicholas alone, and Nicholas hated that more than anything. He could see a future where Danny would have his own life, well away from his weirdo older brother, and what would he do then? Would it be only him and Mum, sitting inside their disgusting house together, both hating each other a bit more every day?

No, Danny wouldn't leave him. Danny knew Nicholas needed him. During those long-ago nights spent hidden under their bunk bed, while their mother crashed around and shouted and cried, they'd made whispered promises that they'd always take care of each other.

"See ya, Danny," a couple of the other boys called to his brother as they left the school and made their way home. No one said goodbye to Nicholas.

They reached their street, and both slowed automatically. It was always a crapshoot as to what sort of state their mother would be in by the time they got home. With any luck, she'd be passed out on the sofa and they could go about making their own dinner—assuming there was anything in the fridge. The worst days were when she was angry. It was never any one thing in particular that she raged against—she was angry at the world, and everything was always someone else's fault. Accepting responsibility for her own actions was something she didn't understand. She liked to take out her fury on Nicholas. Sometimes she got angry with Danny as well, but more and more recently, it was her eldest son who bore the brunt. She never failed to tell him how she wished she'd never had him, how everything would have been all right if only she hadn't got knocked up. How she couldn't bear to look at him and his hideous face.

"I'm starving," Danny said, approaching the front door. "I hope she's got some food in."

"Yeah, there might be some money in her purse if she hasn't. We can go down the chippy."

"Now you're talking."

Danny put his key in the lock and opened the door. Instinctively, Nicholas braced himself.

Everything was quiet, and there was a bad smell in the air—even worse than normal. It had been a long time since the place had been properly cleaned. The bins went out on the odd occasion, when either their mother or one of them remembered the right day and which colour bin it was supposed to be, but the house stank of old rubbish.

Most children might call out that they were home, announcing their arrival and determining the location of their parent, but they weren't most children. If she was asleep, they certainly wouldn't do anything to wake her.

The boys exchanged a glance.

"Let's see what's to eat," Danny whispered, heading for the kitchen.

The atmosphere was all wrong. Was it possible she wasn't home? Alarm bells jangled in his head, his nerve endings lighting up and his skin crawling. He felt as though he was suddenly uncomfortable but wasn't sure why—like when he read something bad and then forgot about it but was still left with that same sense of unease, without quite knowing where it originated from.

They stepped into the kitchen, Danny leading the way. He came to a sudden halt, and Nicholas almost walked right into the back of him.

"Mum?"

Nicholas stepped around Danny.

Their mother lay on her back in the middle of the kitchen. On the worksurface was a plate and an open loaf of sliced white bread, and a cheap packet of ham. A knife sat on the floor to one side. A bite had been taken out of the bread.

Her eyes were open, she stared at the kitchen ceiling, but there was no life in them. The eyeballs seemed dry and foggy, and almost as though they weren't real at all. The stink of piss and shit that Nicholas had picked up on when entering the house suddenly grew stronger, and he realised where it originated.

"She must have choked." Danny's voice was devoid of emotion. "Stupid cow was trying to make herself a sandwich and she was probably so pissed she forgot how to chew." He snorted. "At least we've got food in the house."

Nicholas didn't think he'd ever be able to eat a ham sandwich again.

No, no, no, no, no, no.

A buzzing sounded in his ears, his heart racing, his breath suddenly coming short and fast.

Why was Danny being so calm about all of this?

They needed to call the police or an ambulance. They needed to get someone here to help them. But stupidly, in his panic, he couldn't remember where they kept the house phone.

"We need to call someone. The police," he managed to blurt.

But Danny's hand wrapped around his arm, and he glanced down at the spot where his brother's fingers encircled his wrist. His grip was hard, squeezing tight, creating a red ring on his skin.

"No, we can't."

Nicholas's mouth fell open. "What are you talking about? She's dead, Danny! We have to tell someone."

"Then what do you think is going to happen to us? Do you think they're going to let us keep living here together? No, they won't. They'll send us away. We'll be put into care, and teenage boys in care don't do so well. Those people take in teenage boys because they're perverts. You want to be diddled with, Nicholas? Because that's what's going to happen."

"No." He shook his head. "They're not all like that."

"Even if they're not, there's no way they'll let us stay together. We probably won't even be at the same school. No one takes in two teenage brothers. They'll separate us and send us to two different ends of the country. We might never see each other again."

"They can't do that..."

But his resolve was wavering.

"You're super smart in some areas, Nicholas, but not this one. You're not street smart. I'm the one who knows what goes on in real life, and you need to believe me when I say we can't let anyone else know about this."

He was still hanging on to Nicholas's wrist, his hold getting tighter and tighter with every word.

"But... But we can't just leave her there." He could barely tear his eyes away from his mother's lifeless body. Had he loved her? Was he supposed to mourn? Right now, he didn't feel anything other than shock.

Finally, Danny's hold loosened. "We won't. We'll figure this out."

Dirty dishes were stacked high in the sink. A single fly buzzed around the pile then flew lower to settle on their mother's face where it turned in a circle and headed towards her still open mouth.

Nicholas let out a cry of horror and darted forward, waving his hands to shoo away the insect. It lifted into the air, circled another couple of times, before flying into the kitchen window and bumping against the glass.

He shook his head, frantic. "We can't leave her here."

He couldn't get his thoughts away from the fly. Dead bodies attracted flies, and this was only a few hours since she'd died—he assumed. Within a day or two, there would be more, and she'd start to smell. He couldn't handle that.

"We won't." Danny looked around. "Maybe we can bury her in the back garden."

"Danny, no!"

He couldn't deal with this. His thoughts were bright darts of panic, pinging around inside his skull, trying to find a way out. He tried to suck in a lungful of air, but his chest refused to expand. Blood pounded through his ears.

Nicholas stumbled away, folding at the waist, his hands covering his head. This had to be some terrible nightmare, didn't it? He'd come home as normal and gone to bed, and now he was having a nightmare? Or maybe this whole day had been a dream, and he'd never gone to school that morning, and he was actually still in bed. Anything would be better than this.

A hand shoved his shoulder. "Go!"

Danny's voice felt distant, but the shove had snapped him back to at least a thread of reality. He didn't want to see their mother's body. It made him cold and hot, and dizzy and sick, all at the same time.

"I said go, Nicholas. Get out of here. I'll deal with this."

Deal with this? This wasn't some kid at school who'd been giving Nicholas a hard time. Their mother was dead on the kitchen floor. How did Danny think he was going to deal with it?

"I'll have to wait until it gets dark. We're too overlooked to bury her in the daytime."

He was actually planning on burying their mother in the back garden. This was insane.

Unable to handle it any longer, he staggered from the kitchen and ran for the stairs. There was only one place in the house where he'd ever felt remotely safe, and he ran for that place now.

Nicholas stumbled into the bedroom he shared with his brother—both of them still sleeping in the set of bunk beds, their feet hanging over the ends—and he sank down in the corner of the room, his back against the wall.

Nicholas tried to picture a future that no longer had their mother in it.

There had been occasions when she'd been good to them. One time, she'd spotted a giant chocolate birthday cake that had been reduced in the supermarket. She'd brought it home for them and covered it in candles which they took turns relighting and blowing out all over again, even though it was nowhere near any of their birthdays. It was moments like that where he felt like he got a glimpse of what life could have been like if she hadn't fallen head-first into a bottle of vodka. They could have been a happy, normal, fun family.

But even when she was happy, she was still drinking. He could see the change in her when she'd finally reached that point where she turned nasty. It was as though a wave hit her, the alcohol reaching her bloodstream, and she went from fun to nasty in a split second.

Yes, he would miss her, but there was also another emotion he didn't want to give too much thought to. Relief. What kind of person did that make him?

This was all too much for him, the pressure building inside his head, and he feared his brain would explode, sending his skull shattering outwards. A whine pealed from between his lips, and he hunched down, drawing his elbows into his sides, his knees up to his chest. If he could make himself small enough, maybe he would disappear altogether. But it wasn't working. He was trapped, caught inside this hideous body, with no way of escaping. He clenched his fists and brought them to his head. The first punch against his skull felt good—a release, of sorts—and without consciously thinking about what he was doing, he did it again. And again. And again. Soon he was pummelling his head, hitting and hitting and hitting. It felt as though he would never be able to stop, but eventually his arms grew tired. Plus, his head hurt.

He didn't know how much time had passed, but darkness fell outside.

Nicholas sat with his hands over his ears, trying to block out the sound of the spade hitting dirt, the rustle of Danny wrapping their mother's body in black bags, the sliding of him dragging her across the floor, the groans and curses of exertion as Danny struggled.

Danny was a big fourteen-year-old. He looked older and was developed for his age. Their mother had wasted away over the last few years, barely eating, surviving on the calories from alcohol. It was one thing that was going in their favour—at least she was easier to move.

Nicholas knew he should offer to help, but he couldn't bring himself to do it. If he'd been smaller, he'd have crawled back beneath the bunk beds and hidden until it was all over. Instead, he sat in the corner of their bedroom, his fists clenched and held to his head.

"Nicholas?"

He lifted his head at Danny's voice.

"It's done, Nicholas." His brother put out his hand to help him up. "Come and see."

Nicholas noted the dirt crusted beneath Danny's nails, but he took his brother's hand and allowed him to haul him to his feet. He was still lightheaded, and shivery, as though the cold had worked right into his bones.

"I don't want to," he muttered, keeping his gaze trained on the floor.

"Don't be an idiot. You have to come down to the kitchen some time."

He was right, but Nicholas was still worried about what he was going to see. If he had his way, he'd remain hiding in the bedroom and try to pretend none of this had happened, but he knew Danny wasn't going to let him get away with that. He allowed Danny to lead him back down the stairs. At the bottom, he sucked in a breath and squeezed his eyes shut for a second before stepping into the kitchen.

He didn't know what he thought he was going to see—maybe her ghost still lying in place on the floor—but the kitchen looked like it always did. If he hadn't been covering his ears for the past two hours, trying to hide the noise of her being buried, he'd have thought he'd imagined the whole thing.

Danny crossed the space, walking right over the spot where their mother's body had been a couple of hours earlier, and reached the back door. The key was sticking out of the lock, and Danny turned it with a click.

"There." He pulled the key out then opened a drawer and threw it inside. "Locked. We don't ever need to go out into the back garden again."

Nicholas stared at the back door, picturing the mound of earth that covered the body. "What if someone else goes out there? What if a fox or a dog tries to dig her up or something?"

"It's all walled off. No one else is going to go in the garden. And I made sure I dug the hole deep, so nothing is going to dig her up."

Nicholas shuddered. He didn't want to picture his mother's body, beneath the earth, with dogs or foxes scrabbling in the dirt, trying to get to the meat below.

"What about everything else? How are we going to feed ourselves? We need money, Danny. We can't live on air."

"She gets her dole money paid into her bank account every two weeks, and I know the PIN for her card. We'll go and withdraw it and use that to buy food. We'll probably eat better than we have in years now that she won't be drinking the money away."

He heard the bitterness in Danny's voice. Did his brother not feel bad at all that their mother was dead?

"What about bills and stuff?"

"They all come in the post. We'll open the letters and do whatever we need to." He locked his gaze on Nicholas, his eyes bright with something Nicholas didn't quite recognise. "It'll be better, just the two of us. We'll be fine. No one ever sees Mum anyway. All she did was sit in the house and drink. No one has to know."

"But what about Mum?"

Danny's jaw tightened. "What about her? She's dead. It's not like she gave a shit about us while she was alive, anyway. She was the worst to you, Nicholas. You should be happy she's dead!"

Nicholas hitched a breath. "She was still our mum."

"She was a crap mum. The worst. We're better off without her, and we don't owe her shit, okay?" His tone changed, growing harder. "I said *okay*?"

"Yeah, yeah. Okay."

It was done now. Nicholas didn't have any choice but to do what his brother said.

Chapter Eight

By the time Erica got back, Shawn was sitting at his desk, situated opposite hers.

"How did it go?" he asked, referring to things back home.

"As I thought it would. I'm going to have to make some hard decisions, but I really can't see any other way around it. My dad isn't going to get any better, and I can't expect Chris and Poppy to have to cope with him. It would be different if I was there, but..." She gestured around at the office, the busy buzz of all the various detectives working on different cases.

Could she give this up to stay at home with her father and take care of him twenty-four-seven? She wrestled with herself internally, not wanting to admit the truth to herself. Maybe she was being selfish, finding it easier and more fulfilling being out working than staying at home.

After she'd had Poppy and taken six months' maternity leave, she'd thought she might lose her mind spending another day doing nothing other than feedings, nappy changes, walks to the park, and mother and baby groups. She loved Poppy fiercely, adored the scent of the top of her baby-soft head, the cute little gurgles she made, the way she'd flap her arms and legs if she was excited. It wasn't that she hadn't bonded with her daughter, but there were times when she'd sat in those groups, with Poppy in her arms, listening to everyone talk about cluster feedings and reusable nappies, when she'd thought she might scream. It was as though all these women who probably had careers of their own before becoming mothers had stopped existing and had turned into these one-track-mind stereotypes. She felt horrible thinking it, and she'd smiled and tried her best to pretend she was interested as well, but the truth was she'd probably have crumbled if things had gone on that way.

Luckily, she had Chris, and he understood this was a partnership. He didn't view taking care of Poppy as babysitting or any of the other crap she heard from some mothers about the fathers of their children. With Erica going back to work, he was happy to work from home on his website design and online marketing business, and he had enjoyed getting to spend time there with Poppy.

It wasn't that she loved Poppy any less than any other mother—she adored her daughter and hoped she'd provide a role model for her that would show her that she could do or be anyone she wanted—but staying at home day in, day out, simply wasn't good for her mental health.

The same thing applied now with her dad. The idea of staying home with him crushed her soul.

Besides, it was a practical thing, too. It wasn't all about *her* needs. They needed the money as a family, and she was the main breadwinner. Even if Christopher went back full time, he still wouldn't be covering anything close to her income.

"So," Shawn said, changing the subject, "you want to see who our man is?"

"That's why I'm here."

He leaned past her to bring up the details on her computer. "Meet Lewis Jacobs. Nineteen years old, from Hackney. He's got one hell of an impressive rap sheet.

Arrested for drug possession on two occasions. Once for assault. He was sentenced to six months for robbery but got out in three."

She raised an eyebrow. "Only three months' jail time after all of that?"

He shrugged and exhaled a breath. "Prisons are bursting at the seams. Plus, the robbery was the only one he was charged with as an adult. All the others were before he turned eighteen."

"So, there's a chance this is gang related? He pissed off the wrong people, and this was payback?"

"Seems kind of extreme, but yeah, it's possible."

"The gangs are ruthless these days. So much violence on TV or video games, or online. The kids are getting immune to it."

Shawn raised both eyebrows. "Even so, taking out his eyes is insane. London is getting more violent, but I've never seen anything like this before. He fits the profile for a gangland stabbing, though. All these teenagers carry knives."

"What about his next of kin?" she asked. "Have they been notified yet?"

"We're still trying to track someone down, but right now it's not looking as though he had anyone. His mother died a couple of years ago, and he's been on his own since then. No sign of a father anywhere in the picture, or any siblings. We're trying to get hold of someone on his mother's side—we believe she has a sister in Birmingham—but I doubt Lewis was close to his aunt."

"Bloody hell."

That wasn't the news she wanted. It wasn't only that she felt bad for Lewis Jacobs not having anyone to sit by his bedside to hold his hand. Or that he wouldn't have someone with him over the coming days and weeks and months when he was going to have to navigate this new existence he'd woken in, though all of that was going to be immeasurably harder alone. It was that finding a next of kin who knew Jacobs well would have given them some insight into his life—often into things Jacobs might not have willingly revealed himself. Now they didn't have that treasure trove of information.

Erica pressed her lips together. "This all feels very methodical. This wasn't a crime of passion. Someone has taken their time over this." She thought of something else. "And you said the tox screen came back?"

"Yeah, that's right." Shawn focused on his computer, clicking his mouse to bring up the file. "A drug called Midazolam was in his system, together with alcohol and cannabis."

She frowned, not recognising the name. "Midazolam? What's that used for?"

"It's a sedative that's often used before or after a surgical procedure. It'll make someone sleepy and reduce anxiety, but it also works to decrease any memory of the procedure."

"So, the person who's been injected with it might not put up as much of a fight," she mused, "and then when they've been released, they wouldn't be freaking out, like we'd expect them to."

Shawn nodded in agreement. "Sounds like it fits the description that Becca Bird gave us of how the victim was acting when she came across him."

"It would also mean he might not remember much of what happened to him."

Her mind whirred, trying to piece everything together. While Lewis Jacobs might fit the profile of being the victim of a gangland stabbing, the MO didn't. How many gangs bothered to drug their victims like that? The stabbing tended to be fast and brutal, with the intention of getting the job done then getting the hell out of there, not holding them for any length of time.

Erica was thinking out loud. "So, they've snatched him, drugged him, held him somewhere while they cut out his eyes. But why let him go again? They must realise the victim would be able to speak to us and give us clues as to who took him. Even with the drugs in his system, he still might remember fragments of what had happened. It wasn't as though he was completely unconscious the whole time."

"Sending a message, perhaps," Shawn suggested.

"Or they want to be caught. Perhaps deep down they want to be punished for it. Or else they want to be stopped before they do it again?"

He looked at her in concern. "You think that might happen?"

"Maybe. And they might not let the next one live."

"Jesus." Shawn shook his head. "I'm not sure I'd *want* to live. Can you imagine waking up and discovering that someone's cut out your eyes?"

She pulled a face. "I'd rather not."

They were both silent for a moment. Unable to help herself, Erica pictured the horror of what Lewis Jacobs would go through when he woke. Would he have any memory of what had happened?

Shawn broke the silence. "I know where the gangs tend to hang out in that area. Think we should go down and have a chat? See if anyone knows or has seen anything? His friends might be aware of a spat he had with someone else."

Erica nodded. "Let me check if the victim is awake yet. If he's not, we'll go and have that chat."

• • • •

ERICA HAD MADE THE call to the hospital, but the victim was still unconscious and therefore was still unable to tell them anything. They had both her and Shawn's numbers and had promised to give them a call the moment the victim woke up.

She parked the unmarked Ford Mondeo on the street near Lewis Jacobs's home address. Around them rose tall grey high-rise blocks of flats. In the centre was a paved square lined by a handful of shops that had long since closed. Their signs, now covered in graffiti, still hung above the doors, indicating they'd once been a newsagent's, a fish and chip shop, and a charity shop. Poverty, and possibly the gangs that liked to think they owned this area, had run the businesses out of town, and now their windows were papered over and covered in peeling flyers. Several panes of glass were cracked.

In the middle of the square, a group of youths, aged anywhere from seventeen to twenty-one, hung out, parked up beside yet more graffiti-covered benches. The arrival of the unmarked car had caught their attention, and they'd stopped what they were doing to look over.

Erica took a breath. She never wanted to feel intimidated by anyone and hated that this group of lads made her feel that way. She was the one in charge here. But it was sensible to be cautious. More and more recently lately, these gangs proved just how dangerous they could be. All the extra funding in the world at police level didn't mean anything when they didn't have the funding to tackle the root causes. These young men were growing up in a society that told them this was their future practically from day one. The schools lacked decent teachers because anyone who was any good at their job quickly moved on from these areas. Youth clubs had been shut down, so there was nowhere for them to go in the evenings. Even their own homes in the high-rises were proving to be dangerous, and no one was doing anything about it. There was always a level of responsibility when it came to the choices of an individual, but it was difficult with the undercurrent of fear and violence in these communities. To these young men, it seemed to be a kill-or-be-killed situation.

"Ready?" she asked Shawn.

"As I'll ever be."

He swung open the car door, and she followed, pressing the button on the key fob to lock the door after them. She didn't think the gang would steal an unmarked police car from right under their noses, but she wouldn't put it past them.

Shawn looked tough, like he could have been one of the gang ten years ago. He had that air about him, that same kind of swagger. In a different life, if he'd made a few other choices and followed another path, he most likely would have ended up like one of these youths.

Erica hung back slightly, allowing him to take the lead.

"You guys got a sec?" Shawn called out to them.

It took them a minute, suspicion in their eyes, perhaps momentarily wondering if he was from a different part of the city. But then they spotted Erica lurking in the background, and the penny dropped.

"Fucking pigs," one of them spat. "We ain't done nothin.'"

Shawn lifted both hands. "Relax. We only want to talk."

One of the men squared his shoulders and stepped forward. "We don't have to talk to you."

Erica sniffed the air and glanced to Shawn. "You smell that?"

Shawn nodded, seeing where she was going. "I think we have enough reason to carry out a stop and search."

Erica took her turn. "And if we happen to find something illegal on your persons, that will give us enough cause to arrest you and take you down to the station. You'll have to talk to us there."

The man who'd stepped forward looked between them. "This is fucking bullshit."

"Is it?" Erica raised her eyebrows.

"Or you could just tell us what we want to know," Shawn suggested. "Save all of us a whole heap of trouble."

The young man's shoulders slumped.

"Yeah, all right. What do you want to know about?"

"Do you know Lewis Jacobs?" Erica asked.

The young men exchanged glances. The raised eyebrows and widened eyes suggested they did.

"Told you he was probably banged up," one of them hissed to the other.

"Shut the fuck up, Fitz," the man who'd stepped forward snapped.

"You shut up, Morgan," the one named Fitz said to him. "He'd better not have turned into a grass."

"He's in hospital," Shawn butted in. "That's why we need to talk to you."

The young man frowned. "Hospital? Why, what's happened?"

"That's what we're hoping you can help us figure out. He's been badly attacked. We think it's highly doubtful that he did it to himself, so we want to find out who did."

Morgan scowled. "Can't he tell you?"

"He's unconscious right now," Erica stepped forward, "so he can't tell us anything."

The men gave her that flick of their eyes, from head to foot, as though trying to assess if she was someone they'd either want to fuck with or to fuck. She'd come across plenty of their kind before. They were young, immature, full of bravado, but would take a life without thinking of the consequences if someone rubbed them up the wrong way. They also had zero respect for anyone in authority.

"We need to know, when was the last time you saw him?"

They passed a look between them, and then Morgan, the one who seemed to be the ringleader, shrugged. "Dunno. A couple of nights ago, at least."

"I assume you guys see a fair amount of each other."

That same shrug again. "Yeah, we hang out. No law against that."

No, but there is against what it is you do while you're hanging out. She managed to keep her mouth shut. They weren't here to arrest anyone for possession or even conspiracy to supply. They were here to find out the last known movements of the victim.

"Did you try to call him?"

"Yeah, but he wasn't answering." Morgan frowned as he tried to remember. "It didn't even ring, just went through to answerphone."

"You didn't think to search for him when he didn't show up or answer his phone?" Shawn asked.

"Nah, not really. Figured he'd got himself into something he shouldn't have."

"He's a lucky bloke to have such a caring group of friends." She couldn't help the sarcasm lacing her tone.

He shot her a narrow-eyed glare. "Lewis is a big boy. He can do whatever the fuck he likes."

"But he was in trouble," she persisted. "If you'd raised the alert sooner, maybe we could have done something to prevent what happened."

He snorted in derision. "Seriously? You think if we'd contacted the cops and told him one of our boys was missing they'd have paid the slightest bit of attention? They'd assume he'd got himself into a bit of trouble, and that he probably deserved everything he was getting."

There was an element of truth in what he said.

"Okay." Shawn nodded his thanks. "Appreciate your time."

Erica took that as her cue for them to leave, and she turned and headed back to the car, happy to be out of there. A press on the key fob sent the Mondeo's lights flashing and the clunk of the doors unlocking.

"They didn't know anything," Shawn said as he climbed back into the passenger seat.

She was happy to be back in the sanctuary of the car. "Not that they'd tell us anything if they did."

Erica started the car and pulled away from the group of youths, still watching their progress, perhaps wanting to make sure they actually left.

Shawn rubbed his stomach. "I'm bloody starving. You want to grab something to eat?"

She'd only managed that piece of toast so far today and realised she was ravenous as well. It was well past lunchtime.

"Absolutely. I think we've earned it."

She made sure she'd put enough distance between them and the gang before she spotted a small greasy spoon café and pulled into the nearest parking spot. They climbed back out and headed inside, the air thick with the aroma of coffee and frying grease.

Her stomach rumbled.

They took a seat by the window.

Coffee, black," she ordered, "and a bacon roll."

"I'll have the same," Shawn said, "only make the coffee white, thanks."

The waitress smiled at them.

Shawn leaned back in his seat, his long legs spread either side of the small table. It was something that would normally piss Erica off, but she was only five feet three and didn't need much space. Besides, she was used to Shawn.

Their order arrived, and Erica reached into her bag and took out a miniature bottle of hot sauce. Strong tastes had always been her thing.

Shawn rolled his eyes at her shaking it over her bacon roll. "I'm surprised you haven't added that to your coffee."

She threw him a grin. "Who says I haven't?"

He laughed. "What a way to wake up."

Erica rubbed her hands over her face. "I'll try anything lately. I'm feeling old."

He knew better than to mention her upcoming birthday. "You're not old at all."

She lifted her face from her hands. "What would you know? You're still in your twenties."

He rolled his eyes. "And you're not much older."

"Come on, I'm practically a whole generation older than you."

"No, you're not! You're what," he thought for a moment, "six years older."

"Six years might not seem like a lot, but by the time you've got married and had a kid, and you're stuck between an ageing father and your young daughter, it certainly feels like a lot."

"Yeah, well, I wouldn't know much about all of that."

The reproach in his tone surprised her. Shawn had always been the easy-going, single, happy-to-be-on-his-own kind of bloke, and he'd never given her any sign that he wanted anything different. He hadn't even had a long-term girlfriend in the time she'd known him. Sure, he'd mentioned the occasional names of women he'd met in the pub at weekends, or even online, but no one he'd ever taken seriously. He was still young, after all. It was different with men, though, wasn't it? They often waited until they were older before they settled down.

She needed to get her thoughts away from her personal life and back to the case.

"Anyway," she said, "where are we on the case?"

"I don't think it's gang related."

She took a sip of her coffee, burning her mouth. "Me either. The use of the drugs points towards it being someone who has some experience of a medical setting, and the fact they took the victim's eyes keeps playing on my mind. Why would they do that?"

"To stop someone seeing," Shawn offered. "Maybe they don't like people looking at them."

She pointed her bacon roll at him. "Exactly. And why don't people like being looked at?"

He shrugged. "I don't know. Maybe they have something they're ashamed of. A deformity of some kind."

"So, someone with a deformity, who possibly works in the medical profession, and who doesn't like people looking at them. Jesus. What kind of lunatic are we dealing with?"

A buzzing came from Shawn's pocket, and he pulled out his mobile phone and swiped the screen to answer. He listened for a few moments then said, "Yeah, we'll be right there."

He ended the call and raised his eyebrows at Erica. "Lewis Jacobs is awake."

Chapter Nine

PC Stephen Buckley was still in charge of watching over the victim. He rose wearily from his chair as the two detectives entered the hospital room, his palm pressed to his spine as though sitting in one spot for so long had given him a backache.

"Mr Jacobs," the officer said to the man lying in the bed. "Two detectives are here to talk to you."

Lewis Jacobs didn't respond. He was in the same position as he'd been when they'd left him, his face turned towards the window. The top half of his face was wrapped in bandages.

"I'm DI Swift," Erica told Jacobs, "and I have DS Turner with me."

Lewis Jacobs still didn't say anything, and Buckley gave Erica a tight-lipped smile as though to say, 'good luck.'

"You look like you could use a break," Erica told the officer.

She imagined he must be getting fed up of sitting in a room, but until they got a statement off the victim, she hadn't wanted anyone else attempting to influence Lewis Jacobs's recollection of events. Plus, they'd needed to have someone available to take notes should Jacobs have said anything before they'd arrived that might be useful in the case. She noted how Jacobs's bedside had been ominously free of visitors. How sad that Jacobs didn't have anyone in his life who cared enough about him to visit him in hospital.

Buckley nodded. "Yeah, I could use a coffee and some fresh air. I won't be too long."

"I'll just step out with you," she said.

Buckley nodded at Shawn then moved past him. Erica followed him out so she could speak to the officer in the hallway without the victim overhearing.

"Has he said anything since he woke up?" she asked Buckley when the door had swung shut behind them.

Buckley pursed his lips and shook his head. "Nothing of any relevance, sorry. The staff have only just managed to calm him down. Understandably, he was extremely distressed. The doctor was talking about sedating him again, but I managed to convince him not to until after you'd spoken to him. Luckily, Jacobs calmed down after that, but it's like he's gone the other way, and is barely responsive at all. I'm not sure how much you're going to get out of him."

"Okay, thank you. I'll try to speak with the doctor as well. Was it the same one as before?"

"Yes, Ms Arora."

Erica left Buckley to go and get his coffee and hit of fresh air, and she re-entered the room.

The ICU Staff Nurse with the impressive shelf of a bosom, Jeanne Hay, had followed them in. "Take it easy on him," she said to Erica. "He's been through a lot, and he's probably still in shock. It's a lot to cope with."

Erica nodded. "I'm sure he'll want us to find whoever did this as much as we do."

Though Jacobs was facing the window, it occurred to Erica that he wouldn't have any idea there was a window there, or that the late sunlight filtered through the slats of the blind. It wasn't the bandages preventing him from seeing the light. There was nothing beneath the dressing other than twin holes—or would his eyelids have been sewed up? She didn't even know. Many people who were legally blind still had some idea of light or dark, some even were still able to make out shapes. There was no possibility of him ever regaining his sight. He'd never see the sunlight again.

"Mr Jacobs?" she said gently. "We're hoping to ask you a few questions about what happened to you. Is that all right?"

At first, she didn't think he'd heard her, that perhaps he'd gone back to sleep. It was hard to tell. But then he gave an almost imperceptible nod.

"What do you remember about what happened to you?" she asked.

"Not much." His voice was gruff, as though he hadn't spoken for a long time. "I remember the woman in the street—the one who helped me. I remember the ambulance arriving, and the police. But not much either before or after that."

His hands tightened in the hospital bedsheets, wringing them out, his knuckles white.

"That's okay. Some of it might come back to you as we go along." She checked her notes and read out the address they'd had on file for him. "Is that where you live, Mr Jacobs?"

He nodded. "Yes, it is."

"Do you live with anyone else?"

"No, I live on my own. It's a council flat."

"Have you got a girlfriend? Any children?"

"No. I'm only nineteen. What the fuck would I want with kids?"

Erica smiled reassuringly but then realised he wouldn't be able to see it. She hoped he'd hear the smile in her tone. "What about work? Do you have a job, or study?"

He scoffed laughter. "Study? No chance. I left school the first moment I got. Couldn't wait to get out of there. I work, when I can. Tends to be contract stuff on building sites."

"And you've done that since you left school."

"Yeah, on and off."

Erica remembered his rap sheet. "The times where you weren't working, was that when you were in jail?"

His lips tightened. "That's right."

"Do you know if you made any enemies during your time inside, or even on the outside? Anyone who would have wanted to do this to you?"

He gave a small shrug. "I'm always pissing off someone or another, but for someone to have done this..." He lifted his hand to his face, hovering his fingers above the bandages as though he couldn't quite bring himself to touch them. "Nah, I don't know anyone I would have pissed off enough to want to have done this to me."

"Even so, if you could give us a list of names, we'll go and have a chat with those people, just to make sure on our end."

Erica glanced over her shoulder to where Shawn stood with his pen and paper, making notes of everything that was being said.

Jacobs reeled off a list of names, and Shawn jotted them down. Erica didn't know how truthful Jacobs was being.

There was a possibility he knew who'd done this and was too afraid to tell them.

She moved on to the day in question. "Tell me about what happened that day. Let's start with you getting up that morning. Talk me through it."

"It was just a normal day. I was working most of it, then hung out with some mates after."

"What are the names of the people you hung out with?"

He told her, and she recognised some of the names from the gang she and Shawn had spoken to.

"What did you do when you 'hung out?'" she asked.

"We went down the pub for a couple of beers."

"Which pub?"

"The Crown and Anchor," he told her.

"What time did you arrive, and when did you leave?"

"We got there around nine, I think, and then I left just after kick-out, so I guess that would have been about quarter past eleven."

Erica nodded. "Okay, and did you leave on your own?"

"Yeah, I did. The others were talking about going on somewhere else, but I was knackered from working all day, and I was pretty broke as well, so I thought I'd just go home and crash in front of the TV."

"Good. You're doing really well, Mr Jacobs. I'm sorry we're having to go into so much detail. Let me know if I can get you anything—a drink of water, perhaps."

He let out a sigh. "I don't want anything."

"Okay." Erica continued, "And then, on your way home, do you remember what happened?"

"I remember walking home from the pub. I thought someone was following me, but I wasn't bothered. I can handle myself, you know, or at least I've always been able to before. But he came up behind me, and I think he must have injected me with something. I felt this sharp pain in my neck, and then when I tried to turn around, my legs wouldn't work properly. I was dizzy, and I remember falling. Someone was standing over me, but I didn't get a look at him. He was just a shape. Then the next time I woke up, I was somewhere dark."

"Did you recognise anything?" she asked.

"No. All I remember was that it was dark and the floor was hard. I think he must have injected me again, 'cause everything fades out from then until I came back round on the street."

"What about your other senses? Could you hear or smell anything?"

He thought for a moment. "I think I heard a rumbling, like a train, but I don't know if I was dreaming."

"Any alarms? Sirens?" she pressed.

He shook his head.

"What about the person who took you? What did they sound like?"

"Male. Young."

She nodded, though Lewis Jacobs couldn't see her. "What about an accent? Did they have one?"

"Local, I guess. London, but not strong."

"Okay, that's good," Erica encouraged him. A young male from the local area didn't give them much to go on, but it was something. "Let's narrow things down a little. Did you recognise the voice? Do you think it might have been someone you know?"

"No one I know would dare to do this to me." There was anger in his tone now.

She didn't want to rile him further, but she needed to ask. "We know a little about your background, Mr Jacobs. You have a history. If this was some kind of deal gone wrong, we need to know about it."

He twisted his face towards her, even though he was unable to see her. "This wasn't a deal gone wrong. Who the fuck even does this to another person?"

"That's what we're trying to find out, Mr Jacobs."

To her dismay, he broke down, a great shuddering sob shaking his body. He covered his face with both hands, and the noise that came out of him was enough to break hearts.

The nurse stepped in again. "I think we're done for today." She increased her volume, as though he was deaf instead of blind. "It's okay, Lewis. Try to calm down. I'm going to give you something to help you sleep." She injected something from a vial into the bottom of the bag of fluids that led to the drip threading into a vein in his arm.

Even though Lewis Jacobs was the kind of man who would normally be Erica's enemy on the street, it was impossible not to feel sorry for him. His life had changed beyond all recognition. All the things he'd taken for granted no longer existed. She hadn't seen any sign of any of his so-called friends coming to see him. It wasn't as though they'd made much of an effort when they'd realised he was missing, either. His blindness was a massive vulnerability, and being vulnerable in their world was never a good thing.

He wouldn't be able to slip back into his old life. Everything had changed.

"We'll leave you to rest," she said. "Thank you for your time."

She exchanged a glance with Shawn, who gave her a closed-lipped smile. They left the room to find Buckley on his way back.

Was there a risk of whoever had done this to Lewis Jacobs coming back and finishing the job? She didn't think so. The culprit had plenty of opportunity to kill Jacobs, and he'd chosen not to.

"How did it go?" Buckley asked.

"We got what we could from him," Erica said. "I can't see any more reason for you needing to stay any longer. Thanks for your help."

He nodded his gratitude, clearly relieved to be able to make his escape. He turned back down the hospital corridor, his shoes squeaking on the shiny floor.

She sighed again and turned back to her sergeant. "What do you think?"

"Someone clearly planned this, and they knew who they were going after. They would have needed to know what dosage of the drug they'd need in order to render him unconscious long enough to move him."

"He was moved twice," she pointed out. "Once to the location where he was held, and then away from that location to be left on the street. If he was moved, he must have been caught on CCTV at some point." She paused, mentally going over everything Jacobs had told her. "We need to go to the Crown and Anchor, speak to whoever was tending bar that night, and also see if they've got CCTV installed. I need to know if DC Howard and Rudd have spoken with the park warden as well. They might have found out something that we can go on."

"I'll check with them," Shawn said.

She let out a sigh. "Thanks. I have something I need to deal with at home, so I'm going to leave you to it."

He flashed her a smile. "Leave it in my capable hands, you mean?"

"Yeah, something like that. I'll catch up with you later."

There was a call she had to make that had nothing to do with the case. As much as she wanted to work all night, she had other responsibilities.

• • • •

ERICA STARED DOWN AT her phone, wishing there was a way around this but knowing there wasn't. It didn't help that she was exhausted now as well. She needed to get some sleep before her next shift started, and if her dad was having a bad night, sleep was going to be hard to come by. But she'd made a promise to Chris that things would change, and she had to keep to that promise. As hard as it was, they couldn't keep going like this.

With a heavy heart, she dialled the number.

"You've reached Willow Glade Care Home. How can I help?"

"Yes, hello. My name is Erica Swift. I have contacted you before about my dad. I was putting out some feelers at the time, because he's not been well, but we were hoping to still be able to take care of him at home, only..."

"Things haven't been going well?" the woman on the other end of the line filled in for her.

"No, they haven't. Not at all. We're all struggling to cope. My husband—" She suddenly found herself close to tears and reined herself back in. "My husband has been great, but he's home all day with my dad, and my dad doesn't really recognise or remember him half the time."

Willow Glade Care Home specialised in dementia care. It wasn't going to be cheap, but what choice did they have?

"Would you like to bring your dad in for a visit? See what he thinks of the place?"

"Yes, I guess so. Sorry I'm not more enthusiastic. I'm just struggling with the decision."

"Everyone feels like you do, Mrs Swift. That's if the patient is lucky enough to have someone so caring in their lives. You feel bad because you love your dad, but you're making the right choice for him. There are a lot of elderly people out there who don't have that."

She sniffed. "Thank you. It's not easy."

"It never is. How about you bring him in at nine tomorrow morning, and we'll see what you all think of the place?"

"Yes, okay. I'll do that."

She still felt horrible, but there was a shred of relief as well. She'd started the process, and even though she dreaded it, at least she'd finally stepped onto the path.

How her dad was going to react, however, was a whole different ball game.

Chapter Ten: Ten Years Earlier

Jeering and shouts of encouragement drew Nicholas's attention.

It was lunchtime, and he had found himself a spot behind one of the school's Portakabins that were currently acting as additional classrooms until more permanent ones could be built.

No one knew their mother was dead.

Money was tight, but it appeared in her account with surprising regularity. Danny pointed out that some of it was child benefit money anyway, so it was basically theirs to do with as they wished. They lived on toast and cereal and pasta, but that was fine by them. As long as they had food in their bellies, they'd survive.

Nicholas normally ignored any signs of a fight, knowing that looking how he did was a sure-fire way of giving someone an excuse to get him involved. He didn't fare well in fights. But something about the yells and heckling sent swirls of unease spiralling around his stomach, and he found himself forgetting his lunch and rising to his feet.

A crowd was gathered in a circle, their attention focused on someone in the middle. He didn't know what instinct made him so sure it was his brother who was in trouble, but deep in his gut, he knew it was.

"Hey!" Nicholas pushed his way through the crowd, using his elbows and shoulders to barge people out of the way. He received a couple of shouts of annoyance but ignored them, his only focus on getting to his brother.

Danny stood between two other lads, his fists balled, his upper lip curled in anger. Blood was smeared from his nostrils, and his left eye was swollen and already darkening. Danny's attention darted from one of the boys to the other, trying to assess who was going to throw the next punch. The lads didn't look like they'd got off lightly either, one with a graze across his cheek and the other with a fat lip. But there were still two of them, and only one of his brother.

"What the fuck?" Nicholas declared, muscling between them to stand at his brother's side. "Two of you against one. Real fair."

Nicholas never showed his anger or stood up to anyone. He lived by the rule of keeping his head down and hoping no one even noticed he existed. But there was no way he was going to stand there and do nothing while two of them beat up his younger brother.

One of the other boys, who Nicholas thought was called Theo, but who was the year below, so he didn't know well—not that Nicholas really knew anyone at school well—pointed at Danny.

"He asked for it! Said he'd be able to take two of us on at once. He was the one who started it."

Nicholas turned to Danny. "That true? Did you start it?"

Danny scowled at the ground. "What the fuck does it matter?"

"Of course it matters," he snapped. "You know it fucking matters."

He was bracing himself for the shout of a teacher, demanding to know what was going on here and for them to break it up. But the fight was over now—almost as though it was a fight the other two boys hadn't really wanted to be involved in in the first place. Some of the onlookers had sensed things were finished with and were already wandering off, bored and in search of the next bit of entertainment.

Nicholas grabbed Danny's elbow and yanked him through the remaining spectators. He was surprised no one had used the opportunity to throw a few insults at him, but maybe they were frightened of Danny's reaction. He was clearly geared up for a fight.

When he got far enough away from the others to avoid them overhearing, he let go of Danny's elbow and spun to face him.

"What the fuck do you think you're doing?"

"Nothing." Danny's lower lip jutted out, and he refused to meet Nicholas's eye.

In that flash of a moment, Nicholas saw him for the fifteen-year-old boy he was and not the little brother he'd admired all his life. Nicholas was sixteen now and was about to sit his GCSEs, and this time next year, he wouldn't be here to watch out for Danny. He planned on getting a job, though he had no idea what he'd be doing. His maths predicted grade was an A, as was his physics, but he'd be lucky to get a grade at all in most of his other subjects, including English, that would have allowed him to continue with his education. Not that getting A-levels or anything else was even an option. He needed to find a job as soon as he'd finished his exams in a couple of months. Who would want to employ him, though? With his face, it wasn't as though he could do a job where he had to deal with customers, and he wasn't any good with people, anyway. He could never bring himself to look anyone in the eye, and if someone he didn't know tried to talk to him, he blushed to the roots of his hair. But he wasn't exactly practical either, and doubted he'd be able to work on a building site or pick up a trade.

Whatever it was, he needed to do *something*. The other week, they'd had a letter from the government asking for proof that his mother had been actively seeking work, and he was pretty sure when she didn't turn up to some meeting or other, they'd cut off the benefits. They'd still get the child benefit money—the small amount of research he'd done told him they'd get that money whether or not she was in employment—but she wouldn't get it if they found out she was dead. That the house was owned by the council worried him, too. What if the people in charge of the benefit money talked to the council, and they started putting two and two together?

If they got found out, they'd already decided they'd tell people she'd gone out drinking and simply hadn't come home one day. They'd be honest and say it had happened months ago but would try to be vague about the date. They didn't want any nosy neighbours remembering a specific date and saying they hadn't seen her leaving the house or anything like that. That was the trouble with a lie—someone was always trying to catch you out.

"You can't get in trouble, Danny!" Nicholas focused his attention on his brother. "You're going to draw too much attention to us. You know we need to keep our heads down."

"I have been. That wasn't my fault. Those pricks were talking shit about us, saying we stink and stuff."

"Then you just have to let them. What if the head had seen you fighting? What if he'd wanted to get Mum in here to talk it over? How would we explain that?"

Danny's shoulders sank, and he scuffed the ground with his foot. "Yeah, all right. I get it."

Nicholas allowed himself to breathe. "Good."

His brother had changed since that day they'd come home and found their mother. Nicholas knew he should have helped Danny bury her. He let his younger brother shoulder that responsibility alone, and it had changed him. Danny had moved into their mother's bedroom, so they no longer shared the set of bunk beds. He locked himself away, listening to music and not speaking to Nicholas, even when Nicholas banged on the bedroom door and asked him if everything was okay.

Everything wasn't okay. Their mother's corpse was decomposing in the back garden. Neither of them had been out there since that day, and the patches of grass were getting high. Had her body started to smell? They didn't even dare open the windows at the rear of the house out of fear that they'd catch a whiff of her.

One time, Nicholas had mentioned to Danny about the possibility of her corpse smelling and the neighbours noticing, but Danny had told him not to be such a dickhead. He pointed out that graveyards didn't smell, even though they had loads of bodies buried in them. Nicholas didn't say that maybe that was because something was done to the bodies in the funeral home and that they had caskets and were buried six feet deep. But he kept his mouth shut.

Mentioning all those things wasn't going to help or change anything.

Before this had happened, even when they'd had to deal with their mother's drinking, Danny had been the sunshine child. He'd been confident and reasonably happy, despite their horrendous home life.

Now, even Danny's skin seemed to have reacted to his emotional turmoil, and his normally clear complexion was now peppered with spots. Maybe it was his age, and his skin would have flared up even if their mother hadn't died, but Nicholas couldn't help feeling it was more.

The end of school finally arrived, and the two boys walked home as normal.

Nicholas had always hated coming home because he'd never known what he was going to walk into, but even with their mother dead, he still felt the same way. He was on edge all the time, waiting for this all to blow up. Plus, it was impossible to be anywhere near their house without constantly picturing her body beneath the ground. He'd done his best to avoid anything that might get him thinking about what sort of condition her body would be in by now, but he'd watched enough horror films in his time to be able to picture it with a clarity that was all too sharp.

Danny locked himself in the bathroom, and seconds later, the thunder of the shower echoed through the door.

Nicholas paused outside the bathroom then glanced over to the room that had once been their mother's. He hadn't been in there since it had all happened, even after Danny had taken it over. But something now told him he needed to go in there and learn what was becoming of his brother. He didn't know if he could help, but he knew he had to at least try. He hadn't helped Danny when he should have done, but he was going to now, if he could.

Tentatively, he pushed open the door.

He reared back at the stink of stale sweat and something else, sweet but sour. He recognised the smell, and his heart sank.

Rubbish had been stuffed under the bed, and Nicholas bent down to pick up one of the items.

An empty plastic bottle.

A two-litre bottle of cider. It wasn't something their mother ever drank. She'd preferred vodka and wine. Nicholas knew this empty bottle belonged to Danny. It was the cheapest money could buy. He guessed that was a good thing. It wasn't as though they had spare money to waste on booze, but the presence of the empty bottle left Nicholas sick with worry. Was this going to be Danny's future? Was he going to go the same way as their mother, and one day Nicholas would come home to discover his brother's body on the kitchen floor? He'd be all alone. He'd come to rely on his brother so much that now he couldn't imagine a world where Danny was no longer in it. What would become of him then?

I should have helped Danny, he berated himself for the thousandth time. He should have gone through burying their mother's body with him instead of hiding in his bedroom. Maybe then Danny would feel he had someone who understood the terrible secret he was forced to bear, the horrific memories, the nightmares. Nicholas heard him when he woke up screaming in the night, though Danny shouted for him to go away if Nicholas tried to ask if he was all right.

In the bathroom, the shower turned off again, and Nicholas quickly dropped the bottle and backed out of the room. He made it down the hallway before Danny emerged from the bathroom, a threadbare towel wrapped around his narrow waist.

"All right?" Danny threw a suspicious glance in Nicholas's direction.

Nicholas nodded, all his resolve to confront Danny melting away. "Yeah, fine."

Danny was the only person he had left. What if he challenged Danny about the drinking, and his questions and concern pissed Danny off, and he decided to leave, too?

It was safer to keep his mouth shut.

Chapter Eleven

The group of young men stumbled out of the bar on the back street of Whitechapel.

The cool London air hit Mitchell Walters, and he suddenly realised how drunk he was. They'd come straight out, drinking as soon as they'd finished work, and he hadn't had anything to eat since a greasy steak bake from Greggs at lunchtime. He was sure he was going to regret drinking so much tomorrow morning. Spending a day in the office with a stinking hangover was not his idea of fun, but it was too late now. The damage was done.

He staggered, the ground tilting on its axis for a moment before righting itself.

His friends noticed.

"You are such a fucking lightweight, Mitchell," Simon teased. "I swear you were going to throw up after that last shot."

"Get screwed," he threw back. "I can hold my drink better than you can. I remember when you puked all over my sofa when you crashed at mine a couple of years ago. You're not one to talk."

Not that they were friends, really. They were work colleagues. If Mitchell had a problem and needed to speak to someone, he'd never even consider picking up the phone to one of these arseholes. They were fine to share a couple of beers with, but that was all.

Simon threw both hands in the air and laughed. "I told you, it must have been a bad kebab."

The other bloke they were with, Paul, rolled his eyes. "Yeah, yeah. Like we haven't heard that before."

Something caught Mitch's eye, and he slowed, squinting in the direction of a shape in the doorway of one of the shops that had closed for the night. "What's he doing?"

"Leave it, dude." Simon shook his head. "It's just another homeless guy. They're all over the city now. You can barely cross the road without someone asking you for change."

Paul wrinkled his nose. "They really need to get a job and sort their lives out."

Mitch cocked an eyebrow. "Fucking hell. Got much empathy, there, Paul? It's not always their fault they end up homeless. Marriages break down, or they have gambling issues."

"Yeah." Simon snorted. "That could be you in a few years, Paul, after your missus chucks you out."

"He's got to get a missus first," Mitch retorted, enjoying taking Paul down a peg or two.

The bloke had some seriously messed up views about people. Just because he'd come from a decent background and had had everything handed to him on a plate—from his private education, to the banking job his dad had lined up for him—he thought he was entitled to look down on everyone else.

Paul grabbed his crotch and thrust it out. "I don't need one woman holding me back. I've got a whole row of birds out there desperate for my cock."

Mitchell chuckled. "The only desperate one is you."

"Fuck you, Mitch."

"I'll pass, thanks."

His attention was once more drawn to the bundle in the doorway. Maybe Simon was right, and it was a homeless person who probably wanted to be left alone, but something about them didn't seem right. They were on their knees and huddled over, with their hands over their head. They were clearly in distress, and just because they were homeless didn't mean they were any less likely to be in need of help. He hoped if he were ever needing help, someone would be kind enough to stop and see if he was all right.

Mitch came from a different background to Simon and Paul. He'd come from a rough area, where he was used to finding people sleeping on his doorstep. His parents had often struggled for money, and they'd all shared a tiny two-bedroom flat that was rented and often cold and damp. Food banks hadn't really been around when he'd been a kid, but he could understand how easy it was to find yourself ending up needing to use one. The majority of people were only a couple of months paycheques away from being homeless themselves.

Of course, Paul could always run back to Daddy, so he didn't care.

Mitchell took a couple of steps towards the homeless man.

"Leave it, Mitchell," Simon called after him. "He's probably wasted or something."

A security light was in the shop window. Mitchell frowned. The man in the doorway sported a pair of black brogues, not the normal holey trainers he'd expected to see. The trousers looked tidy as well. What was a smartly dressed man doing hunched in a shop doorway, his arms over his head, rocking back and forth?

Had something happened to him?

Mitchell couldn't help himself. He took another step closer. "Hey, mate? Are you all right?"

"For fuck's sake, Mitch," Paul said from behind him, a hint of panic to his tone.

Simon joined in. "Yeah, come on. Let's go."

But Mitchell couldn't walk away. He scanned the doorway for empty cans of cheap cider, or maybe an empty bottle of vodka, even a syringe or two, something to make him understand what was happening here. But the space was free of anything like that. There weren't even any squashed down cardboard boxes for the homeless man to sit on, or any blankets or other belongings, for that matter.

That's because he's not homeless. Something is wrong with him.

It wasn't like him to be this nervous of someone. His heart was racing too fast, his mouth suddenly dry, his tongue coated with a sour fur of stale alcohol. The sense of everything being off balance returned, bringing with it a bout of vertigo, and he found himself wanting to follow the advice of his work colleagues and put as much distance between himself and the man in the doorway as possible.

"Did something happen to you?" he asked the possibly homeless man. "Do you need me to call the police or an ambulance?"

The man in the doorway lifted his head.

The sight of him hit Mitchell like a punch to the chest. Instead of eyes, his sockets were gaping holes wadded with bloody cotton or tissue. In the faint overhead illumination of the security light, he appeared to be a talking skull.

"Help me," the man croaked. "I think I'm blind."

Mitchell let out a yelp and staggered backwards, into the arms of his colleagues.

"What?" Paul asked. "What is it?"

They'd been too far back to see, Mitchell's body blocking the view. He didn't want to deal with this, his mind reeling. Had he seen what he thought he had, or had he had too much to drink, like Simon had said? Maybe it had been a trick of the light? There was no way a man was sitting in the doorway with his eyes missing. That was the stuff of horror films and nightmares.

His colleagues, clearly glad Mitch had come away from what they assumed to be a wasted homeless man, had already looped their arms around his shoulders, guiding him away. The three of them were joined in a swaying, staggering, four-legged race.

Mitchell dared to glance over his shoulder to where they'd left the man. His head was back down, his arms covering his face.

Yeah, he'd imagined things. A trick of the light. Too much to drink.

All those things made more sense than the truth.

Chapter Twelve

Erica woke with her stomach a knot of anxiety.

She'd worked late into the night and had finally come home to crawl into bed for a few hours. Howard and Rudd hadn't turned up any new leads by talking to the park warden, and because of the area—off the high street, and with no adjacent houses or businesses—there hadn't been any CCTV footage. An intensive search of the cemetery hadn't revealed any new victims, but it also hadn't revealed anywhere that the incident had happened either.

She'd hoped they'd get more from the search, but it had quite literally proved to be a dead end.

A couple of other detectives had gone to the Crown and Anchor and spoken to the young woman who'd been tending the bar the night Jacobs had been taken, but she hadn't noticed anything unusual, and, frustratingly, the CCTV hadn't been working that night. Apparently, the bartender had commented that the cameras were mostly for show anyway and were rarely actually running.

She had to put the case out of her mind. For the next few hours, at least, she had to be Erica the daughter, instead of Erica the detective.

She shrank inside at the prospect of what lay ahead.

It was crazy. She dealt with drug dealers and wife beaters and child abusers—the absolute scum of society—in her everyday life, but the thought of getting her stubborn, fiercely independent father into a home to be looked after made her more nervous than any of those things.

It broke her heart that she was having to do this.

They were only visiting today, but, assuming all went well, they'd be taking her dad back again, to stay this time, in another couple of days. Right now, she couldn't imagine how this was going to go well. It was bad enough when they'd moved him from his home into her place, and it wasn't as though he didn't know her house. It was already familiar to him, and he'd still been confused and angry. Now they were taking him to somewhere he didn't know in the slightest.

Chris was already in the shower, the water thundering onto the porcelain, and so she quickly checked her phone to see if there were any messages or updates on the case. She hadn't heard anything. It must have been quiet overnight. Luckily, Frank had had a good night, so at least they were all rested.

He was fine last night, the little voice in her head that liked to control her guilt whispered. *Are you sure you're doing the right thing? He might still be okay living here?*

No, that was an anomaly. They couldn't base their futures on one decent night. Besides, her dad wasn't going to get any better.

She forced herself to get up and dressed and went through the morning routine of making breakfast for everyone. Poppy bounced into the kitchen, blissfully unaware of her mother's inner turmoil, and Chris, fresh from the shower, approached her with a little more caution.

Of course, this wasn't normally *her* morning routine, it was Chris's. More often than not, she'd have already been out the door, on her way back to the office or heading to a new crime scene or to speak to witnesses. Being home in this domestic situation wasn't normal at all.

The heavy, slow footfall of her dad sounded from the stairs. He'd had a bit of a fall a week or so ago, and now he was cautious on them. That was another reason to find him somewhere else to live. The stairs were dangerous for him now.

"Morning, Dad," she said as he came into the kitchen. "Sit down. I've made you some breakfast."

She was relieved to see he was already dressed. At least that was one less battle she'd have to go through.

"Where's Yvonne?" he asked, mentioning Erica's mother's name. "She makes breakfast."

"I'm making it for you today." She guided him into his chair. "Here you go." She slid a plate of toast and a bowl of chopped fruit and yogurt onto the table in front of him.

Frank frowned down at the food. "I don't like this."

She forced a smile. It was the same breakfast he ate practically every morning. "Try it, okay, Dad? For me?"

Poppy leaned across the table and whispered to her granddad, "I like pancakes better."

He nodded in agreement but picked up the spoon to eat the fruit and yogurt. "Me, too."

At least he was eating. She exchanged a glance with her husband, and to her surprise, found herself blinking back tears. It was easier to build up her walls while she was working, but it was different when things were personal. This was her dad, for God's sake. What kind of person would she be if she wasn't emotional?

"Daddy, can we go to Sophie's house after school today?" Poppy said. "She invited me, remember?"

Chris frowned. "Oh, it's not a good day today, sweetheart. Maybe another day."

Poppy pouted. "Please. Sophie's mummy said that you could come as well. She said you could have a cup of tea while we played."

Erica raised an eyebrow. "Did she, now?"

Who is Sophie's mum? She tried to picture the other woman in her head. Young, long dark hair. Always looked like she made an effort for the school run.

Chris squeezed Poppy's shoulder. "We'll chat about it another time, okay?"

"Okay," their daughter relented sullenly.

They finished breakfast, and then Chris got Poppy dressed and off to school. It wouldn't take him long, and they'd already agreed that he would follow behind in his own car.

Erica turned her attention to Frank.

"I'm taking you out today, Dad." She forced her voice to be bright and pasted on a smile.

"Where? Where are we going?"

"To take a look at a place and meet some people."

His lips tightened. "I don't want to meet any people. I want to go home."

"I know, Dad. I know you do."

She grabbed his coat and guided him towards the front door, praying he wasn't going to resist her. He might be almost seventy, but he was still strong, and she desperately wanted to avoid any kind of physical altercation. But today—for the moment, anyway—he allowed himself to be showed towards her car sitting on the driveway. She opened the passenger door for him, and he climbed in without complaint.

The care home was only a twenty-minute drive from their house, which meant she'd be able to visit every day. The day would come when Frank might not even recognise who she was anymore, but even then, she was determined to visit. He might not know who she was, but she still knew who *he* was, and that was what mattered. She hoped Natasha would make the effort to see him. She understood that her sister had her hands full with three kids, but it wasn't as though Erica wasn't busy as well.

After the short drive, she pulled up into the car park. A weeping willow tumbled green fronds onto the start of a garden that wrapped around the large property. A seating area had been positioned under a wooden pergola which offered a view out onto the garden.

Behind them, Chris's car appeared in the entrance to the driveway. He parked in the empty spot beside hers, and her heart swelled with gratitude at his presence.

Erica threw Frank an anxious smile. "Looks nice, doesn't it, Dad?"

"Lawns need a good mow," he muttered before reaching for the handle and swinging the door open.

Erica exhaled a breath and climbed out after him. So far, so good.

They went to the front door, and she rang a buzzer on the door then spoke into the little intercom. "My name is

Erica Swift. I've brought Frank Haswell—my father—for a look around."

The buzzer went again, and she pushed the door open.

"Come on, then," she said to Frank, the smile starting to feel like it had been painted on.

Her husband was a couple of steps behind, ready to block the way should Frank suddenly decide to make a bolt for it.

An odour of old people and bleach, and an underlying odour of boiled cabbage, taking her back to her school dinner days, filled her nostrils. Did all care homes smell this way? Despite the aroma, the place was bright and airy, with high ceilings and colourful paintings on the cream walls. Ahead of them, a reception desk was boxed in, and to their right, a wooden staircase curved around the outer wall, leading to the first floor.

A woman in her fifties with dyed black hair that was decidedly white at the roots and a stocky frame with no discernible waistline approached them. She smiled, her face transforming from stern to warm, and put out her hand to Erica.

"I'm Monica Roux, the manager here at Willow Glade Care Home." She glanced over Erica's shoulder and spoke directly to her father. "You must be Mr Haswell." She lifted her tone slightly. "Or may I call you Frank? How would you prefer to be addressed?"

"You can call me Frank," he said gruffly. "That's my name, isn't it?"

Monica smiled, apparently unaffected by Frank's lack of friendliness. "Well, it's lovely to meet you, Frank. Let's show you around." She guided him into a dayroom, Erica and Chris following dutifully behind. "We have plenty of staff here to take care of our residents. They're all trained in first aid, health and safety, infection control, and food safety."

Staff in identical outfits of black trousers and a green, short-sleeved polo shirt with *Willow Glade* embroidered across the breast flitted around in the background. One helped an older lady from a wheelchair into a more comfortable high-backed chair, while another cleared away some cups and a couple of plates from a table. They each gave them a welcome smile as they walked around, clearly aware they were prospective clients.

"This place is full of old people," Frank muttered.

"We all get old, Dad," she said. She did her best to remind herself not to be confrontational with him.

She was doing her best, but it was fucking hard. Much like when you first had a child, there was a massive learning curve to how to react to someone with dementia. Patience was one of the first things she had to learn, and it was probably the hardest. She was far from being a patient person. Having Poppy had helped her with that, and then she'd been able to convert some of that patience over to her dad, but it hadn't been easy, and she still got it wrong. Sometimes it felt like she'd said or done the wrong thing every single day.

Chris was better at it than she was. Maybe that was his nature, or perhaps it was simply that he was one step removed from it all. He didn't experience the same kind of pain she did when Frank yelled at her that he hated her and everything was her fault. Of course, Chris got frustrated and angry in return, but he was better at hiding his feelings than she was.

"We have activities every day," Monica said, "and as you can see, we benefit from these beautiful grounds as well. It's good for our residents to get outside into the fresh air." She added, with a smile, "Or at least as fresh as it can get in the middle of London."

"It's beautiful," Erica said honestly.

If it wasn't for the smell or that they were outnumbered by the elderly by about five to one, she could have kidded herself that her dad was going to stay in a hotel. A hotel would still feel so impersonal, though. No matter how much she tried to kid herself, she was always going to feel as though she was washing her hands of her only living parent.

"We do encourage you to bring things in to make the place feel more homely, such as his own bedding and other soft furnishings, books, a radio or television, and of course, pictures of family and things like that."

Erica had already been expecting that, but it was still good to hear it being encouraged. Maybe her dad would start to think of the place as being home. She wanted to imagine that he might even make friends here.

"So, what do you think, Frank?" Monica asked brightly. "Would you like to come and stay with us awhile, and see how you get on?"

"There's more space for you here than there is at my house, Dad. And company, too. I think you'll like it." She wanted to be encouraging, but she could already tell he wasn't impressed.

Frank frowned. "Why can't I go back to my house?"

She exhaled a sigh. "You know you can't. It's not safe for you there now." She exchanged a glance with the care home manager, knowing she needed to speak with the other woman in private, and then turned back to her husband. "Chris, can you take Dad out into the gardens and show him around?" She smiled at her father. "Maybe you can give them some advice about how to tend the flowerbeds."

Frank grunted but raised his chin in a nod of agreement.

She turned to Monica. "Dad always loved his garden. If he wasn't working, he was out pottering around in it."

She caught herself talking about him in the past tense, but she didn't mean it like that. It wasn't *him* who was dead, it was his life before now. That was the part that felt as though it had passed away. That life was lost to him, and with the sale of the house to pay for his care, would be lost to them all.

Chris seemed to take the hint that she needed to speak with the care home manager alone, and he led Frank outside, chatting amiably about the weather.

"So, what do you think?" Monica asked, leading her into her office.

"It's lovely here, and it's close enough to allow both me and my sister to visit regularly."

She switched on her computer. "Of course. How soon are you looking at getting him in?"

"If Dad is willing, we'd like to book him a space as soon as possible." She fought another wave of guilt. "It's not easy at home. I work awkward hours, and so it means my husband is having to take care of Dad all the time. We have a four-year-old as well. None of us are getting any sleep, and it frightens Poppy when Dad gets confused and starts shouting." Tears threatened again, and she angled her face away, wanting to hide them from the other woman. She was a stranger, and Erica wasn't used to showing emotions to people she didn't know—hell, she struggled to show them to the ones she loved.

"I completely understand." Monica gave her another kind smile. "Any caring family member would feel the same way. It's perfectly natural." She paused and glanced back at the computer. "I hate to rush you into any decisions, but rooms don't come up too often here, and we do have a couple of other people interested. Like I said, I don't want to rush you, but..." She shrugged apologetically.

"That's okay. Message heard, loud and clear." Monica might not want to rush her, but if they didn't put her dad's name down for the room, someone else was likely to swoop in and snatch it right out from under them. "I'll let you know for sure as soon as possible."

"Thank you."

The decision wasn't only down to her or Frank. She had to call her sister and talk it over with her. While her dad was occupied by Chris and the gardens, Erica stepped outside and fished her mobile phone from her handbag. She swiped the screen to bring up Natasha's name and then hit Call.

Natasha answered within a couple of rings. "I was just thinking about you. How's it going?"

"Okay. I'm at the care home now. It's really nice, and Dad seems to like it, though he's complaining about all the old people here."

Natasha laughed. "Sounds like him."

"It's not cheap, though, Tash. We're going to have to sell the house to pay for his care."

Her sister sucked in a breath. "Mum and Dad's house?"

"Yes, of course." She did her best to tamp down her irritation and failed. "I can hardly sell mine, can I? We need somewhere to live as well, and I don't see you volunteering to put your family out on the street."

"I wasn't suggesting that, Erica. It's just so sad, that's all. We grew up in that house, and I can't imagine it no longer being in our family. Dad wouldn't want this either. He was always proud that we'd have the house as our inheritance."

"Yeah, I know, but we don't have any choice. We need to be able to pay for his care. I certainly can't afford to pay for it out of my wages. It's going to cost six hundred quid a week."

"Jesus. That's insane. Isn't the government supposed to help in some way?"

"Not when he's got assets of his own. It's all means tested."

"And there's no way he can continue living with you?" Natasha said, clearly still hopeful.

It was so hard to explain to her sister just how bad things had got. Unless you were living in the middle of it, it was impossible to fully understand. It was natural for Natasha to think that Erica was overreacting or blowing things up.

"I'm hardly ever home, Tash. Chris already looks after Poppy, and now we're both expecting him to look after Dad as well. It's too much. We might not want to sell our family home to pay for it, but I can't expect my husband to sacrifice everything instead."

"I know." She sighed. "I wish there was another option."

"Me, too. Honestly, if there was any other way, I'd do it."

"It feels like we're losing them, Erica. Not only Mum, but Dad as well, all over again."

A painful lump blocked her throat, and she struggled to swallow. She glanced over her shoulder to see Chris guiding Frank over towards her, and she lifted her hand in a wave.

"He's still here, Tash," she said. "Dad's right here. We haven't lost him yet."

Chapter Thirteen

She hung up to focus her attention on her dad and Chris, but her phone buzzed again, and she glanced down.

Gibbs.

Her boss's surname appeared on the screen, and she quickly swiped to answer. She'd taken this time off work to deal with her dad, but she couldn't ignore it forever.

Gibbs spoke before she even had the chance to say hello. "There's been another one."

"What?"

She lifted her gaze to Chris and raised a finger to tell him she'd only be a minute. He understood and nodded, steering her father away again by pointing out one of the weeping willow trees that must have given the care home its name.

"A second man was found in Whitechapel around an hour ago. The shopkeeper whose doorway he was found in called it in. She thought he was a homeless man who was just asleep, but then she tried to wake him up and realised he was dead. He's missing his eyes as well. We need you at the scene."

He rattled off an address.

"Jesus Christ. I'll be right there."

She hung up and turned to Chris. "Are you okay to get Dad home? I'm so sorry, but there's been an emergency, and I'm needed in work."

"Yes, of course." Chris looked to her father. "That's okay with you, Frank, isn't it? If Erica needs to get into work."

Frank shrugged. "I don't care, as long as you're not going to make me walk back."

"I'm driving, so no worries there."

She mouthed *thank you* at Chris and hurried to her car.

Her heart raced, adrenaline surging through her. Her thoughts instantly left her father, focusing on the case instead. She never wanted innocent people to get hurt, but finding the bad guy gave her drive and motivation. The truth was that she enjoyed what she did, and she didn't see why she always felt the need to apologise for it.

• • • •

BY THE TIME SHE ARRIVED at the crime scene, SOCO were already there, the area cordoned off. A privacy tent had been erected to hide the body from any curious passers-by or photographers who might decide to snap a picture and upload to social media.

She spotted the figure of Lee Mattocks, who headed up SOCO for their borough. He was a tall, lanky man with slicked-back dark hair, who always wore a charcoal-grey suit. In another life, she imagined he would have been an undertaker. He was a man of few words but had a keen eye for detail, and there was nothing he wouldn't do to gather something he might consider to be evidence. A strong stomach was a must in that job, but Mattocks had one made of iron.

Shawn had beaten her there as well, and he lifted his hand in a half wave as she approached.

So far, there weren't any signs of the press, but she doubted that would last for long. With two victims sustaining the same injuries, word was bound to get out. The press would soon be buzzing around here like flies on a corpse, eager to use the gruesome nature of the two men's injuries to sell more copies of their papers.

"So, this is a murder investigation now," she said to Shawn, without bothering to say good morning. "I'd say there's a good chance that whoever did this is connected or related to the Jacobs case."

"No chance of it being a coincidence?" Shawn suggested, playing devil's advocate.

She cocked an eyebrow. "Do you think there is?"

"Let's hope not. I'd rather not give any thought to the possibility that we have two eye-stealing psychopaths running around the city. Trying to catch one is proving hard enough."

"How long has he been dead?"

"Ballpark guess of a couple of hours."

"Dammit. If only we'd got to him sooner."

They couldn't interview a dead victim. This man might have been able to tell them something about whoever had done this to him. Now, they'd have to rely on his body to give the pathologist some clues.

The doorway was that of a small Asian grocery store. "Did the owner of the shop see anything other than finding the body?"

"No, she didn't. And she isn't happy about not being able to open either, but there's nothing we could do about that, other than reassure her that we'd work as quickly as possible."

"She needs to be brought in for questioning. We all need to find out if she has any CCTV fitted in the shop that might have caught something." Erica glanced up at the doorway, but there was nothing obvious. "Are there any other possible witnesses?"

"A bar owner from across the road said he saw a group of young men who'd left the pub around one in the morning giving the guy a hard time. He said he didn't think anything of it while it was happening—unfortunately, getting hassled by pissheads is part of life for those on the street—but obviously he didn't know the man was going to die at that point."

"So, he was still alive at one this morning?" she double-checked.

Shawn nodded. "Yes, seems that way."

"We need to find that group of men, see if the man said or did anything that might help us."

"Already on it," Shawn said.

One of the SOCO team handed her protective clothing and boots which she pulled on. She ducked under the cordon then entered the privacy tent, Shawn right behind her.

"Jesus Christ."

The body of the man sat slumped in the doorway, his chin on his chest. Blood was smeared across his face.

Mattocks was talking to a sergeant in charge of the scene, but they both fell silent as she stepped in.

"DI Swift," she introduced herself.

"Mark Coggins," the sergeant said, giving her a nod.

"Where are we up to? Do we know who he is yet?"

Coggins nodded. "Yes. Fifty-two-year-old Patrick Ronson. He owns a small chain of corner shops. Not married, no children, that we're aware of. In fact, he doesn't seem to have any close relatives."

"We need to find out how he's connected to Lewis Jacobs, the other victim who was found with his eyes cut out earlier this week. I highly doubt this was completely random. There will be something, other than them both being men, that's linking them together. We're going to need to bring more people in on this. DCI Gibbs is going to want to set up a task force and get some additional resources."

"I've already got my officers canvassing the neighbourhood," Coggins said.

"Good. We're going to need all the people we can get."

She turned her attention to the head of SOCO.

"Have you found anything?" she asked Mattocks.

He straightened, a clear bag with some kind of swab inside held in one hand. "Some blood from the victim, but that's all. This is a high footfall traffic area, which hasn't helped. Doesn't look as though there's enough blood for the injuries to have occurred here, though."

"You think he was moved?"

"He died here, we know that from the statement of the bar owner across the street, but he was most likely moved here after the injuries were sustained. We'll know more once the autopsy has been carried out."

Erica dropped to a crouch to get a better view of the victim's face. It was the stuff of nightmares. Where his eyes should have been, there were two gaping holes smeared with dried black blood instead.

Remembering what the doctor had said about the puncture wound in Jacobs's neck, she reached out with a gloved hand and tilted his head to one side to give her a better view. Sure enough, there was the dot of a puncture mark.

She signalled for photographs to be taken.

Erica let out a steady breath and rose back to her feet.

Shawn spoke up. "We have a name of one of the men who went over to the victim in the early hours. He paid for drinks using his credit card, and the bar owner was able to give us the name. Mitchell Webster."

"Do we have an address for him?"

"Yes," Shawn said. "He lives in Shoreditch."

"Not far from here, then. Let's finish up here, and then go and pay Mr Webster a visit."

Chapter Fourteen

Mitchell Webster lived in a block of new-build flats with blacked out, glass front doors leading onto the lobby.

Erica hit the buzzer for Webster's flat, and she and Shawn waited expectantly.

There was no answer.

"Do you think he might be at work?" Shawn suggested.

To afford to live anywhere this decent cost a pretty penny in this part of London, so there was no way Webster wasn't earning. Already, Erica was getting a picture in her mind about the sort of person they were about to visit. It was mid-week and also mid-morning now.

"Yeah, we might need to pay him a visit there instead."

As they were about to give up, a voice came through the speaker. "Hello?"

She and Shawn exchanged a glance. He was home in the middle of the day. Why was that?

"Is that Mr Webster?"

"Yeah, it is."

"Mr Webster, I'm DI Swift, and I have DS Turner with me. We'd like to talk to you about an incident that happened in the early hours of this morning."

"Oh, right. Come on up." The buzzer went, and the front door to the building clicked open.

Erica remained cautious, but she pushed her way inside. A single lift was at the back of the lobby, and they walked over and hit the button for Webster's floor. No one else was around, and the lift arrived quickly, the doors sliding open. They stood shoulder to shoulder and rode up to Webster's floor.

He was already at the door to his flat when they arrived.

"Sorry. I was putting on some trousers." He motioned them inside then stepped out of the way to let them both in, closing the door behind them. "Can I get you a drink? Coffee?"

"No, we're fine, thanks," she said, right as Shawn said, "Coffee."

She shot him a look, and he shook his head.

He changed his answer. "I mean we're fine."

Webster gestured for them both to take a seat, and they perched on the leather sofa while Webster sat in an armchair opposite. The flat was small and had that typical bachelor vibe—all glass and chrome, with hardly a plant or picture frame or throw cushion in sight.

"No work today?" she enquired.

Mitchell's cheeks grew pink, and he glanced at the floor. "Oh, I called in sick."

She raised an eyebrow. "You're ill?"

"No, I'm hungover. Went for a few drinks after work with a couple of the guys, and it all got a bit out of hand."

"Out of hand how, exactly?"

"You know, getting the shots in and stuff." He paused and frowned. "What's this about? I'm sure you're not here because I called in sick to work."

"No, Mr Webster, we're not. We're here because a man died last night, and we believe you may have been one of the last people to see him alive. We're going to need to ask you to come down to the station for an interview."

His mouth dropped open, and he quickly covered it with his hand. "Jesus Christ. You mean the man in the shop doorway, don't you?"

She clasped her hands between her knees and leaned forward. "Yes, I do. You remember him?"

The colour fell out of Mitchell's face. "Yeah, he was a bit hard to forget. You mean he's dead? How?"

She didn't intend to give this man too much information. They didn't know the full extent of his involvement yet. "He had injuries to his face, which he died of. We believe he had those injuries when you saw him. Like I said, we're going to need you to answer some questions at the station. Are you okay to come with us now?"

He looked between them both. "I'm not in any trouble, am I?"

"Not at all. We'd simply prefer to do this in a more formal setting. You could have information that might help us find his killer."

He got to his feet. "Of course. We can go now."

Erica rose with him. "We'll drive you."

• • • •

ERICA REMAINED STANDING as Mitchell Webster slid into the plastic chair in the interview room.

"Can we get you anything?" she asked him. "Coffee? Water?"

It was an inversion of what had happened at the flat, when he'd offered them a drink.

He clasped his hands on the table between them. "Yeah, I'll have a coffee, thanks. Late night and all that." He smiled, but the expression didn't reach his eyes.

Shawn nodded and slipped from the room to get the coffee.

Erica went through the routine of letting Mitchell Webster know that the interview was being recorded.

A knock came at the door signalling Shawn's return with the coffee. He set the paper cup in front of Webster. "It's from a machine and tastes like crap," he said apologetically, "but it has caffeine."

Webster pulled the cup closer. "Thanks."

Erica took the seat opposite him. "Are you ready to start?"

The witness nodded.

She spoke the names of everyone present, together with the time, date, and location of the station, out loud to be recorded and began the interview.

"What is it you do for a living, Mr Webster?"

"Call me Mitchell, please. Mr Webster makes me sound like my dad."

She smiled. "Of course. Mitchell it is."

"Umm, I work in the city as a Wealth Management Analyst."

"Sounds interesting. How long have you been doing that for?"

"About five years now. It's a good job. The guys I was out with last night are colleagues."

She would have moved on to that, but since he was handing the information over himself, she decided to run with it. "I'd like the names of everyone you were with. We'll need to speak with them as well."

"Err, yeah, of course." His gaze flicked to Shawn, who was already prepared with a notepad and pen. "Simon McCallum, and Paul Brent."

"Thank you. Did you go out straight after work?"

"Yeah. It was only supposed to be one drink, but you know what it's like. One drink turned into two and then three, and then before I knew it, it was gone midnight."

"Was the pub across the road from where you saw the victim the only one you went to?"

"No." He shook his head. "We went to a few places before that."

"I'm going to need the names of each of the establishments."

Mitchell thought for a minute, and then rattled off a list.

"Thanks," Erica said. "Now talk me through what happened when you left the pub."

"We left thinking everything was fine. We were messing around, you know, ribbing each other, like blokes do. Then I saw the man sitting in the doorway." Mitchell looked between them, his features taut with worry. "I thought I was imagining things. I figured it was a trick of the light or something. You know when you catch movement from the corner of your eye, and you're sure there's something there, but there isn't? That's what it felt like. I was drunk, and my friends kept telling me to leave the guy alone."

"Why did you approach him in the first place?"

"I could tell something wasn't quite right. Normally, with these rough sleepers, they at least have pieces of cardboard or a blanket, or a couple of bottles of something around them, but this guy didn't have anything like that, and he was well dressed, too."

Erica frowned. "But you didn't think to call anyone for help?"

He twisted his lips and glanced away, embarrassed. "Like I said, I was drunk."

"I need you to think hard now," she said. "We believe he wasn't hurt in the same place he died, which means he was moved. There's the possibility that whoever did this to him was still around after you came across him. Can you remember seeing anyone else? Anyone hanging around who caught your attention?"

He thought for a moment and shook his head. "No, not at all. It was quiet for that time in the morning." His forehead furrowed. "I mean, there might have been some cars that drove past, but I wasn't really paying any attention."

"Are you sure?" she pressed him.

He nodded resolutely. "Yes, I'm sure."

"Okay. Now, tell me exactly what time you left your office to go out for drinks."

"Umm, about six thirty, I think."

Erica took a breath and prepared to go over every detail.

• • • •

GIBBS HAD CALLED A briefing.

Erica went straight from the interview and slipped into the room, which was already filled with her team. She noted several new faces as well. As she'd expected, extra detectives had been brought in to work on the case. One of the people turned to glance at her and offered her a nod.

She smiled and nodded in return.

DI Andrew Price was a good detective, and he'd brought some of his DCs along with him as well. She was pleased to see him there. There was no way they'd be able to handle this on their own.

Gibbs had named himself Senior Investigating Officer on the case. He stood at the front of the room and cleared his throat, and the murmur of conversation that had been going through the room when she'd entered fell silent.

Gibbs ran through who was present and thanked everyone for being there then brought them up to speed with where they were on the case. "We suspect we're looking for a white male, local, young and strong enough to abduct grown men, possibly with some kind of facial deformity, which is why he has this obsession with taking out people's eyes. He doesn't want anyone looking at him."

"Most people would make do with a blindfold," one of the DCs called out, and a ripple of laughter went around the room.

"I believe the removal of their eyes is the main reason he's taking them, though," he continued when the laughter died down, ignoring the comment. "He's not intending to kill them."

"The last victim died," Price said.

Gibbs nodded. "Yes, but not directly at his hands. He was alive when he was released, and the suspect had done his best to stop the blood flow from his wounds. Which brings me to another point. There's a possibility he has some kind of medical training. It looks as though both victims were injected with a sedative, so he knows his drugs."

"We've just interviewed Mitchell Webster," Erica said, "the man we believe was the last person to see the second victim alive. It doesn't look as though he saw anything or anyone suspicious, but he's given us the names of the two men he was with as well, so we're going to need to send someone to speak with them."

"The woman who owns the shop has also been interviewed," DI Price said, "but so far it doesn't look as though she's seen anything of any relevance, other than finding the body, of course."

Gibbs huffed out a breath of frustration. "No one's seen anything, then. What is this guy, a ghost?"

"I think we should also check our databases for any other cases where the eyes have been deliberately disfigured," Erica suggested, "or even incidents where a suspect has attempted to go for the eyes and might have failed."

"I can do that," offered Rudd. "How far back should I check?"

Erica glanced over at her DC. "Start with ten years and see if that pulls anything up."

She gave a curt nod. "Got it."

"We're waiting on the CCTV footage from the shop to come in as well," Erica continued. "And we need to go back to the hospital and interview the first victim, see if he knew the second one."

Gibbs nodded. "Good. I'll leave that in your hands."

They finished up the briefing, and Erica left the room. She took a seat at her desk and switched on her computer.

DC Hannah Rudd approached.

"That CCTV footage from the shop is in," she said. "Thought you might want to know."

"Thanks, Rudd," she told the other police officer. "Appreciate it."

"No rest for the wicked." Shawn raised an eyebrow from where his desk was positioned opposite hers.

Going through CCTV footage could often be a long and tedious process, but it needed to be done. She got antsy sitting in one spot hour after hour. She'd never be able to handle a desk job.

Shawn knew how she felt about being tied to a desk. "How about you take the first half," he offered, "and I'll take the rest?"

She nodded in agreement. "Sounds like a plan to me."

At least if they broke it down, they would get through it quicker.

Armed with coffee, she got to work, going through the footage from that night, watching for anything suspicious. It was a busy area, with numerous people and vehicles passing the shop doorway.

After about forty minutes, Shawn got her attention. "You might want to see this."

She rose from her chair and went around to Shawn's desk. He clicked his mouse and brought up the same scene she'd been staring at for the past hour. He hit Play.

"Here he comes. Watch."

On screen, a figure stumbled down the street, his hands held out in front of him. To any outside observer, he would have looked as though he was drunk, and Erica remembered what Rebecca Bird, the other witness, had said about thinking the first victim had been inebriated. She made a mental note to check this victim's tox screen for the same drug Lewis Jacobs had been given. The Midazolam was supposed to reduce anxiety and memory, so did Patrick Ronson not really understand what was happening to him? Why else would either victim not have shouted for help the moment they'd found themselves free?

There was no sign of anyone else.

With his hands outstretched, the victim patted down the window of the shop. When he reached the indent of the doorway, he fell into it. He landed on his knees then dropped to his backside, where he stayed. With his back pressed up against the doorway, he covered his head with his arms and rocked back and forth.

Whoever had done this to him hadn't led him to the doorway. He'd made it there by himself.

Shawn rubbed his hand over his mouth. "Shit. We need to get a bigger picture. He came from somewhere, and he can't have got far, not in his condition."

Erica exhaled a long breath, realising they were going to need to spend more time sitting in front of the computer. "We're going to need to request all CCTV from the direction he came from. He's going to appear at some point, and when he does, we'll get the bastard who did this."

He nodded slowly. "Let's hope so, because right now we've got nothing."

"I'd better let Gibbs know."

She went to her DCI's office and knocked on the door.

He glanced up from his desk. "Swift? Got any further on this eye thief case?"

She cocked an eyebrow at the name. "The *what* case?"

"That's what the newspapers and social media are calling these...incidents."

He couldn't call them murders. After all, the first victim had lived—so far, anyway.

"Eye thief." She suppressed a smile. "Thought they'd think of something *cornea*!"

"You're going to make me roll my eyes," Gibbs said with a smirk.

They both laughed.

"So, tell me you've made some progress." He grew serious again. "I can't have some other poor bastard stumbling around East London missing his eyes."

"We need to get some more CCTV coverage, but we have the second victim on camera. He must have come from somewhere. We know what direction he came from, so all we need is to get more footage, and I'm sure we're going to get a licence plate from a vehicle that he must have been thrown out of."

Gibbs folded his arms across his chest. "You think whoever did this drove him into the area and kicked him out of a car?"

"I doubt he just wandered out of someone's front door. Something is tying them to this location, though, because the first victim wasn't found too far away."

"If we can get eyes on the car, then we should be able to figure out who's driving it," Gibbs said

Erica nodded. "Exactly."

Her DCI huffed air out through his nose. "Okay, good. Get on with it, then."

Erica turned and went back to her desk.

Her phone rang, and she checked the screen. She didn't recognise the number but swiped to answer the call. "Swift."

"Hi, this is Monica Roux from the nursing home. I wondered if you'd given any thought to how you'd like to proceed with your father?" She added, hurriedly, as though feeling bad about pursuing her, "I don't mean to push you, but we get a lot of enquiries. If you think you're going to pass, then it would be good to know sooner rather than later so we can offer the care to someone else who needs it."

Adrenaline rose inside her at the idea of losing the room. It wasn't going to be easy to convince Frank it was the right thing to do, but she was sick with worry at the thought of losing the space and being back to square one. There were plenty of other nursing homes in the area, but not all of them offered specialist dementia care, which her dad needed, and they wouldn't have those lovely grounds for Frank to walk in.

"I think the place is lovely, and yes, I'd like to take that room, if it's still possible."

"Wonderful. That is good news. I'm sure Frank will be very happy here."

"Yes, I hope so."

She ended the call and threw her phone down on the desk. "Shit."

"Everything okay, boss?" Shawn asked.

"Yeah, just stuff with my dad. He's got a place at the care home we liked, but it means I'm going to need to take some time to move him in. It's not the best timing. I still need to go back to the hospital and speak with Lewis Jacobs again."

"Can't you put it off for a while, at least until we get a bit further on the case?"

She sighed. "It's not that easy. They say the rooms are in high demand, and they want to fill it."

"Won't paying for it be enough, and then you can move him in later?"

"I think it's about more than the money. They know they can be helping someone if the room is filled, and throwing money at it means someone who actually needs the spot is going without."

He rubbed his hand across his mouth. "I see. That makes things more difficult. But look, I can cover for you if you need a few hours. I'll go and speak with Jacobs, and I'll call you if we make any progress or anything else changes."

She sagged with relief. "Thanks, Turner. You're the best."

He glanced away, as though she'd embarrassed him. "Hey, anytime."

Chapter Fifteen: Ten Years Earlier

Heavy banging came at the front door.
Nicholas sat at the top of the stairs and crouched down so he could see.

Uniformed police officers! He recognised the blurry colours through the frosted glass in the door.

Shit.

He leaned back to get a view of the bedroom that had once belonged to their mother.

"Danny!" he hissed at the closed bedroom door. Was his brother drunk again? He hoped not. He was going to need him to be sober if they were going to have to deal with the cops. "Danny, the fucking pigs are here."

The bedroom door opened, and Danny emerged, his blond hair stuck up on one side and dull with dirt. "What?"

"There are police at the front door."

Announcing their presence one more time, the police officers hammered again, the bangs thumping through the house.

"We should just ignore them," Danny whispered.

"What if they break down the door? We look guilty by not answering."

"Shit."

Both boys glanced back to the front door.

Nicholas thought of something else. "They might come around the back if we don't answer."

He didn't need to vocalise the part he was worried about. Even though the back garden was overgrown with weeds, there was still a starkly bare mound of earth beneath which lay their mother's body.

Nicholas shot to his feet. "I'm answering it."

He took Danny's silence as agreement and hurried down the stairs. Out of habit, he pulled the hood of his sweatshirt up and over his face. He reached for the lock, his hand shaking, and opened the door.

"Hello, son," the male police officer said. "Mind if we come in for a chat?"

A woman in a suit stood behind the police. Nicholas recognised her for what she was—child protective services. Some arsehole must have reported their suspicions that he and Danny were here alone—one of the neighbours or someone from the school, maybe. Fuck.

Nicholas stood his ground. "What for?"

"Like I said, just a chat. Is your mother home?"

Nicholas didn't let go of the door, making sure it wasn't wide open. It was a false sense of security, since the police could force him to let them in. He sensed Danny lurking behind him.

"No, she's popped out for a bit."

His expression didn't change. "Can you tell us when she'll be back? We need to speak with her."

He shrugged one shoulder. "Dunno. Couple of hours, probably."

He wanted to tell them that she was out for the night and he didn't know when she'd be home, but even saying that might be enough for the woman from the social to decide they weren't safe.

"Mind if we come in and wait?" the police officer suggested.

Danny stepped forward to join Nicholas's side. "There's no point. We don't know when she'll be back."

He cocked an eyebrow. "Are you boys often left on your own, not knowing when your mother will come home?"

Nicholas wanted to kick Danny. "No, but we're not exactly little kids, are we? I leave school this year. I could probably move out myself, if I wanted to. It's no big deal."

"So, she *does* leave you here alone often?"

Nicholas scowled, unhappy this man seemed to be catching him out at every turn. "That's not what I said."

The woman in the suit moved closer to the house. "I think you should let us in so we can speak with you properly. It's Nicholas, right?" She glanced over Nicholas's shoulder. "And you must be Daniel."

"It's Danny," Danny muttered.

"My name is Delia Casey, and I'm from social services. We've had reports that you boys have been left here alone for much longer than a few hours. I know you're not small children, but that's still against the law. We don't want to make this any more difficult for you than I'm sure it's already been, but we're not going to walk away from here without talking to you both and making sure everything is all right."

Nicholas had the sense that they already knew everything wasn't all right.

"Fine," he relented, stepping back from the door to let them through.

The male police officer entered first, followed by Delia Casey, and then the woman officer.

"Can you take your hood down, son?" the male officer asked.

Nicholas scowled again but reluctantly pulled his hood away from his face. He waited for exclamations of shock or disgust, or for them to either stare or no longer be able to look at him, but they all hid their feelings well. Maybe they'd been prewarned before they'd got here.

Wanting to keep them away from the kitchen door and what it led out onto, Nicholas went into the lounge, Danny following behind. He was horribly conscious of how filthy it was in here. Neither of them had done any cleaning since it had all happened. Dirty mugs and plates were stacked up on the coffee table, and there were fingerprints in the dust on the television. The house had always smelled musty, but it was even worse now. There was no way either the police officers or the social worker hadn't noticed.

Awkwardly, they found places to sit, the social worker perching on the arm of the sofa, while the male police officer remained standing.

"My name is PC Faulks," the male officer said. "I want you both to understand that we're here to help you. We're not the enemy."

Nicholas shot a look to Danny. He knew what his brother was thinking—the police *were* the enemy, in their minds.

"Can you remember the last time you saw your mother?"

Nicholas screwed up his lips then said, "Can't remember."

"So, it's been that long since you last saw her that you can't remember exactly when it was?"

Nicholas remained silent.

"How have you been spending your days since she's been gone?"

Nicholas stared at the floor. "Just the usual stuff. School. Watching TV. Hanging out."

"You get up and go to school each morning?"

"Yeah, of course." He wasn't going to tell PC Faulks that they deliberately kept going to school, knowing if they didn't, the exact situation they were currently in would have happened far sooner.

"What about food? How are you feeding yourselves?"

Danny rolled his eyes. "Same way everyone else does. We go to the shops."

PC Faulks smiled at Danny. "Where do you get the money to buy food from the shops."

"We have our own money," Danny said sullenly.

They couldn't tell the PC that they were using their mother's money. If they did that, they'd also have to explain why their mother didn't need her own money anymore, and that would lead to even more difficult questions.

A creak came from a floorboard overhead, and Nicholas suddenly realised they were one person short. The female police officer hadn't come into the lounge with them, and Nicholas's heart lurched into his throat.

What's she doing up there?" he demanded. "We never said she could go up there."

At least she hadn't gone out the back. It was a small relief, but it was something. But then he realised if she peered out one of the back bedroom windows, she would get a view straight down onto the mound of earth that marked their mother's grave.

"Taking a quick look around," Faulks said.

"Aren't you supposed to have a warrant or something to do that?"

"Not if we believe someone might be in danger."

"She isn't in danger," he blurted. "She's a drunk, that's all."

The policeman's lips pressed into a thin line, his eyebrows drawing together. "I was talking about you boys. You're the ones who might be in danger."

Delia stepped in. "Your mother hasn't been here for some time, has she? Please, be honest with us and tell us when you last saw her, and don't say that you can't remember. You must have some ballpark idea. Guess, if you have to." Delia offered them a kind smile, but Nicholas knew it was full of lies. "We're only trying to help you."

"I dunno. A few days," he muttered, staring down at his hands which were clasped between his knees.

"A few days? So, last Tuesday?" she guessed.

He shrugged. "Yeah, maybe."

She leaned forward slightly, as though trying to catch his eye. "Because your neighbour says they haven't seen her for weeks."

Nicholas screwed up his lips into what his brother would have referred to as a cat's arse. "Not my fault if they're blind."

The female officer who'd been poking around stuck her head into the lounge. "There's something of interest out the back. The ground has been disturbed. Recently, too."

The male officer glanced back at them. "Do you know anything about this, boys?"

Nicholas exchanged a glance with Danny, silently warning his brother to stay quiet. If he made a fuss now, the cops would know they were trying to hide something. It was bad enough that they were clearly here alone. The last thing they needed was the police finding the body as well. But Danny had gone completely pale. His knee bounced up and down, his hands twisting together.

"Anything you want to tell us, Daniel—Danny?" The woman officer corrected herself.

Shit. The police had picked up on his nervousness.

Danny shook his head but didn't look up.

Nicholas gritted his teeth and kept his head down. "We don't go into the back garden."

She cocked an eyebrow. "You don't go out there? What, never? You don't go out and kick a ball around?"

"Do you see any footballs around?"

They might have found one if they searched hard enough—deflated and sad behind an overgrown hedge. Nicholas and Danny had used to play out there when they were little—it had been a good escape from their mum—but neither of them had set a foot out there since that day.

The police officer's eyes narrowed. "You're telling me you never go into the garden?"

"He said no!" Danny blurted. "Why's that so fucking hard to understand?"

Delia lifted both hands in a stop sign. "Okay, I think everyone needs to take a breath."

The police officer addressed Nicholas. "You understand that if your mother is missing, we're going to need to file that as a missing person's report? It isn't something we can simply forget about. We have a responsibility to try to figure out what's happened to her. What if she's in some kind of trouble, or she's hurt? You boys don't seem terribly concerned about her welfare."

"She was never too concerned about ours," Danny said.

Nicholas thought he had a point, but obviously that wasn't the reason they weren't worried about her. They knew exactly where she was—buried under that mound of earth that now appeared startlingly like an unmarked grave.

"I think you boys are going to need to come with me," Delia Casey said. "I know somewhere safe where you can spend the night. Pack a couple of things to take with you, and I'll drive you there now."

Nicholas exchanged a glance with Danny and gave him a small nod to tell him to do what she said. It would mean leaving the police in the house, but what choice did they have?

• • • •

THE SOCIAL WORKER PULLED up outside the front of a tatty terraced house. The door was already open, and, in the doorway, a skinny woman tugged an equally tatty grey cardigan tighter around her body as they approached.

"This is Mrs Winchester," the social worker introduced. "She's a foster carer. I'll leave you in her capable hands."

Without another word, she turned and got back into her car, leaving them in the care of a stranger.

Mrs Winchester didn't even crack a smile. She led them into the house and shut the door behind her.

"This is your room," she said, her voice flat. "There's a downstairs shower room through the kitchen, which is what you're to use. The upstairs is for family use only. There's a small television in your room as well, so you won't feel the need to come into the living room. Meals are at seven-thirty a.m., one p.m., and six p.m. You're expected to eat whatever is given to you without complaint. There won't be any special meals made, or snacks if you're still hungry. We don't pander to fussy children here."

Nicholas was tempted to tell her that they'd lived on toast and cereal for weeks now and had been forced to scavenge out of the bin to get something to eat when they were younger. They'd eat anything.

• • • •

THEY ONLY SPENT ONE night in that foster home. Perhaps it should have been a relief, but it wasn't.

A familiar banging came at the front door early the following morning. It was followed by Mrs Winchester, mean-faced, opening the bedroom door. "Get up, both of you. The police are here to see you."

It was a different police officer, one in plain clothing who introduced himself as DI Johnson.

"Nicholas Bailey and Daniel Bailey, you are both under suspicion of unlawfully burying a body and concealing a death. You will be questioned with an appropriate adult, which will most likely be your social worker, and given the opportunity of legal representation. You do not have to say anything. But it may harm your defence if you do not mention when questioned something which you later rely on in court. Anything you do say may be given in evidence."

Nicholas turned to Danny. "We didn't do anything," he told his brother. "Remember that, no matter what." He didn't want Danny to take the fall for this.

They were taken in separate police cars to the station. Nicholas found himself sitting in a cramped room with a table and a handful of chairs that didn't even match. Was he going to see his brother again?

The social worker, Delia Casey, showed up, but instead of a kind smile and reassurance, the woman could barely meet his eye. Then an older man with a belly like that of a nine-months-pregnant woman, his shirt buttons ready to ping off against the strain, arrived and introduced himself as Nicholas's solicitor.

Maybe he should have been more worried about himself, but all Nicholas could think about was his brother. Was anyone sitting with him right now, or was he in a room like this, all alone and frightened about what was going to happen to them?

DI Johnson arrived into the room and nodded good morning to the other adults before turning his attention to Nicholas.

"This interview is going to be recorded, Nicholas, okay?"

Nicholas shrugged.

It wasn't as though he had an actual choice.

Johnson clicked on a recorder and spoke into it. "Detective Inspector Johnson conducting an interview with Nicholas Bailey." He gave the location of the interview room, who was in attendance, the time and date, then got started. "Nicholas, I want you to remember that we're all here to help you. From what I've gathered so far, you and your brother haven't had an easy upbringing, and it's the job of all the people in this room to protect you both."

Nicholas didn't say anything.

"Can I get you something to eat or drink? Did you manage to have any breakfast? You must be hungry."

His stomach rumbled treacherously, but he kept his lips clamped together. All this talk of them protecting him was bullshit. He knew exactly how this worked. They would make out like they were friends, but it was all a trap.

Johnson exhaled a steady breath through his nostrils. "Is that a no, then, Nicholas?" He got no response. "Well, if you change your mind, or you want to take a break, just let us know."

Nicholas gritted his teeth.

"You live at home with your mother, Felicity, and your brother, Daniel."

"Danny," Nicholas corrected him. It always sounded weird when people called him Daniel.

Johnson smiled. "Of course, Danny. What about your father? Do you have any contact with him at all?"

"I don't even know who he is."

"Okay. What about other family members? Is there anyone on your mother's side?"

Nicholas shook his head. "Not that I know of."

"That must have been hard, it just being the three of you."

"It was fine," he lied.

"You mentioned yesterday that your mother had a drinking problem?"

"Yeah, she did. I mean, she does," he corrected himself, realising he'd used the past tense.

"But I assume you became pretty self-sufficient, the two of you, if your mother was unable to cope."

"We managed."

"So, you've been looking after yourselves lately, too."

"Yeah, of course. We're practically adults. We were doing okay."

He didn't mention his brother's drinking or how there was a part of Danny that Nicholas was afraid of now.

"And when was the last time you saw your mother, Felicity Bailey?"

Nicholas twisted his fingers together, staring down at them, not wanting to meet the detective's eye. "Not sure, really. A couple of weeks ago."

"It's been a couple of weeks, but you never thought to report her missing?"

"We didn't want to be put into care," he replied truthfully. "We were old enough to take care of ourselves, probably better than she ever did. We both know what happens to boys in care."

Johnson folded his hands on the table. "Nicholas, I regret to inform you that your mother's body was found last night. She was buried in your back garden. Did you know that?"

He wondered if he should act surprised at the news she was dead, but discovered he didn't have it in him. "No, of course not."

"How do you feel about your mother being dead?"

"I don't know. I guess I'm not surprised. I figured something bad had happened to her."

"Do you know if your mother has any enemies? Anyone who might have wanted to hurt her?"

He shook his head.

"You're going to have to say it out loud." Johnson pointed to the recorder.

"No, but she was always meeting dodgy men at the pub."

"Weren't you worried about her?"

Still, he couldn't look up. "Not really. She was always getting herself in trouble. She drank vodka for breakfast. She was a shit mum. We did better when it was only the two of us and would have stayed that way if people hadn't come poking around."

"Was she ever violent towards you boys?"

He shrugged. "Sometimes. She'd drag us in or out of our room or smack us if she felt we weren't doing something right. If she happened to have something in her hand when she felt the need to do that, then she'd hit us with whatever that was. But it wasn't bad."

How could he tell the truth, not only about what had actually happened, but how she made him feel? How could he tell this policeman that when his mother was sober, she could make his whole body light up with love if she gave him a simple smile or kind word? But when she was drunk, she acted as though he didn't even deserve to be alive. Perhaps the physical violence could have been worse. She'd left bruises but had never broken bones. It never got bad enough that social services had threatened to take them away. Maybe things would have been better if they had been put in care when they'd been little. Their mother might even still be alive today. It might have been that final nudge, that rock bottom, that would have pushed her into getting help.

But she was dead, and there was no point in wishing things had been different.

"Did you notice the disturbance in the garden after she went missing?"

He shrugged. "We never went out there. It was a shithole, anyway. Just a patch of weeds."

"You're saying you never went into the garden?"

"No, I didn't go out there," he repeated stubbornly.

"Nicholas, did you know your mother's body was buried in your back garden?"

A cold fist clenched around his heart. "No."

The detective sighed. "Here's what I'm thinking. The two of you came home one day, and maybe there was a fight and something happened and she got badly hurt—hurt enough to kill her—and then you and your brother buried her in the garden and pretended like everything was fine."

Fire rose inside him at the accusation. "No! We didn't hurt her. She was a horrible parent, but we'd never have done that. Never!"

"Okay," he said slowly, "so maybe you came home and found her like that, and because you didn't want to be put into care, you buried her body."

He clasped his fingers together on the table and shook his head. "I already told you, she simply didn't come home one day." He forced himself to lift his gaze to meet the steely focus of the detective. "Do you really think we could have lived in that house all that time if we'd known her body was out there?" He shuddered, and he hadn't even needed to fake it. "I might look like one, but I'm not a monster."

Johnson frowned slightly. "No one is saying you're a monster. I think you might have just been two frightened boys who got in over their heads."

"Or our mum was a drunk who got involved with the wrong person. It didn't have anything to do with me or my brother."

"Nicholas, we're still waiting for the autopsy report to come back, which will determine your mother's cause of death, but you need to know that we found your brother's fingerprints on the black bin bags her body was wrapped in. Care to explain that?"

The autopsy. Of course. The police would be able to see that they hadn't hurt her. That she'd been drunk, and she'd choked. Maybe they wouldn't get in too much trouble for hiding her body. Surely, the authorities would understand. For one crazed moment, he was tempted to tell the truth, to let the secret he'd been living with for longer than he wanted to remember spill from his lips and become someone else's problem. But then he remembered his brother, and how Danny was the one who'd buried her while he'd hidden in his bedroom like a coward. This wasn't his arse on the line, it was his brother's.

"The bin bags were in the house," he replied sullenly. "We always had to change the bin."

So long as Danny stuck to the same story, they couldn't prove a thing.

Chapter Sixteen

Poppy appeared in the kitchen doorway, her dark hair—like Chris's, and nothing like Erica's strawberry-blonde colouring—ruffled from sleep, rubbing her eyes with her hand. She was bundled up in a fluffy pink dressing gown, and Erica put out her arms to let her daughter stumble into them.

"Good morning, baby-girl."

Erica had woken early and been unable to fall asleep again, too many thoughts tumbling around her head, so she'd got up and come downstairs while the rest of the house was still quiet and sat and drunk her coffee at the kitchen table. The mug she'd been drinking her coffee from had World's Best Mummy scrawled across it—a gift on a Mother's Day a couple of years ago. It felt ironic to be drinking from it when she felt anything but the world's best mum.

She'd already checked her phone for any updates about the case that might have happened overnight, but it seemed everything had been on the quiet front. She guessed that was a good thing.

"Mummy. You're not at work yet."

Erica kissed the top of her head, the soft hair against her lips, inhaling the scent of her. "No, not yet. We're moving Granddad to his new home today, remember?"

"Does that mean he won't be shouting in the night anymore?"

Her heart contracted. "No, sweetheart, he won't. We're going to visit him lots, though, aren't we?"

"Every day?" she said brightly.

"Maybe not every day, because you've got school, but almost every day."

"Can you take me to school today, Mummy?" She gazed up at her with wide blue eyes.

Erica bopped her lightly on her upturned nose with the tip of her finger. "I can't, sweetheart. I need to get Granddad ready. But I will next time, I promise."

Poppy twisted her lips but nodded. "Okay."

Her heart swelled with love for her daughter. She was still so small and yet was more accepting of things than most adults would be.

Chris came down. "Morning." He kissed her on the head. "How are you feeling?"

"Nervous," she admitted. "It's not going to be easy."

"No, it's not. But it's the right thing, for all of us."

She bit her lower lip and nodded. "I know."

Chris must have sensed her hesitation, and he squeezed her shoulder. "Hey, he's lucky to have you. There are plenty of children who don't give a shit about their parents. I mean, your sister has hardly been involved, has she?"

She bristled, naturally defensive of her sister. "Tash is busy with the kids. You know what it's like."

"We're all busy, Erica. We still manage to find time."

Her sister hadn't even been to see the place, trusting Erica to make those choices on her behalf. Erica did find it frustrating, but what could she do? She wasn't going to fall out with her. Even though Natasha was older than Erica,

Erica had still always felt like the one who had to arrange everything. Natasha had left home at a young age and had always been independent, wanting to distance herself from their parents.

A little voice came from beside her. "Don't fight, Mummy."

She forced a smile. "No one is fighting, sweetheart. Come on, what do you want for breakfast?"

"Choco-hoops!" Poppy declared.

"Full of sugar." She ruffled Poppy's hair. "But okay, then." Erica turned to Chris. "I'm going to make a tray up for Dad as well and take it up to him."

Frank had been up during the night and had been awake when Erica had got back, her eyes tired and gritty from staring at the computer screen, going over the CCTV footage, making sure they hadn't missed anything. Her heart had sunk when she'd realised he was awake, selfishly wishing she could crawl into bed and leave him to it. Luckily, he hadn't seemed too disorientated, and she'd been able to give him a glass of water and send him back to bed again.

She left Poppy downstairs with Chris and took a tray of tea and toast upstairs to Frank. She opened the door with her elbow, careful not to spill anything. It was still early—only just past seven—but it was better that he get a couple of hours to prepare rather than her wake him up and hustle him out of the house.

"Morning, Dad. How are you feeling today?"

He was already sitting up, his glasses on, a paperback in his hand.

"I'm okay." He spotted the tea and toast. "Oh, you are a good girl, Natasha."

She tried not to feel hurt that he thought she was her sister. "It's Erica, remember, Dad?"

"Yes, Erica. Of course. That's what I said."

She didn't push him, knowing it wouldn't end well. "Do you remember what we're going to do today? We're going to take you for a little trip to that lovely place we visited."

"Oh, yes, the place with the beautiful gardens."

"That's right." She smiled, pleased he remembered.

It was hard when he was confused and distressed and either crying or shouting. Seeing her proud, intelligent, strong father crying hurt like nothing she'd ever known before.

"And all the old people," he finished, sounding less impressed.

She smiled. "Yes, those, too."

Chris had packed some of Frank's belongings the previous day and had already put them in the boot of the car, so it didn't feel so final to Frank when they were leaving. The care home manager had told her that they treated it as though he was having a little holiday, rather than overwhelm them with what was really happening. Of course, he'd still need to pack his clothes and toiletries. It all still felt incredibly cold and brutal, moving him out like this. She wasn't sure she'd ever get over the guilt.

"Well, finish your breakfast and then get dressed, and we'll get going."

Frank lifted his chin, and she noted that it was bristly and in need of a shave. It wasn't the sort of thing he thought of doing anymore, and she would have to do for him. Who would help him with shaving when he was in the home? Perhaps it would be better if he grew a beard, but then she'd never known him to have a beard, and a part of her was worried that he might not even recognise himself in the mirror if she allowed one to grow. She would probably have to come back up in half an hour and help him dress, since he'd most likely have forgotten that they were going anywhere. She didn't mind. Considering she was handing him over to someone else to take care of, it felt like the least she could do.

"Everything okay?" Chris asked as she went back into the kitchen.

"As good as can be expected." She looked to Poppy, who was almost done with her chocolate hoops. "Time to get dressed for school now, kiddo."

Poppy hopped to her feet and ran back upstairs. She'd probably come down with her shirt mis-buttoned and her shoes on the wrong feet, but again, Erica was happy to help.

At twenty past eight, Chris took Poppy off to school. Erica found herself squeezing her daughter even tighter than normal, needing the emotional strength she took from her love for her.

"I'll be back in half an hour," Chris said, kissing her on the cheek. "You don't have to do this alone."

She gave him a smile of gratitude and let them both go. She waved at the living room window as they walked away, Poppy bouncing with excitement at the prospect of another school day ahead of her. They vanished around the corner, and Erica turned from the window. With a heavy heart, she made her way back up the stairs and went back to the room that would cease to be her father's after today.

She knocked lightly on the door and let herself in. Her dad was sitting on the edge of the bed, dressed, with his bag at his feet.

He looked up at her as she walked in. "We're going somewhere today, aren't we? I can remember that, but I can't for the life of me remember where."

She smiled, but it felt strained. "That's right. The place with the beautiful gardens."

He seemed so old and frail, when he wasn't even that elderly, and it broke her heart.

She picked up his bag and quickly checked that he'd packed what he needed. She figured as long as he had the basics, together with the stuff they'd already put in the car, she could always drop anything else off to him tomorrow.

She would rather be at work than sitting at home, worrying about how he was getting on. The thought of him distressed and frightened, and not knowing where he was, and her not being there to help, sickened her.

He didn't know where he was in our house, either, the sensible part of her brain told her. She knew that, but it was still hard.

By the time she got her dad ready to go, Chris was back from dropping Poppy off at school. Even though he'd offered to help, Frank was surprisingly lucid this morning, and she felt as though she could handle things.

"It might be better if I do this on my own," she told Chris. "He's calm for the moment, and I don't want him to feel as though we're ganging up on him."

"Of course. Whatever you want. But you know you can call me if you need me."

"I do, thank you."

She added Frank's bag to the car and helped him into the passenger side. Then she drove the short distance to Willow Glade Care Home.

Monica Roux came out to meet them, greeting them warmly. "Frank, it's so lovely to have you with us."

Frank frowned at the building. "I've been here before."

"That's right, Dad. We came here yesterday to look around."

"Let's get you inside," Monica said. "We're just about to have tea and cake in the dayroom. How about we get you some refreshments while your daughter gets everything set up for you?"

To Erica's relief, Frank allowed himself to be guided inside the house.

One of the other staff members, a young woman in her early twenties with an accent Erica placed as being Eastern European, came out to help Erica carry Frank's things inside.

"I will show you to your father's room," she said with a kind smile.

Erica had made sure to bring soft furnishings from Frank's house, not her own—a table lamp, some cushions, his pillow and bedding, some photographs of him and Erica's mother when they'd been younger, and of Erica and her sister. She and the staff member went to and from the car, bringing everything in and setting it up for Frank.

With the room ready, Erica went back out into the dayroom to find her dad. He was sitting in one of the high-back chairs, eating a plate of custard creams and chatting to a white-haired woman—who also appeared to be one of the residents—beside him.

"Hi, Dad." She almost didn't want to interrupt. "How are you getting on?"

"Fine, I suppose. How long are we staying?"

"For a bit longer. Do you want to see your room?"

His eyes narrowed. "My room is here?"

"Yes, because you're staying, remember?" She put her hand out to him. "Come on, I think you'll be really pleased."

He grunted. "I'll see about that."

She showed her dad into the ground floor bedroom that was now his. The window offered a view out onto the gardens—a feature she thought he would like.

Frank looked around with a frown. "When's Yvonne getting here? She won't like those cushions on the chair like that."

She bit down on her urge to tell him his wife had died a long time ago. There was no point. It would only upset him in the short run, and then he'd simply forget again. Reminding him of his wife's death years ago didn't achieve anything.

"I'm not sure, Dad. You can always rearrange things if you want."

"I'm going to have to." He sounded exasperated. "I can't leave them like that."

"You can do whatever you want to make this feel like home, Frank," Monica said from the doorway. "We want you to feel comfortable here."

The phone buzzed in her jacket pocket again, and she felt that tug of responsibility, pulling her between the different roles she had in life.

She leaned in and kissed her dad on the cheek. "I'll pop back later, Dad, okay? Try to enjoy yourself until then."

Frank was focused on rearranging how she'd set everything out, and so she backed out of the room, Monica coming with her.

"He'll be fine," she said kindly. "And if he's not, we're all trained here to deal with those episodes as well. He's in a safe place now, and we'll care for him as though he's our own."

He's not, though, is he?

She managed not to voice her thoughts.

They were standing out by the reception desk, facing each other as they talked.

Erica sensed the weight of a stranger's gaze on her and turned to find a young man exiting one of the bathrooms, pushing along a wheeled bucket, a mop in his other hand. His head was down now, but she was sure he'd been looking at her. Probably just wondering who the new arrival was.

"Who's that?" she asked Monica, nodding to the man.

"Oh, that's one of our cleaners. Don't worry, he has all the same training as the rest of our care staff. It's important everyone who has contact with our residents are all fully trained."

"That's good to know."

Erica really had to get back to work. She checked her phone. Sure enough, there were a couple of messages from Shawn, letting her know the pathologist had her report for the second victim ready.

Chapter Seventeen

His heart pounded hard, the beat thumping in his ears. Nicholas had been frozen, just as he had been that day. It had all come back to him, hitting him as though he was experiencing that terrible moment all over again. His breath left his lungs, and the room spun around him.

It was her!

What was she doing here?

That was a stupid question. Clearly, she'd brought a relative—he assumed the old man was her dad—in to stay in the home. If she cared for her father, that meant she would be back again, and often, and their paths were going to keep crossing.

He'd often wondered if he'd ever see her again. For a long time afterwards, he'd thought every woman with that distinctive wavy, reddish-blonde hair was her, and in his mind, he'd rehearsed exactly what he was going to say to her.

He would make her *see* just how badly she'd failed.

She'd caught him staring at her, and that jolt of eye contact brought him back to the present. He'd ducked his head again, focusing on the mop and bucket. He wasn't allowed to wear his hoodie here, even though he was sure all the old people would feel more comfortable if he did. Instead, he had to wear the branded polo shirt and black trousers that was the uniform for the home. He must seem like some kind of disfigured hunchback shuffling around this place—a monster that lurked in the shadows—though he'd never done any of these residents any harm. He told himself that many of them were half blind anyway and didn't really see his face, but that didn't stop him from keeping his head bent. If anything, he preferred to be around the dementia patients more than he did everyone else. They never judged him. Most of them were happy to have someone around who would actually listen to them—properly listen to what they had to say instead of dismissing them because they were old and starting to lose their marbles. These people deserved far more respect, in his mind, than the majority of so called 'ordinary' people out there. Those people only treated him like shit, looking at him as though he was nothing more than a smear of dog shit on the bottom of their shoe. The patients here weren't like that.

They were safe.

He knew he'd probably been given this job out of pity. But he was smarter than they gave him credit for. He stood by and watched and listened and learned, soaking in every little bit of detail. People thought he wasn't worth any more than cleaning toilets and wiping out bedpans, but they were wrong. He knew far more than they thought.

He'd always been treated badly, and perhaps he deserved it, but lately he'd been filled with a new emotion.

Anger.

He wanted to teach them a lesson. All of them. They thought he didn't notice the way they stared at him, the whispers behind the backs of their hands, the nervous laughter or sneers of disdain.

He hated how they stared at him. He couldn't help his appearance.

Now he was teaching them a lesson, and he couldn't help but wonder if he should put the female police officer on his list.

Chapter Eighteen

She did her best to pull her thoughts away from having left her dad, though she'd shed a tear in the car on the way to the station. Chris had texted her as well, asking how everything had gone. She'd replied that it had gone better than she'd expected, knowing he would be relieved to hear it. He was worried about her, and she understood that, but she also suspected he was worried she'd have changed her mind, especially if Frank had refused to go in, and that she'd have ended up driving him back home again.

With a second victim, and with them still no closer to finding out who was doing this, she knew her DCI was going to want to have a briefing to make sure they were all heading in the right direction. He wouldn't like that she was late in that morning either.

Killers didn't care about detectives with family problems.

The briefing was already underway when she slipped into the office. She found a spot at the back of the room, but of course, it didn't go unnoticed. It wasn't as though she could hide, anyway, not when she had a job to do.

"Nice of you to join us," Gibbs said with a tight smile.

"Sorry, family stuff," she muttered, hating that her cheeks burned.

It didn't matter to Gibbs that she'd been here until midnight, had gone home and climbed into bed, and then was up again at six to deal with her dad and daughter. He'd never had to worry about a work-life balance. His wife—a meek woman who'd been more than happy to stay at home to take care of their two sons—did everything for him, and probably rarely nagged him about how much time he spent in the office. Theirs was a far more traditional, or perhaps she should say backward, job-role.

There were several people in the room, including DC Howard and Rudd, and Shawn as well, who'd offered her a sympathetic smile as she'd entered. There were also officers from other divisions who were there to offer help.

"So," Gibbs clapped his hands together in front of his body, "where are we on this today?"

"The pathologist has the report ready on our second victim," Shawn called out.

"Good." Gibbs nodded. "You and Swift go down and speak to her, see what she's found out. Hopefully, this arsehole has fucked up and left a couple of prints on the body. We need something substantial we can work with."

"The press are gathering outside," Erica said. She'd had to muscle her way through them on the way in, while they'd shouted questions at her, and a couple had snapped photographs. "Word is getting around that there's a serial offender, and potentially a serial killer, on our streets."

Gibbs frowned and folded his arms across his chest. "We don't want there to be a panic. You know how people overreact to these things. I'll speak with them."

"We have more CCTV footage from the area that's going to need to be gone through as well," she mentioned.

"I can do that, boss," Rudd offered.

"Great." Erica smiled gratefully at the other woman. "Something's bound to show up. It happened in the city, and he didn't just appear out of nowhere."

"Good, so, you've all got work to do." Gibbs was already turning back to his office. "Get on with it."

Erica was happy to see him go.

Everyone stood and filed out of the room.

"How did it go?" Shawn asked from beside her.

He knew all about her taking her dad into the care home that morning.

"As well as can be expected. I still feel like a piece of shit about it, though."

"It's not your fault."

She sighed. "I know. I guess there's a part of me that thinks maybe he deserved a different kind of daughter. Perhaps if I'd been one of those women who liked to be at home and take care of others, then he'd have someone who'd be there for him."

Shawn cocked an eyebrow. "Doesn't your sister do that?"

He had a point.

"Anyway," he continued, "your dad was in this game, and he raised you to want to be as well. I'm sure he's extremely proud of you and would never want you to give up your career for him."

A painful lump tightened in her throat. "Okay, you've got to stop being nice to me." There was no way in hell she was going to cry in front of her sergeant. "Let's go and look at a dead body instead."

• • • •

THIRTY MINUTES LATER, they arrived at the coroner's office.

The pathologist, Lucy Kim, was there to meet them.

Erica liked Kim. It was hard not to. She certainly wasn't the type you'd normally expect to find working among the dead. She was tall and whip-thin, with one side of her head shaved in an undercut, and a sleeve of tattoos down one arm. She was always enthusiastic about her job, and Erica had never had an encounter with the other woman where she'd seemed in any way tired or bored of what she was doing.

"Good morning," Kim greeted them. "I have a report for you."

Erica returned her smile. "That's why we're here."

She jerked her head towards the closed doors. "Come on through."

They helped themselves to protective clothing before entering the examination room. The space was laid out much as any regular surgical room would be, only without the need of lifesaving equipment such as ventilators or vital signs monitors. There was no bringing these patients back.

Beneath a sheet lay the body of Patrick Ronson. Erica didn't need to pull back the covering to know his chest cavity would have been opened up, his ribs cracked like a lobster tail. His internal organs removed and weighed.

"It's definitely the same guy you're looking for. There's a puncture wound from a hypodermic needle in the back of his neck." Kim's dark eyes brightened with excitement, and she tilted the head to reveal the mark Erica had already spotted at the scene. "The tox screen came back showing Midazolam in his system, the same drug that was used for the first victim. There are ligature marks around his wrists and ankles, though I believe they were caused by tape rather than rope or cuffs. I was able to sample some tacky substance from the areas. The way the eyes have been removed—with a sharp knife—was identical, and then I found filaments I believe are from cotton wool in the eye cavity."

"He stuffed the eye sockets before he let them go?" Erica confirmed.

"Looks as though that's what happened. My guess is that he wanted to stop the bleeding."

Shawn frowned. "He didn't want to kill them."

Kim pursed her lips and shook her head. "I don't believe so, no."

Erica walked around the operating table. "So, what did Ronson die from?"

"His heart gave out on him. It was hardly surprising, really, considering his age and what he'd gone through. The shock alone would have been enough to cause his heart to fail, but if you add in blood loss and the drugs as well…" She shrugged. "Perhaps whoever did this hadn't planned for him to die, but there's little doubt in my mind that going through what he did was what killed him."

"The cotton you found in the eye sockets. Any chance it's from some rare cotton retailer that only sells to one chemist in the whole of London?"

Kim pulled a face. "Sorry. I believe it's standard use medical cotton wool."

"Okay, thanks. What about anything else? Any other fibres, hair strands, or prints from his skin?"

"No prints other than his. There was some brick dust embedded into his skin. Looks like it's from where he was lying. Not sure what use that's going to be to you, though."

Her heart sank. Shit. She'd hoped she was going to come back with something more substantial, if only to keep Gibbs off her back.

"Well, if you find anything else, please let us know ASAP."

Kim nodded. "Of course, will do."

They left, ridding themselves of the protective clothing as they went.

"At least we know we're after the same guy," Shawn offered, trying to perk her up. He would have known that she'd have hoped to get more out of the report.

"We already suspected that much. All it's done is confirmed it. Same with the cotton wool. He's got access to medical supplies, but anyone who can use the internet can get hold of them these days."

Shawn pressed his lips into a thin line. "True."

"Maybe something will show up on the rest of the CCTV footage," she said, though she wasn't feeling too hopeful.

It was as though both the killer and the victims had appeared out of thin air, only for the killer to vanish again.

Chapter Nineteen

Gibbs was busy when they arrived back at the office, so at least she had some breathing room before she needed to update him about the coroner's report.

She switched on her computer and tried not to think about how her dad was getting on. She glanced at her phone. Would it be okay to call and ask? A part of her wanted to, but the other part worried that if it wasn't going well, it would only give her more to stress about. She needed to focus on her job.

Rudd approached her desk. "I checked files from years ago, going over old cases, and I found something."

The news perked Erica up. "Tell me."

"Seven years ago, a body was found with one of his eyes stabbed out. Nineteen-year-old Bobby Finn. His body was found in the canal at Limehouse, but the body was badly decomposed. The murder weapon was found when the canal was dredged, but there wasn't any evidence that could be preserved. The knife wound had penetrated the brain, but water was found in the victim's lungs, so he was still alive when he went into the canal."

"Hmm. Could be a coincidence, though the location is right. Did they get anyone for it?"

The DC shook her head. "No. Some people were questioned, but no one was charged."

"Get me the names of the people they'd suspected."

"Already done." She slipped a folder across the desk. "One of them was a Daniel Bailey, but we're going to have trouble speaking to him again."

She looked up sharply. "Why's that?"

"He's dead."

Erica opened the folder. On top was a photograph of the man in question.

Her stomach dropped. She recognised him immediately. That had been a day when she'd almost changed her career path for good. Of course, she'd seen death before. She'd been at the aftermath of car accidents, where people, including children, had been cut from destroyed vehicles. She'd been to house fires and witnessed burned bodies being removed from the houses. She'd seen death and had believed herself to have hardened to it over the years.

But to have it happen right in front of her, the utter shock and helplessness, had left her reeling. She'd thought she was winning, had really hoped she'd made a difference, and then it had all been snatched away in a matter of a split second.

God, it was the anniversary soon. Not that she could ever have forgotten, considering what day it had coincided with.

She did her best to cover her reaction. "If he's dead, he's clearly not responsible for what we're dealing with now."

"No, he's not."

"Okay, I'll give this a look over and see if there's anything that could tie in that murder to this case. Maybe the detectives at the time missed something."

"If they never charged anyone for the murder, there is a chance it's our guy," Rudd continued hopefully.

Erica sucked in a breath. "Yes, you're right. What about the CCTV footage? Did that bring up anything else?"

"No, we lost him in a blind spot."

"Could he have got out of a car there?"

"It's possible. A number of vehicles were caught on CCTV cameras around that time, but that's to be expected. It was a road, and this is London." Rudd shrugged as though she felt bad for the natural business of the city, even in the early hours of the morning.

"Let's track them down. If nothing else, the drivers of the cars might have seen something. Patrick Ronson had to have come from somewhere. He didn't magically appear in a cloud of smoke."

Rudd nodded. "Yes, boss."

She turned and left, and Erica sat forward, her elbows on her desk, needing a minute. She ran her hand over her mouth, surprisingly shaken at being reminded of something that had happened so long ago. She felt as though someone had punched her in the gut, winding her, her adrenaline soaring.

Triggered. That was what all the young people seemed to be calling it these days. Seeing his photograph had taken her right back to that time and place, her body reacting as though she was experiencing it all over again.

It was just a coincidence that the man brought in and questioned about this case was the same one she'd encountered in her early years on the force. She'd always worked in this part of the city, and troubled young men were bound to show up repeatedly. The vast majority of offenders went on to offend again.

Not that it mattered. There was no possibility this was the man they were after since a dead man couldn't abduct or assault anyone.

She looked around for Shawn but didn't see him anywhere. She wanted to update him about the case Rudd had found. While she was at it, she should probably update Gibbs as well—not that she wanted to. But she couldn't let her own personal feelings get in the way of doing her job.

Erica pushed back her chair and went to Gibbs's office. The door was open a crack, and she stood in the doorway, her hand poised in position to knock, but her DCI's voice filtered out to her.

"That's the problem with having women on the force. Always having to run off to some family crisis or another. You never see the blokes having to do that. They're one hundred percent focused on the job."

Her face flushed with heat, and her heart thumped. Who was he talking to? She peeped through the gap to see Shawn standing in front of Gibbs's desk.

Was her sergeant in there bad-mouthing her as well? She'd never have thought Shawn was like that.

She wanted to burst in there and defend herself. What could she say? That Gibbs was lucky to have his wife at home to be able to deal with everything on his behalf? But even that felt wrong. After all, she had Christopher at home, taking care of Poppy and looking after the house. It didn't stop her feeling guilty, though, and she was sure it was a guilt the men wouldn't understand. Even though she was the main breadwinner for their family, and kept a roof over their heads and food in their bellies, she did feel horrible about not being there for every bedtime, and having to miss school plays and sports days because she was working. It was hard not to feel like she was not enough for all the different aspects of her life—a bad mum for not being around all the time, and a bad detective because she sometimes had to take time to be with her family.

She guessed all working mothers lived with this internal struggle, no matter what their jobs.

Shawn stuck up for her. "She lives for this job, sir. Erica is one hundred percent committed, and she's one of the best people I work with. I like that she gives a shit. She brings a different perspective to this job."

Gibbs rolled his eyes. "She's got you under the thumb, too, I see."

Erica cleared her throat to make sure they were aware of her standing there and then stepped into the room. "Wanted to give you an update on what we'd found."

"DS Turner was just doing that," Gibbs said.

She didn't think she imagined the guilt crossing Shawn's face.

He gestured helplessly. "I got called in."

Erica understood. If their DCI asked for an update, Shawn could hardly refuse.

"That's fine," she said. "DC Rudd came across an old case that might fit in with ours. I thought you would want to know."

Gibbs pursed his lips. "Rudd found it, eh? What about you, Swift? How are *you* lately?"

She knew the comment was to do with her personal life, and she gritted her teeth.

"Thumbs are a bit achy. But that's to be expected considering how many people I apparently have trapped under them." She kept her tone jovial—just a bit of office banter—but she wanted him to know she'd overheard what he'd said.

Gibbs at least had the decency to glance away. He muttered something and shuffled paperwork around on his desk.

In her head, she added, *and in case you were wondering, I did a fifteen-hour shift yesterday, and will probably do that same today, though I'm sure you wouldn't dream of doing anything less than twenty-four.*

DCI Gibbs had left the office hours before she had the previous evening, and he must have known it. It wasn't easy being a woman in what was mainly a male environment. For the most part, she liked to keep her head down and get on with her job, but sometimes she wished she could take Gibbs down a peg or two.

But she was still his subordinate, and she knew she wouldn't get away with being disrespectful towards a superior officer. There would be consequences, and she'd been lucky to get away with the thumb comment.

Chapter Twenty: Seven Years Earlier

The police had never been able to prove that they'd been the ones to bury their mother's body.

At eighteen, Nicholas left foster care and was moved into a tiny council flat. He wasn't afraid of hard work, though his appearance and background made it hard for him to get employment.

A year later, Danny also got out of foster care and moved back in with his brother. Danny was still drinking whenever he could. Even though he was essentially bunking with Nicholas, he showed Nicholas zero respect or gratitude. While Nicholas worked all the hours he could, Danny lazed around the flat, drinking and gaming, and rarely doing anything to help out.

Despite Danny's behaviour, Nicholas was still happy to have him back. His had been a lonely existence, and finally he was no longer alone.

But Danny was a tortured soul. He was plagued with nightmares, either sleeping for days on end, or else Nicholas heard him pacing the tiny hallway in the middle of the night, unable to sleep. He barely left the flat. Sometimes, he went a week or more without even speaking to Nicholas.

On a rare day off, Nicholas decided it would do them both good to get out of the flat. The walls had been closing in, and it was no fun being stuck inside with Danny, amid the mess and the stale stench of filth.

"Come on. Let's get out of here," he suggested. "We can go for a beer somewhere. I'll treat you to a pint."

Nicholas didn't drink often—if hardly at all—but if it meant getting Danny out of the flat, he'd have a beer with him.

The promise of free booze got Danny's attention. "Where do you want to go?"

"I dunno. Down by the canal, maybe."

Danny shrugged. "If you throw in a packet of crisps, you're on."

"Deal."

They walked side by side, Nicholas with his hood pulled up, covering his face, despite the warm weather, and Danny with his swagger and brooding expression. But Nicholas was still pleased to spend time with his brother outside of the flat. The area they were in was rough, anyway, so it wasn't as though they didn't look the part. No one hung around here unless they were some kind of trouble, or else had got lost, and anyone who was lost would want to find their way back to a safer area quickly.

They found a pub that had a couple of benches out the front. They were flaking and leaned to one side when the brothers sat, but they would do. Nicholas went into the dark interior of the pub, blinking to adjust his eyes. The stink of cigarette smoke and stale beer filled his nostrils, but it was no worse than he was used to at home. He ordered a couple of lagers from the bloke behind the bar, and a packet of cheese and onion crisps for Danny, then carried them back out again.

Danny downed his pint almost as soon as Nicholas had put it on the table. "Lend us a tenner, and I'll get the next ones." He motioned with his fingers for Nicholas to hand some money over.

Nicholas didn't argue and gave him a tenner. Danny disappeared back into the pub and returned with another two pints, even though Nicholas had barely touched his first one.

Danny drank the second one, then pointed to the third pint he'd bought—the one Nicholas hadn't touched yet. "You gonna drink that?"

Nicholas shook his head.

Danny spent the rest of the money on another pint and drank that, too. Nicholas was still nursing his first, and it had gone flat and warm.

It was getting dark now.

"I'm out of cash," he told Danny. "Guess it's time to head back."

"Yeah, whatever." He got to his feet and swung his arm around Nicholas's shoulders. "You know I love you, bro, don't you?" He kissed the top of Nicholas's head. "We went through a lot of shit, didn't we, but we turned out all right."

Nicholas didn't think either of them had really turned out all right, but it was good to see Danny happy, even if it was only drunk happy.

The two of them staggered alongside the canal, Danny's arm still hooked around Nicholas's shoulders, perhaps needing his support to keep him upright.

Another young man was walking towards them. He caught sight of the brothers and slowed, moving to one side, closer to the canal, to make way for them.

At Nicholas's side, Danny stiffened.

Fuck.

The young man had deliberately glanced away, as though he was finding something interesting in the graffiti scrawled across the concrete walls on the other side of the canal path. His body language was all about minimising himself, drawing his shoulders in, his head tucked down.

By contrast, Danny did the exact opposite. "What the fuck are you looking at?" he threw at the man.

Nicholas's chest tightened in panic. "Leave it, Danny. He's not doing anything."

"Yes, he is. Fucking prick."

Nicholas tugged his hood higher, ducking into the safety of the shadows. He wanted to vanish from the moment. Danny had had too much to drink and was spoiling for a fight.

"He thinks we're a pair of freaks." Danny had deliberately raised his voice so the other bloke would hear. "You can see the way he's looking at us. Maybe he thinks we're a couple of homos. I reckon we need to teach him a lesson."

Nicholas's gaze darted around, desperately hoping to spot someone else, but other than them, the canal path was empty. There were only a few feet between them and the other man now, though he hadn't said anything, wisely keeping his head down and mouth shut, hoping he might be able to slip past them without there being any trouble.

From seemingly out of nowhere, a knife appeared in Danny's hand.

Nicholas had a moment to think *where the fuck did that come from?* Then Danny darted forward, the knife held high.

The man reared back and lifted both hands to shield his face, but he wasn't fast enough. Danny plunged the knife downwards, and the sharp point of the blade met with the man's eye. It sank deep, and the man screamed, but Danny didn't stop there. He twisted the knife and yanked it back out again—Nicholas tried not to think about the quivering matter on the silver blade—then he grabbed the man's shoulder and shoved him hard to the side.

It all happened so fast—a matter of seconds—too fast for Nicholas to react. The man staggered to one side. The edge of the canal path was right there, and he toppled over. He hit the water hard and sank beneath almost instantly.

A bubble of blood reached the surface and popped, sending ripples out in a circle, and then everything was still.

Danny wiped the handle of the knife on his t-shirt, then using his t-shirt to hold it, he tossed the weapon out into the water. It hit the surface with a small *plop* and vanished into the darkness.

Nicholas stood, rooted to the spot, staring at the place where the man had sunk beneath the water. He was waiting for him to burst to the surface, splashing and coughing and calling for help, but nothing happened.

They were alone on the canal path once again. It was as though the man had never been here.

He finally found his voice. "What the fuck, Danny?"

Danny shrugged. "People who dare look at us like that need to be taught a lesson, Nicholas. They need to learn some respect."

That bloke wasn't going to be learning anything. He was dead.

"But...but...you stabbed him in the fucking eye."

Danny shrugged again and continued to swagger down the canal path as though nothing had happened. "If they can't keep their eyes to themselves, they don't deserve to keep them."

Chapter Twenty-One

Christopher Swift sat in the silence of his house and breathed a sigh of relief. Maybe it made him a complete arsehole for enjoying being alone in his house for the first time in weeks, but he couldn't help it. Recently, he'd struggled to concentrate on work, always conscious that he also had to keep an ear out for his father-in-law.

He appreciated what Erica did for a living. Not only was she out there, keeping people safe, her role also meant that he was able to do the job he enjoyed from home, and he'd be perfectly content doing the school runs and then coming home to work for a few hours until it was time to pick Poppy up again. He didn't even mind all the playground mums that Erica found so hard to be around—they'd always been perfectly friendly towards him.

But then Frank had moved in, and their easy-going life had changed dramatically. He'd even worried about going to pick up Poppy for fear of coming home and finding Frank had set fire to the house trying to boil himself an egg.

His work had taken a hit while he'd been distracted with taking care of Frank. At first, he'd done his best to minimise the effect in Erica's eyes. She had enough on her plate without having to worry about his job as well, but in the end, it had been impossible to keep it from her. She was far from stupid, and she knew they were all exhausted and that everything was getting on top of him.

He liked Frank, and it was a tragic shame this was his life now. He'd been a tough, no-nonsense kind of guy up until a few years ago, when the signs first started showing. They tried to laugh it off at first, hoping things would get better on their own, but of course, they only got worse. Eventually, Erica took her father to a doctor's appointment, and they got the news they didn't want to hear. Frank had been put on medication that was supposed to slow the onset of the dementia, but it hadn't worked. Or maybe it had, and his dementia would have come on even faster without the meds. Who knew?

Something outside the window caught his eye, and Chris frowned.

A man was lurking on the street opposite his house. He had a slight build, with his hands in his pockets, and his hood pulled up to shield his face. There were a couple of parked cars on the road, and the man wandered between them. At first Chris thought he was checking out the cars, perhaps seeing if any had been left unlocked, or if there was anything left inside them that was worth breaking a window for, but then the man stopped and lifted his head to look directly at their house.

What was he doing? He definitely appeared to be scoping the place. This wasn't a particularly rough area, but there weren't any areas of London that were completely free from crime. Still, this particular person must be pretty dumb to be checking out the home of a detective.

The stranger must have spotted Chris at the window, as he quickly ducked his head and took off at a fast walk down the street.

Chris sat back in his chair. That was strange. He should probably mention it to Erica when she got home, though he didn't want to give her something else to worry about. No doubt, she'd be worried sick and feeling guilty about her dad.

He went back to enjoying the quiet, and the thought of the hooded youth went completely out of his head.

Chapter Twenty-Two

It was getting late, but Erica still wasn't done.

The brick dust residue found on the second victim's skin was playing on her mind.

"Lewis Jacobs said he heard rumbling while he was being held, and that he thought it might have been a train," she said, half to herself, but loud enough for her sergeant to hear. "Do you think he might have heard a Tube train?"

Sitting across from her at his desk, Shawn lifted his head and frowned. "You think our guy took the victims on the Tube?"

"No, but wherever he did hold them might have been *near* the Tube, and there's a chance he was kept on a brick flooring or was leaning up against a brick wall."

Shawn suggested, "Like a converted cellar room, maybe?"

Erica remembered a time she'd had a boyfriend who rented a cellar flat in Notting Hill. It had been close to the Tube line, and every time a train went past—which was approximately every three minutes—everything in the flat rattled, and the vibrations went right up through her feet.

That brick dust, though... "Or perhaps it hasn't been converted yet."

There was a corkboard on the wall with a map with pins in the locations where the victims had been found. She stood to take another look at it.

"Where are the nearest Tube stations to where the two victims were found?" she asked.

"Mile End for the first victim and Whitechapel for the second," Shawn said, joining her.

"The stations are all on or near Whitechapel Road, with the central line basically running beneath it. Is it possible he has a place somewhere between the two?"

Shawn nodded. "Worth checking out."

"I want to see planning from the council. Let's find out which properties around that area have had cellars converted into flats."

"It might still only be a cellar," Shawn said. "It might not have been converted yet."

"Yes, you're right. But to have use of a cellar would mean whoever is doing this also has use of the property above. This might be East London, but it's still expensive to live. In the profiling, it was suggested that this person might be disfigured, a bit of a recluse. It's unlikely that he's married or even sharing a property with anyone." She let out a sigh. "But of course, you're right. Let's try to find out which properties are likely to have cellars, and then which ones are closest to the Tube lines to be able to hear the trains. It should narrow things down."

She tapped her finger on her lips, thinking. "I'm going to go back into the hospital and speak with Lewis Jacobs again. He might have thought of something else since we last interviewed him. If we can narrow this location down, we might finally have something substantial to go on."

"Do you want me to come with you?" Shawn offered.

"No, you focus on the planning applications. See what you can come up with."

He tipped his fingers to his head in a salute. "Yes, boss."

• • • •

THE LIFT DOORS SLID open, and she stepped out into the hospital corridor, her boots squeaking on the linoleum floors as she walked. She was relieved to be out of the lift. Though she'd never have admitted it to anyone, she hated being inside those things. It felt inherently wrong to be suspended in a metal box by a piece of wire, and she hated being in such close confines to other people as well, especially when those people were also in a hospital and hacked and coughed over her shoulder.

Erica paused for a moment, getting her bearings. Even though she'd been here before, this whole place felt like one of those fairground attractions where mirrors reflected the same corridor over and over, each of them looking exactly the same. She checked the sign on the wall pointing out each of the different departments on this floor and made sure she saw ICU before following in the direction the sign pointed.

Pushing through the doors onto the ward, the reception area directly ahead of her, she realised she'd entered a commotion.

Somewhere on the ward, an alarm blared, and hospital staff raced past, no one paying any attention to her.

What's going on?

She picked up her pace, her heartbeat tripping. As she hurried down the corridor, the staff vanished into one of the rooms.

Shit. Is that Lewis Jacobs's room?

Erica broke into a run and turned into the room. The space was filled with doctors in white coats and nurses in their scrubs. Several were kneeling on the floor, and the view of their backs blocked the person who was focusing all their attention.

"Call it," one of the doctors announced, and one of the other staff called the time of death.

The doctor exhaled a long sigh. "There was nothing more we could have done."

What the fuck? Lewis Jacobs was dead? What had happened? His injuries hadn't been life-threatening—at least not in the way they had been with Patrick Ronson. Jacobs had been stable when she'd spoken to him last, and Shawn hadn't mentioned anything about Jacobs's condition worsening when he'd come in to question him either.

She suddenly remembered her reason for being there. She'd wanted to ask him some more questions, to try to pin down the location where he'd been held. Her mind jumped to the possibility that the person who'd done this to him had come back to finish the job. Damn it. She'd sent home the PC who'd been watching over him, not believing Jacobs had been in any danger. Had she been wrong?

She realised they were standing in a potential crime scene, and the hospital staff were walking all over it. While preserving life was always going to be her first priority, now the victim was dead, preserving any evidence topped it.

She was going to need some help.

Erica fished her phone from her bag and called her DCI.

He answered after a few rings. "What is it, Swift? I'm in the middle of something."

"You're going to want to hear this. Lewis Jacobs is dead."

"What? How?"

"I'm not sure yet. I called you as soon as I found out. We're going to need to get SOCO in here to process the scene for fingerprints, DNA and do a preliminary exam of the body, and call the coroner's office, too."

"I'll get a local sergeant out to you immediately as well."

"Thank you, sir."

She ended the call.

This was a high-profile case, and very soon this ward was going to be swarming with officers and detectives. But it was going to take time for additional resources to arrive, and in the meantime, she needed to do her job.

Some of the hospital staff had noticed her in the doorway, and she flashed them her ID.

"DI Swift. What's happened here?"

The doctor who'd been working on Lewis Jacobs rose to his feet. "Hung himself with the bedsheets. Guess he couldn't handle the thought of being blind."

Now that people had started to move away, Erica was able to get a view of Jacobs's body. Sure enough, a twisted sheet was wrapped around his throat, though one of the medical team must have loosened it. The bandages were still around the top half of his face, and for that Erica was grateful. She remembered how the second victim had looked with his eyes missing, and it was definitely an image that would haunt her nightmares.

"Hung himself from what?" she asked.

Her gaze flicked down to the name badge on his shirt. *Dr P Avery.*

Dr Avery pointed to the back of the hospital bed. "From the back of the bed. He must have tied the end up and then kneeled forward, off the end of the bed."

"Did anyone see him do it?"

"No, of course not. We'd have stopped him if we'd seen him. One of the nurses came in and found him, and she called for help, and we got him down and started CPR right away. He must have already been dead for a good ten minutes or so, though. We did everything we could, but we couldn't bring him back."

She glanced to the corners of the room. "And you don't have any security cameras in here?"

"No, not in the room. It would be an invasion of the patient's privacy. We have security cameras in the corridors."

"I'm going to need to check them. Make sure no one came in or out of here shortly before he died."

The doctor frowned at her. "You think someone else did this?"

"I think it's convenient that the only witness to two separate attacks is now dead, and I want to make sure no one else was involved."

"Yes, of course."

"Did you see any defensive wounds on the body?" she asked him. "Did it look as though he put up a fight?"

"Not that I'm aware of, but I wasn't looking for that when I worked on him."

"I'm going to need to interview the nurse who discovered him and anyone else who had contact with him, within a few hours before his death. None of the staff, visitors, or patients should leave the ward. They're all going to need to be questioned."

Dr Avery nodded. "Whatever you need."

Erica sighed and shook her head at the body on the floor. Poor bastard. Maybe Dr Avery was right, and Jacobs hadn't been able to handle the idea of living the rest of his life blind. But now Lewis Jacobs was never going to be able to find out if he'd have been able to adjust to his new life.

There was one thing certain about death—it was final.

Chapter Twenty-Three

The following morning, Erica entered her kitchen, a tight knot in her chest. It was a day she was supposed to celebrate but hadn't since the events of six years ago. Her mood wasn't helped by what had happened with Lewis Jacobs last night.

So far, Lewis Jacobs's death looked as though it was suicide. From what they could tell, he'd been alone in the hospital room the whole time. All the interviews of the staff had told the same story, and from the CCTV footage, it didn't look as though anyone had entered or left the room shortly before his death. What a horrible way to go. He hadn't been able to accept living in a world of darkness, so he'd jumped into nothingness forever.

On the way back from the hospital, she'd popped into the care home to see her dad, but he'd been sleeping, and they hadn't wanted to disturb him. She felt bad that she hadn't managed to visit with him properly again that day, but the truth was that he probably wouldn't have remembered anyway, or if he did remember her coming, he wouldn't be able to place what day it had been.

Poppy stood by the kitchen table, beaming brightly. Beside her, on the surface, were a couple of presents wrapped in brightly coloured paper, shiny foil bows stuck to the tops. Taking pride of place in the middle of the table was a chocolate cake with candles, and *Happy Birthday* scrawled across it in white icing.

"Happy birthday, Mummy," Poppy cried.

Erica forced a smile. "Oh, how lovely." She put her arms out to her daughter, and Poppy bundled into them, her small arms wrapping around Erica's waist, her face pressed to her stomach. "You didn't need to do all of this for me."

"Daddy said you'd say that, but I wanted to."

"Did he, now?"

Chris hovered by the oven, sporting a guilty expression.

She unwound Poppy from her waist and crossed the kitchen to plant a kiss on her husband's lips. As she slipped her arms around his neck for a hug, she whispered in his ear, "You know I hate celebrating."

Equally as subtly, he whispered back, "Poppy wanted to. It's for her as much as for you."

He was right. Poppy was excited to celebrate her mummy's birthday.

Erica made all the right noises, *oohing* over a handmade card Poppy had drawn, with a slightly crazed-looking Erica on the front holding a bunch of balloons, and then she unwrapped the gifts of chocolates and some moisturiser. She held up the box. "Is this because I'm getting old?"

Chris kissed her cheek. "Thirty-four is hardly old, and anyway, if you're old, then what does that make me?"

Chris was five years her senior.

"*Really* old," Poppy declared with a giggle.

"Oi, cheeky." He grinned at her and ruffled her hair.

"Does this mean we get to have chocolate cake for breakfast?" Erica asked.

Chris winked at her. "You're the birthday girl. We get to have whatever you want."

Poppy clapped and jumped up and down. "Chocolate cake, chocolate cake."

Erica nodded at her daughter. "Chocolate cake it is."

"Yay! You're the best mummy ever!"

Erica laughed, but the sound felt false. She was doing this for her daughter, taking the memories and weight in the middle of her chest, the heaviness on her shoulders, and pushing it down as far as she could.

It had been seven years since she'd last celebrated her birthday properly. Each year, she thought it would get easier, but it didn't. It would always be there—what had happened on this day, like a ghost clinging to her back.

She finished up her coffee and cake then kissed her family goodbye.

"I have to get to work. Sorry. My DCI has been giving me a hard time about all the hours I've been taking off when we're in the middle of a case."

Chris rolled his eyes. "Erica, you've barely been home before midnight for days. How is that taking time off?"

She sighed. "I know, but that's the way it is. All hands on deck until we find this guy."

"The eye guy?" he double-checked.

She shot a look to Poppy to make sure the little girl wasn't listening. "Yeah, that's the one."

News of the killer was all over the papers and social media. People were warning each other not to go out late at night, and never on their own. East London was in a particular state of panic, since both victims had been found locally. She wished there was a way she could tell the public not to worry—after all, making people feel safe was supposed to be her job—but the truth was that they still didn't know who was responsible.

Chris kissed her again. "Okay, go and catch the bad guy. Stay safe."

"Thanks."

She left her little family finishing up her birthday cake and drove to the office. For once, she got in before Shawn, but Gibbs was already there, poised in his office doorway, glowering at her. She had no intention of mentioning to him that it was her birthday. She doubted he'd have got her a present.

"There you are," he said, as though she'd spent days out of the office rather than a matter of hours. "We're still nowhere close to finding this arsehole, and now our first victim and only real witness has gone and bloody hung himself. Please tell me you have some good news."

"We've narrowed down the area where we think he might be keeping his victims," she told her DCI. "I've got Rudd and Howard covering it today."

She'd sent the two DCs to do a door-to-door on all the houses along Whitechapel road that had cellars, converted or otherwise, to see if anyone had seen or heard anything, or if they came across someone acting suspiciously. It was a tedious job, but it needed to be done.

Gibbs's lips thinned. "We'd better have something substantial by the end of the day. I do not like the idea of this son of a bitch laughing at us."

"Me neither, sir. I want to get him as badly as you."

Gibbs snorted. "Better get on with it, then."

She was relieved to have a reason to distance herself from her DCI. The man had the ability to rub her up the wrong way. She was sure he didn't speak to the men on their team like that.

She got back to her desk to find Shawn already there. He opened his mouth, and she held up her hand.

"Don't even say it."

He pouted. "Not even a little happy b—"

"I said don't say it," she cut him off. "This is one day I do not need reminding about."

"Okay, okay. How are you feeling about last night?"

"Not great, to be honest."

She blamed herself for the death of Lewis Jacobs. "I was the one who sent home the officer who'd been watching over him. If I hadn't done that, he might still be alive today."

Shawn shook his head. "You don't know that. He might have been able to do it anyway."

"Not if someone had been watching him," she insisted.

"If he was going to take his own life, if he knew he couldn't cope, he'd have done it at a later date anyway. You couldn't have had someone watching him for weeks or even months to come."

She shrugged. "He might not have. If he'd had enough time, he could have learned to deal with being blind."

Shawn gave her a sympathetic smile. "You saw the background he came from, the people he considered to be friends. Do you really think he could have adapted to that situation?"

She shook her head and rubbed her hands over her eyes. "I guess we'll never know now. Besides, if he'd waited until a later date, we might have at least been able to question him again and be one step closer to catching the bastard who did this to him."

Her phone rang, and she checked the screen. It was the care home. Her stomach dropped. This was the last thing she needed right now. Was she ever going to catch a break?

She had no choice but to answer. "Erica Swift."

"Yes, hello, Mrs Swift. We're sorry to bother you when you're busy, but your father is a little agitated right now, and we can't seem to calm him down. Are you able to pop in at all? We think it would help for him to see a familiar face."

She was already on her feet, grabbing her bag. "Yes, of course. I'm coming right there." She ended the call and looked to Shawn. "Cover for me? I'll be back as soon as I can. My dad's not happy."

"Yeah, of course. Go."

"Thanks, mate."

God, her poor dad. He was probably confused and frightened, being in a strange place surrounded by people he didn't know. Guilt swept over her in a wave, threatening to drown her. What had she done?

As she hurried from the building, she called Chris. He answered on the first ring.

"Chris, there's a problem with my dad at the care home. They've called me in, and I'm not sure I can handle it by myself if he's upset. Can you meet me there?"

She wasn't a weak woman. Maybe she should have been able to deal with her father by herself, but she found it hard. She took his insults and anger far more personally than

Chris. Chris was her rock, and she honestly didn't know how she'd cope without him.

"Yes, of course. I'm finishing up something, and I'll be right there. It'll be fine, Erica. It's just teething problems, okay?"

She sniffed. "Thanks. I love you."

"Love you, too. I'll see you there."

Chapter Twenty-Four

She drove as fast as she dared.
Within fifteen minutes, she was pulling into the car park outside Willow Glade Care Home. Everything seemed quiet from the outside, but she was sure it would be different when she got into the building.

She hurried to the entrance, not quite breaking into a run, but not far off. She clutched her handbag tight to her shoulder, unsure why she'd even bothered to bring it.

Monica rushed out to meet her. A commotion was going on in the background, and Erica was fairly sure it had something to do with her father.

"I'm sorry to call you in, Mrs Swift. We do normally handle these things by ourselves, but since Frank's only been here for such a short time, and none of our distraction techniques seemed to be working, I thought it was best if he sees a familiar face."

"No, it's fine." She hoped he would recognise her. He did most of the time, though he sometimes got her mixed up with Natasha, or even their mother. "I'd rather you called me."

"He's this way."

She turned to guide her towards the dayroom.

Her dad was standing behind one of the high-back chairs with a walking stick in his hand, which he was using to jab at the staff. Where had he got the walking stick from? It wasn't as though he even used one. He must have grabbed it off one of the other residents. Erica hoped he hadn't done that while the other resident was on their feet.

Was it possible for a dementia patient to be excluded from a care home for bad behaviour? She hoped not, or she had the horrible feeling her dad wasn't going to be welcomed here, six hundred pounds a week or not.

"Hi, Dad." She forced a smile. "What's going on? Why are you so upset?"

"I'm not supposed to be here!"

His face was strained, his jaw rigid, and lips pulled back over his teeth.

"It's okay, Dad. You're staying here for a while. Remember?"

"Where's Yvonne? I was supposed to have taken her to an appointment an hour ago, and I can't find her, and these arseholes won't let me leave."

She tried to take a step towards him, but he swung out with the walking stick, and she darted back again to avoid getting caught by the end. "You don't need to worry about any of that. It's all been taken care of, I promise."

"No! Where's Yvonne? What have you done with her?"

It tore Erica up inside to see him like this. She'd have done anything to wave a magic wand and take this terrible illness away from him. She suddenly realised that with her father's illness, she'd lost the last adult in her life she'd always leaned on. If she had problems, she'd always known her dad would be there for her to help ease her worries, but now that support was gone. Chris was wonderful, but it wasn't the same. Your parent was the one person who would be on your side, regardless.

She tried again. "Everything is fine, Dad. You're staying here for a little while to give yourself a break, remember? Everyone here wants to take care of you, and you can't act like this towards them."

Several of the other residents had also become distressed by the outburst, and some of the other staff were dealing with them, either calming them down where they were or guiding them from the dayroom out to their own rooms or into the gardens.

Had this all been a massive mistake? Maybe she should offer to take Dad home? She'd never wanted for his illness to affect others. But then what would she do about work? She was already skating on thin ice with Gibbs.

Where was Chris? He said he was on his way. She was doing her best to hold it together, but she was starting to feel desperate, and she knew Frank would pick up on that desperation. She appreciated everything the staff at the care home were trying to do, but she could really use someone else who knew both her and Frank.

"Here we go, Frank." One of the carers came bustling along with a cup of tea on a tray, together with a plate of biscuits. "How about you sit down and have a nice cup of tea?"

"Don't you fucking patronise me. I'm not a goddamned child."

"I wouldn't do that," the woman said kindly. "I thought you looked like you could use one."

She set the tray down on a small round table, never taking her eye off the walking stick Frank still had in his hand.

The carer continued in her bright tone. "You can't drink a cup of tea standing up. Why don't you sit down for a while, and we'll see what we can do about that appointment?"

Erica held her breath, praying this was going to work, and that her dad would put down the walking stick and calm down.

Her dad lowered the walking stick and took a step towards the table. He reached for the cup of tea, and she exhaled a sigh of relief, her shoulders sagging. Of course, these people were trained for this. That was the whole point of him being here—that he was around people who knew exactly what to do in these difficult circumstances.

Her dad picked up his cup of tea, but instead of lifting it to his mouth, he threw the cup at the wall. It hit violently, pieces of china shattering, brown liquid flying everywhere.

Erica jerked back. "Dad!"

Monica turned to call over her shoulder. "Bailey, don't just stand there. Go and get a mop and a dustpan and brush. We don't want anyone cutting themselves."

Erica glanced over her shoulder to see who Monica was addressing.

Lurking in the doorway was the cleaner who'd been staring at her the last time she'd been in. He was doing the same thing now, watching her intently, more focused on her than on the chaos happening around them.

Bailey? Where did she know that name from?

There wasn't time to think about it now.

"The mop, Bailey," Monica said again, raising her eyebrows at him, clearly wondering why he was still standing there.

He quickly looked away from Erica and nodded then rushed out of the room. He returned moments later with a mop in one hand and a dustpan in the other and hurried over to the mess.

Erica reached for the dustpan. "Here, let me."

But he snatched the items away as though she was trying to steal them, and he dropped to his knees to sweep up the broken pieces of china. Where he'd seemed unable to tear his eyes from her a moment ago, now he didn't appear to want to make eye contact with her at all.

The breaking of the teacup at least seemed to have taken the last of her father's rage out of him. He dropped the walking stick, and one of the staff darted in and grabbed it, removing it from his reach.

"It's okay, Dad." Erica took his arm to help him into his chair. "Everything is okay."

Frank allowed himself to be helped this time, and he sat heavily.

Movement came from the doorway, and Chris rushed in. "I'm so sorry. I got here as fast as I could. Is everything okay now?"

Erica clutched his arm, needing his support as much as her father had needed hers, and she nodded.

The cleaner had finished picking up the pieces of broken teacup and mopped up the spilt tea. He straightened as Chris joined Erica.

"Hey, I know you, don't I?" Chris said, frowning in the young man's direction.

The cleaner pressed his lips together and ducked his head, staring down at the floor.

Chris pointed a finger as it came to him. "Weren't you on our street the other day?"

"No," the man snapped. "I don't know you."

With his head still down, he shoved past Chris, knocking Chris's shoulder as he went.

Chris didn't say anything, clearly not wanting to make a scene after they'd only just managed to calm everything down, but he threw a concerned glance to Erica, who frowned in return. The man's strange behaviour hadn't escaped her, but she couldn't worry about that now. She still had to make sure Frank was okay.

Erica dropped to a crouch beside her dad's chair and took his hand. "How are you doing, Dad?"

Frank nodded but looked away, staring out of the window into the gardens. It was as though he knew he'd done something wrong and was embarrassed about it, but he couldn't quite figure out what it was—like someone who'd been sleepwalking and only had a vague recollection of wandering around half-naked, but were unsure if it were a dream or real.

"Do you want to go out into the garden?" she asked. "We can take a walk if you like?"

He shook his head. "I'm tired. I think I might have that cup of tea now."

Erica glanced over her shoulder at one of the care workers, who nodded to show she'd understood then hurried off to get a fresh cup of tea. She hoped it wasn't going to end up the same way as the last one.

Before the carer had even made it back, Frank's eyes had already slipped shut, his hold on Erica's hand growing loose.

She gave it a squeeze and rose to her feet. The care home manager had left to deal with other patients now everything had calmed down, but Erica felt she needed to talk with her.

"I'd better find Monica," she told Chris. "See what the fallout of all this is going to be."

Erica found Monica out near reception, talking to someone else, but she turned to Erica as they stepped out of the dayroom.

"Everything settled down now?" Monica asked with a smile.

"Yes, thank you. I'm sorry about that. Is it...has it made you think differently about having him here?"

A look of surprise crossed her face. "Oh, gosh, of course not. He isn't the first to lash out, and he won't be the last. Once he's been here a little longer, we'll start to learn what triggers the episodes, and we can make sure to avoid them. I expect it's because everything is so strange for him at the moment."

"So, you're not going to ask him to leave." She melted inside with relief.

She wasn't sure what she would have done if they'd had to take Frank home. That had been part of her reason for getting Chris to come, in case that had to happen. She'd never have been able to do it alone.

"No, we wouldn't dream of it. We're all becoming rather fond of Frank. Well, possibly not Mrs Wright, since she was the one whose walking stick he stole." Monica threw her a wink.

Erica smiled, pleased that she could see the humour in the situation. Maybe working somewhere like this was similar to working in the police force. You had to keep a bit of dry humour around, so it didn't grind you into the ground.

She remembered the one concern she'd had.

"The man who cleaned up a moment ago," she said hesitantly. "Is everything okay with him?"

"Oh, you mean Bailey," Monica said. "He doesn't talk much. But he's good at his job—thorough—and he treats the patients as though they're his own mother or father, which is what we encourage. We also feel it's good to give those from a more..." she sought for the right word, "challenging background a help up. Wouldn't you agree?"

Erica didn't think Monica had noticed the definite shoulder barge he'd given Chris. She wondered whether to mention it and then decided against it. They'd caused enough problems here already today without adding more.

"Yes, of course. Is he just shy?"

"I think he's what might be referred to these days as being socially anxious. But he's been through the same dementia training as everyone else who works here, which is renewed every year, and he's always passed his exams with flying colours. As long as you don't expect too much small talk from him, you'll all get along fine."

"Of course."

She never meant to imply that there was anything wrong with him in that way, more just why he was staring at her like that. And why had he been so rude to Chris? People were never rude to Chris. Everyone loved him. And what did Chris mean when he'd said that he'd seen the cleaner on their road? It was a coincidence, surely? After all, they didn't exactly live far from here.

Erica quickly checked on her dad again before leaving, but he was still sleeping in the chair, so she left him in peace. Hopefully, he'd be feeling better when he woke. She made a mental note to call the home in a couple of hours and make sure he was okay.

They left the building, Chris at her side.

She looped her arm through his and gave him a squeeze. "I'm sorry for getting you over here when you didn't need to be."

"It's fine. You didn't know how things were going to turn out."

"Do you think we have anything to worry about with the cleaner?"

Chris raked a hand through his hair. "Yeah, that was strange. I'm sure it's a coincidence, though, seeing him like that. I was sitting at my desk and I caught sight of someone hanging around on the other side of the street. At first, I thought they were interested in the parked cars, like maybe they were thinking of breaking into one of them or something, but then I saw him looking at our house. He caught me watching him and took off."

"You're sure it was him?"

"Yeah, it was him. He recognised me, too. I could tell. This look of panic flashed across his face."

"So weird. I caught him staring at me the other day as well."

She wondered if she should report it, but then he hadn't broken any laws. He had as much right to be on their street as anyone else. It wasn't as though she could get him for loitering with intent. Besides, if the bloke was simply someone who had social issues, she didn't want to cause any trouble for him.

She knew that name from somewhere, though, but she couldn't place it. It niggled at the back of her mind, telling her she'd forgotten something.

"I need to get back to work," she told her husband.

"Yeah, me, too." Chris pulled her in for a kiss. "Will you be back for dinner?"

"I'll try. Things are a little crazy with the case at the moment."

"Poppy would like you back for dinner. I know you don't celebrate birthdays anymore, but it still means something to her. She's excited about it being her mummy's birthday."

That stab of guilt again.

She sighed. "I know. I'll try, okay? Even if it's only for an hour."

"An hour would be great."

They parted ways, and Erica got back into her car. Gibbs was going to love that she'd left the office to deal with something personal again.

Still, something bugged her. Where did she know that name? Bailey what? She should have asked the manager for his surname, but again it felt like an intrusion when they were the ones doing her a favour by taking care of Frank. Besides, she had to keep reminding herself that the cleaner hadn't actually done anything wrong.

Sometimes, it was hard not to look at everyone as though they were guilty of something.

Chapter Twenty-Five: Six Years Earlier

"Danny?" Nicholas called out as he arrived home.

The two brothers were still in the crappy, two-bedroom council flat. Maybe it was for the best that they'd lost their mother's house and left all the memories it contained behind, but Nicholas felt like when they'd packed up the couple of boxes of belongings to move, they'd brought their mother's ghost along with them.

His brother should have been home. He rarely went out these days, staying locked in his bedroom, or sometimes sitting on their sagging sofa and scrolling the internet or watching trashy television. He drank unashamedly, and Nicholas didn't dare even mention it, knowing Danny would blow up if he did. His brother's temper was constantly bubbling beneath the surface, waiting for an excuse to boil over.

The confident boy Danny had been when they were at school was gone. The clear complexion was now sallow and grey and prone to outbreaks across his forehead, nose, and chin. There was always a stale, sour stink rising off him, and Nicholas rarely heard the shower running.

Nicholas was filled with guilt about what had become of his younger brother. He'd struggled himself with what they had done, but of course Danny had been the one who'd handled everything. Nicholas would never forgive himself for that. He was the older brother. He should have stepped up. Nicholas suffered from nightmares where his mother wasn't really dead, and he found her back in the kitchen, covered with dirt and demanding to know what the fuck they were playing at—but he imagined it was a hundred times worse for Danny. Danny had been the one who'd dragged her lifeless body across the garden, who'd dug the hole she'd had to go in, who'd pushed her into it and then thrown dirt onto her face as she stared back, unseeing. It was bad enough imagining those things without having experienced them for real.

Neither of them had spoken of the events at the canal, though the police had come sniffing around after the body had been found. They'd been pinpointed as being in the same area as the incident because of the time they'd spent at the pub, but the police hadn't had anything substantial. It was just another horrible secret that hung like a fog between them.

Where was he now?

Danny should have been in. He normally slept for twelve hours a day, only getting up to drink, and occasionally eat, and then going back to sleep again. Nicholas knew his brother was depressed. Danny talked about how peaceful it must be to be dead and had even mentioned on one occasion about how he'd kill himself, if he was going to do it. Nicholas had told him not to be so stupid, but he didn't know how to help his brother.

"Danny?" he called again, moving between the rooms, checking the tiny, filthy kitchen, the adjoining lounge. Not there. He went to Danny's bedroom next, but there was no sign of his brother.

Worry wormed through him. Where was he?

Should he go out looking for him? He wouldn't even know where to start.

He stopped in front of the fridge, a Post-it note stuck to the front catching his eye.

I can't anymore. Sorry. D.

Nicholas froze, his heart stopping. What did that mean? He couldn't do what anymore? Live here? Be his brother? What?

He had a horrible, sinking feeling that he knew exactly what it meant.

Where would he have gone?

Danny's mood had grown darker with every passing day. Would he have done something stupid?

With ice water filling his veins, Nicholas remembered the conversation they'd had a few weeks ago.

"I'd jump in front of a train," Danny had said. "Ruin the day for all those posh pricks trying to get to their high-paid jobs. Maybe they'd even get some of my blood splattered on their suits."

Nicholas had snapped at him. "Don't talk like that, Danny."

He'd laughed, but there was no humour in it. "I'm only screwing with you, Nicholas."

He remembered that conversation with razor-sharp clarity now. Danny wouldn't have done that, would he?

The Tube station was only a five-minute walk from the high-rise block.

Nicholas ran from the flat. He didn't even bother to shut the front door or use the lift, as waiting would take too long. He flew down the stairs, his feet not moving fast enough, and he jumped the final few stairs of each flight, gripping the handrail to swing himself around the corner. His heart raced, his mouth running dry. He was too late; he knew he was. He could feel it in his bones. Danny hadn't been messing around at all when he'd told Nicholas his plans. That was exactly how he'd planned to do it.

For once, Nicholas didn't worry about hiding his face from the public. The hood of his jacket fell down, blown back in the wind his movement was creating. Nicholas ran, barely noticing the people he barged past on the street or the shouts of annoyance as he pushed them out of his way. A young woman with a pram turned to protect her baby with her body, an older man shouted in annoyance, a younger one called him a fucking arsehole.

He knew how he must look. His features, so misshapen and hideous, his expression contorted with panic and fear, lashing out at anyone he passed. Nicholas didn't care. All he was focused on was reaching the Tube station.

A group of people were gathering outside.

Oh, no. God, no.

A man in a suit stepped into his path, but there was no way he was going to let someone stop him. He pushed the man out of the way and hurdled over the barriers. Two at a time, he raced down the stairs. He had to pause a moment, trying to figure out what platform to go towards.

The rumble of an approaching train echoed down the tunnel.

Nicholas allowed himself a moment of hope. He wasn't too late. They'd have stopped the trains if he was, and they hadn't. He tried to piece together in his mind what was happening.

The groups of people standing around were commuters, exactly like Danny had planned for. Some looked worried and anxious, others irritated and rolling their eyes.

Nicholas picked up on bits of their conversations.

"Why can't these people take themselves off somewhere private if they want to kill themselves?"

"Why do they have to make such a scene?"

"It's all for attention."

"What do they have to go ruining everyone else's day for?"

It was all Nicholas could do to stop himself spitting in their faces. *He wants to ruin your days, you stupid fuckheads. That's exactly what he wants to do!*

Nicholas hurried past them and ran out onto the platform.

Danny stood on the edge, well over the yellow line and the warning to 'mind the gap'. He was leaning forward, as though trying to see down the tunnel in the direction the train was going to come.

Several feet away stood a woman with reddish-blonde hair—almost the same shade Danny's had been when he'd been younger and taken care of it. Now it was dull and dirty, sticking up from his head in all directions, held in place with grease.

Though she wasn't in uniform, Nicholas could tell the woman was a police officer of some kind. When you grew up like the brothers had, you got a nose for being able to pick out a member of the fuzz.

The young policewoman was speaking to Danny, but Nicholas couldn't make out the words.

Nicholas was rooted to the spot, frozen in fear. He wanted to open his mouth and shout out to Danny to move back and that he didn't want to do this, not really, but nothing came out.

Below them, a mouse ran across the track, darting one way and then the other, searching for an escape, perhaps, or simply hunting for food one of the commuters may have dropped.

The rumbling rattle and screech of the Tube train hurtling towards them grew louder with every passing second. Danny had made sure to stand as close to the tunnel exit as possible, so the train wouldn't get the chance to slow down as it entered the platform. Hadn't the police officer contacted the driver? Couldn't she have told him to stop? Or did they see this kind of thing all the time and they simply couldn't afford to make all the trains cease running just because of someone threatening to jump? It was a threat, right? That was all. It didn't mean he was going to do it. They must have issues with passengers all over the Underground and couldn't stop the trains running every time they had a potential problem. No, this female police officer thought she was going to talk Danny down, Nicholas could tell. Maybe they'd warned the train driver that there might be trouble up ahead, but they hadn't told him to stop.

Danny! Nicholas wanted to shout. *Stop it, Danny. You don't want to do this.*

But no words made it past his lips.

The policewoman must not have taken Danny seriously. Nicholas bet she thought Danny was just a stupid young man who'd had too much to drink and wanted a bit of extra attention. How could Nicholas tell her that he was very serious? That Danny had done and seen more than any boy ever should? That his mind and soul were broken and would probably never get fixed again?

Murmurs of 'he's going to do it', and 'oh, shit, the train is coming' came from around him.

Nicholas screamed in his head, willing himself to move. It was like being trapped in a nightmare.

The train was almost here.

As though he'd sensed Nicholas standing there, Danny turned his head and locked eyes with his brother. That moment snapped Nicholas's paralysis, right as the lights of the train appeared in the tunnel.

"No!"

He took a solitary step forward, his hand outstretched.

The front of the train burst out through the tunnel.

And Danny jumped.

Screams of horror rose around the platform.

The woman stood in place, her mouth dropped open. A uniformed British Transport Police officer ran down the platform towards her.

Too late.

She should have done more.

She should have told the train to stop.

She should have believed Danny when he said he was going to jump.

He sucked in a shuddery breath and put both hands over his face. When he exhaled, a high-pitched moan escaped his throat. Despair and grief flattened him. *No, not Danny. No, no, no.*

A wave of cold terror washed through Nicholas. He couldn't get involved. The terror of being caught up with the police again, of being made to sit in a room and answer questions, was too much. He couldn't go through it again. At least back then, he'd had the support of his brother, but now he had no one.

They would catch up with him, he was sure. Would there even be enough of Danny left for them to ID? He didn't know, and felt sick and dizzy even thinking about it, but he didn't want to make it any easier for them to track him down. What if they blamed him? What if they said he should have done more?

No, it hadn't been his fault. The policewoman was the one who should have helped Danny, only she hadn't. She'd failed him.

They'd all failed him, and now Danny was dead.

He stumbled away, bouncing off people and walls, only wanting to put as much distance as possible between himself and the body now lying beneath the Underground train. A thin line of snot ran from his nose down to his upper lip. He wanted to go back in time and do things all over again, to have run quicker to get to the station, to have not frozen on the platform, but he couldn't change what had happened.

He'd failed his brother.

Nothing would ever be the same again.

Chapter Twenty-Six

Thankfully, Gibbs hadn't noticed she'd snuck out of the office.

Rudd and Howard were back from their door-to-door, but it wasn't good news. They hadn't unearthed anything that had caught their attention as being suspicious. All their leads were a dead end. She was starting to feel as though they were going to have to wait for the suspect to do it again before they'd have anything more to go on. They hadn't even found anything connecting the two victims, except they were male and now they were both dead.

What about the old case—the one where the body had been found in the canal? She hadn't managed to look fully into that yet. There probably wasn't a connection, but she was at the point of being willing to consider anything.

She suddenly remembered where she'd seen the name Bailey before. Of course. It had been the name of the young man who'd been questioned about the stabbing.

The same one who'd jumped in front of the train exactly six years ago today and had died right in front of her.

Could they be connected?

She knew she was clutching at straws. It was most likely just a coincidence. It didn't mean anything.

Did it?

She trusted her gut on these things.

Erica couldn't help her thoughts going back to the other young man who'd also taken the same route out of this life. It was hard for men. They were always taught to be tough and not feel anything, but the truth was that they were as human as any of the rest of them. They hurt, but they had no outlet for those feelings.

Erica used her computer to check Daniel Bailey's history. The young man had spent the latter half of his childhood under the care of social services. He was arrested once before when he'd been a minor, for unlawfully burying his mother and concealing her death, though he hadn't been charged. But that wasn't the part that interested Erica. He'd had a brother. Nicholas Bailey.

Her heartrate increased.

Could Nicholas Bailey be the same Bailey at her father's care home? She'd assumed Bailey had been his first name, but it could have been his surname that the care home manager was referring to him by. It wasn't that usual—after all, they did exactly the same thing within the police force.

Quickly, she looked up Nicholas Bailey. The face of the cleaner at Willow Glade Care Home appeared on screen. It was definitely him.

She let out a sigh and closed her eyes briefly. So what if he was Daniel Bailey's brother? It didn't mean anything.

She needed to run this by someone else and make sure she wasn't overthinking things.

"Hey, Turner," she said, getting her sergeant's attention. "You know that case Rudd found from years ago, about the body found in the canal with his eye stabbed out?"

Shawn lifted his head from what he was doing to give her his full attention. "Yeah, what about it?"

"Is it strange that I just found out one of the suspects they brought in happens to be the brother of a man who now works at my father's care home?"

He twisted his lips, thinking. "People have relatives," he said eventually. "What are their names?"

"Daniel Bailey was the man questioned. Nicholas Bailey is his brother."

"Has he done anything that makes you think he's up to something?"

She wrestled with the idea of telling him the full story but didn't want to look like she was being paranoid.

"Not really. He was acting a bit strangely when he saw me at the care home, but that's all."

"If he has a bit of a background, the police might make him nervous."

Erica exhaled a breath. "You're right."

There was nothing substantial linking Nicholas Bailey with the two victims. Plus, they'd had a theory that the attacker possibly had some facial deformity, and she'd seen Nicholas close up, and there was nothing wrong with his face. He was a normal man.

Still, it was something to go on, and right now she didn't have much else.

Erica straightened and turned her attention back on the computer to check their records for Nicholas Bailey. Where did he live? If he had a basement flat near a train line, she'd at least have something more than gut instinct and a tenuous link to a seven-year-old crime to go on.

She clicked the mouse to bring up his records.

Dammit. He had a council flat on the eighth floor of a high-rise. It was highly unlikely he was keeping any victims there.

She exhaled a breath and put her head in her hands. Was she heading down the wrong route?

Nicholas Bailey hadn't done anything other than act a little strangely around her. His brother hadn't even been charged with the stabbing. She had nothing to link him to the two men who'd died.

Still, she couldn't seem to tear her thoughts away from the fact the man working in her father's care home was the brother of the man who'd killed himself in front of her exactly six years ago today.

Nicholas Bailey had no idea who she was, of course. Maybe she could go and have a chat with him and see where he was on the nights of the abductions, but she certainly didn't have enough to be considered reasonable grounds for an arrest. That didn't stop her from talking to him, though. She would try to strike up a conversation with him and see if she picked up on any vibes.

She got to her feet and grabbed her jacket.

"Everything okay?" Shawn asked, noticing she'd got up.

"Yeah, fine. I said I'd have dinner with Chris and Poppy tonight, you know, considering what day it is. I thought I might pop in and check on Dad on my way back as well, make sure that he's okay after what happened this afternoon."

"Of course. Take a couple of hours."

"If Gibbs asks, tell him I'm following up on a lead."

Chapter Twenty-Seven

She left the office and went out to her car, slipping into the driver's seat. Maybe she was on a wild goose chase, but she hoped she could be subtle enough not to piss anyone off. Plus, she told herself she was mainly going to check on her dad. Seeing if she could ask Nicholas Bailey a couple of questions was simply a matter of convenience—she was there anyway, so why not?

Her phone rang, and she glanced down at the screen, surprised to see the name of Poppy's school.

She swiped to answer, immediately concerned. The school normally knew to contact Chris if there were any problems. Besides, school had finished by now. Maybe they'd forgotten to pay for a trip or something that was needed urgently.

"Hello, Erica speaking."

"Hi, Mrs Swift. Nothing to worry about, but we've got Poppy sitting in the office. We wondered if someone was going to be with us shortly to pick her up, or did you need her to go into after school club for a little while?"

"Sorry? Her dad didn't get her?"

"No, he didn't."

"Oh, okay." She checked the clock. "Give me fifteen minutes, and I'll be right there."

"Great. See you soon."

She ended the call but immediately scrolled down to find Chris's number. She was more worried than angry. It wasn't like Chris not to pick Poppy up, and on the odd occasion something had come up and he wasn't able to do it, he'd always called her or the school.

Hitting the Call button, she waited for it to connect. She'd expected it to ring, but instead it went straight to answerphone.

"Hi, it's me. The school phoned and said you didn't get Poppy today. I'm going to get her now, but please call me and let me know what's going on. I'm worried."

She hung up again and focused on her driving, pulling the car out of the station car park and into traffic. She drove as fast as she dared, hating to think of poor Poppy sitting alone outside the school office, wondering why her parents had forgotten her.

Fifteen minutes later, she drove into the school's car park. She jumped out of the car and raced to the front door, hitting the buzzer that connected to the school's office.

"Hi, it's Poppy Swift's mum. I'm here to collect her."

The school secretary buzzed her in, and Erica rushed through the building. She caught sight of Poppy sitting on one of the chairs outside of the school office, swinging her legs and looking around anxiously. The office door was open, giving the secretary a view of the little girl waiting there.

Poppy spotted Erica and jumped to her feet. "Mummy!"

Erica swept her up into a hug, pressing her little body against her and kissing the top of her head. "Hello, sweetheart. I'm sorry you didn't get picked up today."

"Why didn't Daddy come?"

"Oh, I think something came up at work and he must have tried to call me, but I missed the message." She could sense the secretary's gaze on her, and she didn't want to say anything that might make them look like irresponsible parents. "Let's get you home, okay?"

"Okay."

Erica flashed the secretary a smile. "Thanks so much. I'll get her home now."

The woman gave Erica a nod, and Erica guided Poppy out of the office and towards the exit.

She got in the car and checked her phone for any missed calls from Chris, but there was still nothing. She wanted to call him again but didn't want to in front of Poppy in case something had happened. She'd get Poppy home and engrossed in some cartoons and with a snack, and then she'd make some calls.

She drove them the short distance home.

Chris's car was still sitting in the driveway. Was he home? If so, why hadn't he answered his phone or collected Poppy? She hadn't thought to call the house phone. She'd assumed that he'd not been there.

A horrible thought jolted through her. What if he'd had an accident—choked on a piece of food or electrocuted himself? Her mind went to the worst possible options. What were they about to walk in on? She didn't want Poppy seeing anything like that.

Erica used her key to open the front door, but it was already open. She deliberately kept Poppy behind her. She stepped into the hallway, using her body to block her daughter's view.

"Chris?" she called. "Are you home?"

There was no answer.

Erica turned to her daughter and dropped to a crouch. "Stay here for me a minute, sweetheart, okay? I won't be a second."

Poppy had clearly picked up that something was wrong. Her small face crumpled. "Okay, Mummy."

"Good girl."

Erica left Poppy standing awkwardly in the hallway while she ran around the house, checking each room for any sign of Chris.

She entered the living room and drew to a halt. At the desk in the corner of the room, a cup of tea had been knocked over, and so had Chris's office chair. That wasn't good. Chris would never leave a mess like that.

Pressing the back of her hand to the cup, she could tell it had been like that for some time. No warmth remained in the porcelain.

Chris wouldn't knock over tea and a chair and then leave the house and not even lock it after him. And where would he have gone? She checked the back door, which was also unlocked.

What the hell was going on?

She hesitated then left the back door open, in case he came back and didn't have his keys and couldn't get into the house.

"Come on, we're going to your Aunty Tasha's."

"Why? Where's Daddy?"

"I think he's just had to do some work." There was no sense in Poppy worrying as well.

"But it's your birthday," Poppy protested. "Why would he work on your birthday?"

"Grownups still have to work on birthdays, sweetheart. I still had to go to work today, didn't I?"

She locked the front door, so the house wasn't completely open to burglars. Leaving the back door open made her anxious, but she was worried about Chris and didn't want to lock him out if he'd only popped out somewhere for an hour.

Back in the car, she drove quickly to her sister's.

She pulled up in front of the house and unclipped Poppy from her car seat. Perhaps she should have called ahead and warned Natasha they were coming, but there hadn't felt like there was time.

Taking Poppy's small hand in hers, she led her to Natasha's front door and rang the bell.

Natasha appeared at the door with her youngest daughter, eighteen-month-old Harper, balanced on her hip. She held a tea towel in her other hand, as though she'd been doing the dishes, multi-tasking.

Her eyes widened at the sight of Erica and Poppy. "Hi! This is a surprise! Happy birthday."

"Don't do the birthday thing," she said. "You know I can't."

"Okay, okay." Natasha knew what had happened that day and why she didn't want to be reminded of it. "What's happened? Is it Dad? Is he okay?"

She didn't have time to berate her sister on how a little more involvement would ensure Natasha already knew how their father was doing.

"Hi, no, Dad's fine," she said in a rush. "I wondered if you could have Poppy for a couple of hours."

Natasha's smile was strained, and she glanced over her shoulder to where the sounds of two other children fighting were coming down the stairs. "Oh, well, I kind of have my hands full right now." She realised who she was speaking in front of and flashed Poppy a smile. "Not that I wouldn't love to spend some time with you Pop-pop."

Poppy clung tighter to Erica's leg. Erica tried not to focus on the pinch of Poppy's mouth, the worry in her eyes.

"Please," Erica begged. "You always have your hands full."

Erica widened her eyes down at Natasha, trying to convey via facial expression alone that she couldn't say exactly what was happening in front of her daughter.

Natasha seemed to understand. "Hey, Poppy. How would you like to go and see your cousins for a bit? They're playing some computer games on their tablets. That's what all the noise is about. Would you like to go and join in?"

Erica wouldn't normally have allowed Poppy to spend time on tablets, and she didn't want to think about what sort of games the two older children were playing, but she didn't have the luxury of being picky right now.

"Claudia! Ethan!" she bellowed up the stairs. "Your cousin is here. Let her join in."

Erica pushed Poppy forward. The girl was still a bit hesitant, but the lure of being able to have a go on a tablet while her mother wasn't looking gave her a little extra courage. Besides, she'd known her cousins her entire life. It wasn't that she was normally afraid of them. Erica thought Poppy had already sensed something being wrong, and that was why she was reluctant to leave Erica's side. Both women remained silent until Poppy had run up the stairs and turned the corner, in the direction of the bedrooms.

With Poppy out of earshot, Natasha turned to Erica. "What's going on?"

"I'm hoping it's nothing, but Chris didn't show up to pick up Poppy from school. He never does that. I've tried calling him, but he's not answering." She chewed at her lower lip. "I'm worried."

"Could he have gone to meet someone? A work colleague, maybe, so he's turned his phone off?"

"I'm not sure. It's really not like him to forget. Plus, his car is still sitting in the driveway, so he hasn't taken it anywhere." She moved from chewing her lower lip to worrying at her thumbnail. "There's something else."

"What?"

"The front door was unlocked, and a half-drunk cup of tea beside his computer had been knocked over. It was spilt all over his desk. Why would Chris spill a drink and then not even bother to clean it up again?"

"If he was leaving in a hurry," she suggested.

"Yes, but what would he be in that much of a hurry for that he wouldn't tell me about?"

Natasha wrinkled her nose. "You don't think..." She hesitated before she blurted the words, "You don't think he might be having an affair?"

"No!"

The idea had never even crossed her mind. Chris wasn't like that at all. He loved her and Poppy. He'd never do anything to put what they had at risk.

"I mean, you leave him alone in the house all day. And there are all those other mums at the school gate who are probably fluttering their eyelashes at him and wondering if he's single. He's not bad-looking, your Chris. Maybe someone decided they might like to have him at home as well."

"He's not having an affair, Tasha!"

She hated that her sister's words had sent a worm of doubt coiling around her gut. How well did you ever really know someone? Chris was her rock, but Natasha was right when she said that Erica left him alone a lot of the time. It wasn't intentional—she was working—but perhaps he had started to get lonely, and one of those younger mums at the school gate had decided to set up a playdate between her child and Poppy in order to get to know Chris better. She remembered Poppy mentioning that one of the other girls in her class had invited Poppy and Chris back to theirs after school.

Could something have happened with a girlfriend? What if she was over there, and they had a fight about something—maybe her—and the other woman stormed out? Would that be enough for Chris to knock over his tea and chair, and chase after her? They could be at the other woman's right now, still fighting, or even worse, making up, while she was worried sick about him.

She was a detective. She needed to get her head on straight and start thinking of this like a case instead of something so personal to her.

What would she normally do if she needed to find someone?

They didn't have any trackers on their phones. They knew couples who did that, and had always laughed about it over a glass of wine, talking about how paranoid and insecure someone would have to be to track their partner's phone. Could he have been lying to her this whole time? Was he secretly relieved she didn't buy into all of that crap so that he could cheat on her?

No, she had to shake that thought from her head.

Where are you, Chris?

He hadn't taken the car, so she couldn't put out a trace on that either. What about security cameras? She didn't have any around their property, but there was a chance one of their neighbours might have one. Those damned doorbells with the cameras on them were becoming more popular these days. She didn't know her neighbours, though, and she was going to have to go door-to-door to ask if they either had cameras or if they'd seen Chris leaving the house earlier. At least that would help to narrow the time down that she'd need to look at.

Erica shouted up the stairs to her daughter. "Poppy, I've got to leave you with Auntie Tasha for a bit, okay? I'll be back after dinner."

A faint, "Okay!" came back to her, and she was relieved Poppy was engrossed in whatever game they were playing. It was easier than her getting upset and clinging to Erica, refusing to let her go.

"I'll feed her dinner," Tasha said. "It's only fish fingers and oven chips, though."

Erica forced a smile. "Poppy loves fish fingers and oven chips. Thanks so much for doing this."

"Don't be silly. After everything you and Chris have done for Dad lately, it's the least I can do."

Erica stepped in and hugged her sister hard then spun away and hurried from the house. She hoped next time she came here it would be with Chris by her side, so they could pick Poppy up together.

Chapter Twenty-Eight

She hurried away from her sister's house, heading back to her car, her phone in her hand.

Should she call the local hospitals and see if Chris had been brought in? Though he seemed fit and healthy on the outside, he might have suffered a stroke or a heart attack, and that was why the cup and chair had been knocked over. Perhaps he'd only just managed to make it to the front door and a neighbour had called an ambulance for him.

But then why would no one have contacted her to let her know?

It didn't make sense.

No, she'd go back to the house first and check it over without having to worry about Poppy. There might have been something obvious she'd missed the first time. He might have even left her a note somewhere explaining, but she'd put herself in a panic and not seen it.

Before she reached the car, she tried Chris's number again, but once more it went straight through to answerphone. "Please call me, Chris. I'm really worried now, and so is Poppy. Call me as soon as you get this."

She ended the call, and immediately the phone vibrated in her hand. Her heart lurched, and she locked her gaze on the screen, praying it would be her husband, but instead it showed the surname of her sergeant.

She answered the call. "Swift."

Shawn's familiar voice came down the line. "I wanted to give you a heads-up that Gibbs has been asking where you are. I wasn't able to tell him what lead you were following up on."

"Honestly, Turner, Gibbs is my least concern right now."

"Why? What's wrong?"

"Chris is missing. I'm trying not to panic, but I can't help thinking the worst."

She could hear the frown in his tone.

"Missing? How do you mean? He's not answering his phone?"

"No, and his car is in the driveway. I've got a horrible feeling, Shawn." She slipped into using his first name now this was about something personal.

"I'm sure it's nothing sinister. Are you at home now?"

She opened her car door and slid behind the wheel. "No, I'm at my sister's, but I'm going to go back there and knock on some of the neighbours' doors and see if anyone heard or saw anything."

"Someone might have security cameras as well."

She exhaled a breath. "Yeah, I already thought of that."

"Okay. I'll meet you there. Try not to worry. We'll find him."

She ended the call and pulled the driver's door shut behind her. Was her home a crime scene now? She couldn't get her mind off that spilt cup of tea. While Chris was far from being OCD about things, he wasn't messy. He wasn't the kind of man who left toothpaste in the sink or his socks on the floor for someone else to pick up.

She'd always thought herself to be incredibly lucky, but what if it was all a guise to hide who he really was? Maybe he was a serial cheater or even worse, and she'd had her head in the clouds, thinking he was some perfect guy.

The idea sat uneasily inside her.

No, she needed to trust her gut, and that was telling her something bad had happened to him.

This was taking her away from the investigation she was supposed to be working on, but her concern was greater than her professionalism at that moment.

Erica started her car and pulled away from the kerb to head back to her house.

She prayed Chris would be home when she got there.

• • • •

ERICA STOPPED THE CAR up in front of her house and climbed out. She stared at her home, hoping to spot a sign that Chris was back and relieve her worried mind, but everything looked exactly as she'd left it.

She reached into her handbag for her keys to open the front door. She could have gone around the back, but she was going to need to open up for Shawn, and possibly other police as well.

She almost hoped she was going to find out that Chris was having an affair. At least then she'd be able to deal with it and move on. This not knowing what had happened to him was the worst. Her husband hadn't even been missing more than a couple of hours. She thought of all the families she'd dealt with over the course of her career who had lost people for months and even years, never knowing what had happened to their loved ones. She suddenly understood what they were going through with a new clarity. What absolute torture that must be.

As she headed to the door, she passed Chris's car still sitting on the driveway.

Erica paused, frowning.

The driver's door wasn't fully shut.

Had it been like that before? She hadn't thought to check his car for any clues about where he might have gone. Perhaps the car hadn't started for some reason, and he'd gone to get jump leads for it

It seemed plausible. Chris might have seen something happen to the car while he'd been sitting at his desk and had jumped to his feet to deal with it, knocking over his chair and spilling his tea. It still didn't explain why he hadn't answered her calls, but it was possible.

Another memory came back to her, that of Chris telling her how he'd seen Nicholas Bailey watching the house. She paused for a moment, staring across the road to the spot where she imagined Bailey must have been standing, watching her house. Did he know she was the one who'd been there the day his brother had died? She couldn't see how he would, but still, it was all feeling a little too strange. Maybe she should get a radio car to go to Nicholas's flat and see if he knew anything.

Dammit. Had she screwed up? Should she have taken the presence of Nicholas Bailey and his strange behaviour towards them both at her father's care home more seriously? As soon as Shawn arrived, she'd run it by him and see what his thoughts were.

Erica turned her attention back to the car, and she reached for the handle. The door opened as normal, and she peered inside.

Movement came from behind her, but before she could react, something hard hit her across the back of her head. Her handbag slipped from her shoulder, and she slumped forward, onto the driver's seat.

And as darkness crept into her vision, something sharp pierced her neck...

Chapter Twenty-Nine: One Week Earlier

Nicholas walked down the street, his hands stuffed into his pockets, his hood pulled up to hide his face. He'd cut through the park to get to his building. The flat was on the eighth floor of the high-rise. The 1960s tower block had been deteriorating for some years now, and the surrounding area, the stairwells and hallways, were all hotspots for antisocial behaviour. Gangs of young men—some of them no more than teenagers—hung out, smoking pot, drinking, openly dealing drugs, and blasting rap music from wireless speakers.

A shout snatched his attention.

He made the mistake of glancing over.

Immediately, one of the lads stepped forward. "What the fuck are you looking at, freak?"

Nicholas put his head back down, his heartrate increasing. He should never have glanced over. Had they seen his face? Maybe they recognised him? He was fairly sure he was known around the estate as being the weirdo with the messed-up face. Maybe they even knew about Danny, and he was also known as the one whose brother had killed himself. Something like that didn't buy you sympathy in a place like this. All it did was create a weapon they could use against you.

He could feel their gazes on him, weighing him down, trying to smother him.

"Stop it," he growled.

The words had escaped his lips before he'd even been aware he was speaking. Instantly, his stomach dropped, his chest tightening, compressing his lungs. Why had he done that? *Stupid, stupid, stupid.*

The leader approached, a swagger rolling his shoulders. "What did you say? Did you talk to me, fuckface?"

Nicholas stuffed his hands deeper into his pockets. Run. He should run. He couldn't take the lift, 'cause they'd be on him before the doors even had the chance to slide shut, and anyway, that lift was hit and miss as to whether it would even be working. Take the stairs two at a time and put as much distance between himself and the gang as possible. None of this was going to end in anything good.

"Hey! I'm talking to you."

That stare. It gnawed at his nerve endings like rats on a sack of grain, leaving him frayed and anxious. They were all looking at him now. All five of them watching his every move. All he wanted was for them to stop. Just to focus on someone or something else. He wanted to vanish. To crumble into dust and blow away in the wind.

"Stop looking at me." His words were a murmur. His fists clenched by his sides.

The leader took a step closer, his buddies right behind him as backup. "What the fuck did you say to me?"

"I said stop looking at me."

"I'll do whatever the fuck I want." He ducked his head slightly, as though to try to get a glimpse of what was hidden beneath Nicholas's hood. "What are you hiding under there anyway?"

"He's talking back to you, Lewis." One of the other group members snorted. "I think you need to teach him a lesson in having some fucking manners."

Laughter rippled around the group. Nicholas huddled in further, trying to withdraw into himself. He couldn't run for the stairs now. He'd left it too late. They were too close. But he didn't even care about getting away now. All he wanted was for them to stop looking at him. He wished Danny was here, missing his brother with a sudden pang of longing. Danny would have stepped in and stopped this. Danny had always been so much braver than him, or he had been before the drink and drugs had taken hold. Danny had been younger, but he had always felt older to Nicholas. He'd been Nicholas's protection against the world. If only he'd realised how much Danny had been struggling, maybe he could have done something. But Danny had always been the one who'd taken care of him, and it had never occurred to him that Danny might have needed taking care of himself.

After it had happened, Nicholas hadn't thought he was going to survive. He couldn't envisage it—a life without Danny in it. They'd always been together, for as long as Nicholas could remember. An empty cavern had opened out in front of him, and he'd been certain he'd end up utterly lost. But somehow, he'd managed to survive.

Someone snatched at the back of his hood, yanking it from his face. Nicholas cried out, curling into himself and covering his face with both hands.

"What the fuck is wrong with you?" The one they'd called Lewis laughed.

A low moan escaped Nicholas's lips. He hunched over, elbows into his stomach, neck bent. If he could make himself small enough, maybe they would forget he was there.

He took a step, hoping to put space between himself and the gang, but one of them stuck out his foot, catching Nicholas's ankle. Nicholas flew forward, the ground rising to meet him. His hands were already in front of his face, protecting his features, but he still hit the ground hard, air bursting from his lungs. He didn't even have time to recover before something slammed into his ribs.

"Take that, freak!"

Figures surrounded him, looming over him on all sides. Something else, solid, with power behind it, struck his waist. They were kicking him. Another person kicked him, and another and another. One lifted his foot and stamped onto his spine, flattening him to the ground.

All he could think to do was keep his face covered. He couldn't move, couldn't even crawl forward—not that it would do any good. They'd only come after him.

Was no one going to interfere? No one going to shout over, demanding to know what they were doing? No, anyone who saw them would pretend they hadn't seen anything at all. People knew when *not* to look when it suited them. It was safer to turn the other way.

Yes, people only looked when they thought it was safe.

Danny wouldn't have put up with this shit. Danny would have taught them a lesson, like he'd taught that bloke on the canal path all those years ago. If his brother was alive today, he'd be ashamed of Nicholas and what he'd become. He was pathetic.

He needed to change. As another boot caught him in the ribs, bursting the air from his lungs, he made a decision.

He would teach them a lesson about what happened to people who looked at him the wrong way. He remembered what Danny had said the day he'd killed that man at the canal...

If they can't keep their eyes to themselves, they don't deserve to keep them...

Chapter Thirty

The roar of a train and the screech of metal on metal lurched Erica into consciousness.

Where was she? What had happened?

Her brain felt foggy and too big for her head, but she tried to piece together what she remembered. Slowly, it came back to her. She'd been on the driveway of her house and had been trying to find Chris. She'd noticed the driver's door standing open an inch and had gone to check the car, thinking Chris might have left some clue in there as to what had happened to him, but before she'd been able to react, someone had attacked her and plunged something sharp into her neck.

From the pounding in her skull, she assumed it had been a needle. She didn't remember much from after that.

Shit, Chris was missing.

And now, she figured, so was she.

Erica tried to focus on the here and now, needing to figure out where she was. She was lying on the ground, her cheek pressed to cold concrete, her body curled in the foetal position. She wanted to lift her hands to her face, but with the impulse came the realisation that her hands were tied behind her back, and her ankles were pressed together, something binding them as well. Tape covered her mouth, sealing her lips shut.

All around her was darkness.

Terror swept through her. *Oh, God. Oh, dear God.* The darkness...did it mean the worst? She had a feeling she knew who'd taken her. It was the same man she'd been looking into, the one who worked at her father's care home.

Nicholas Bailey.

And she already knew what he did to his victims.

Her eyes? Did the darkness surrounding her mean he'd taken her eyes?

She tried to get a feel for it, but her senses were foggy. He drugged his victims with Midazolam so, when he released them, they didn't know what was happening and they weren't in pain right away. Had he done that to her now?

Erica let out a muffled whine of despair. How had this happened? Was she really blind?

But then she became aware of something pressing against the sides of her head and against the back of her skull. Tape, perhaps? Or a blindfold? That didn't mean she still had her eyes, though. He'd packed in the eye sockets of the other victims, filling them with cotton wool to prevent them bleeding out.

There was an ache in her head, and adrenaline tripped her heartrate. Pressure was right there, behind her eye sockets. Was that because they'd been packed with cotton wool, or was it simply the effects of whatever he'd drugged her with to get her here?

Her breath came in fast little sips through her nostrils, and she knew she was hyperventilating. She needed to control herself and focus. Losing it wasn't going to help her or anyone else.

Was she alone in here? Or was he somewhere nearby, sitting or standing, watching her struggle? That sick son of a bitch.

Erica held herself still and tried to focus on her surroundings. The floor was hard and cold beneath her body. The air was warm and cloying. She remembered what had woken her—the roar of a train. The first victim had described hearing a train, but they'd assumed it was more distant. The volume and power of the one she'd heard was like she'd been in the tunnel with it.

The train and the tunnel. The same place Nicholas's younger brother, Daniel, had died. The same death she hadn't managed to prevent.

This was all tied together; everything was linked to Nicholas's younger brother. Did being down here make Nicholas feel closer to his brother somehow? Or did it feel like he was avenging his death or reliving his memory by being close to the place his brother had died?

Chris.

She suddenly remembered her husband. Had he taken Chris as well? Was Chris here with her?

Erica used her elbows to push herself up to sitting. She needed to find out what was around her, and prayed her husband was here with her as well, and that he was still alive. She shuffled around, using her feet and shoulders to feel her way. She was terrified about what she was going to find. What if she came across the person who had done this to her? Would she instinctively be able to tell the difference?

Another train hurtled through a tunnel nearby, and she shivered.

Her thoughts went to Poppy. Their daughter had only recently started school. She was still so young. She needed both her parents. It broke Erica's heart to think of her baby girl losing both of them in such a horrific way. Erica's sister would take in Poppy—they'd already had conversations about who would take care of each other's children should the worst happen, though neither of them envisaged something like this. They'd been thinking of car crashes or even cancer. Not this. Of course, Natasha would do everything she could to make Poppy feel like her own, but it wouldn't be the same. And what about Natasha herself, having to deal with losing her sister, and who would watch out for their dad? Would he understand? Would he even know she was gone?

No, she had to stop thinking like that. She couldn't die. Too many people needed her—including Chris. Decent, selfless Chris. She knew she'd struck gold when she met him, and right now she was terrified to think about what might have happened to him.

He has to still be alive. He has to be.

She couldn't bring herself to imagine a life where she didn't have her husband and Poppy had to live without her dad.

Another wriggle and a shuffle brought her to hard concrete or brick. A wall. It was cold, but she pressed herself against it, trying to get a feel for where she might be. Vibrations rumbled through the wall, molecules of concrete and brick jostling together, and then her ears picked up on the roar and screech of another train.

Brick. She remembered the pathologist's report finding brick dust on the second victim's skin. Was this where it had come from?

Think, Erica. Think.

The trains were so close. From the regular intervals between them and the bone-scraping familiar screech of the wheels on the tracks, she knew she was in the Underground, and not one near the mainland rail. But the Underground was full of people. There were commuters and train drivers and engineers. How would they not have seen her, or the victims who'd come before her?

Using the wall at her back as guidance, she shuffled along. Her hip bumped something soft, halting her movements.

Erica froze, her pulse racing. Blood pounded through her ears.

The solidity, the warmth, all made her think whatever she'd reached was human. Was it Chris? Or the man who'd taken them? Or was it some other unknown factor—another victim she hadn't taken into consideration?

She nudged the solid form again. She wished her hands weren't bound or her eyes and mouth weren't taped. At least then she could use some of her senses to find out who she was sitting beside. Her imagination conjured her worst fears. What if it was the man who'd taken her—the same one who'd cut the eyes out of those men? He could be sitting there, smiling at her in the dark and passing a sharp blade between his fingers as she pressed her hip and shoulder closer.

Torn between an impulse to yank herself away again and wanting to connect with the person in the hope it was her husband, she remained on the spot.

She needed to get her hands free and the tape off her mouth. She waggled her jaw and nose back and forth and ducked her face to scrape the side of her head against her shoulder. She poked out her tongue, sliding it between the thin slit of her lips, conjuring saliva to ruin the adhesive.

The person beside her groaned.

Chris? Was it really him?

She wanted to believe it, her heart banging with renewed adrenaline. If he could moan, it meant he was alive.

The edge of the tape on her mouth caught on her shoulder, loosening. She worked harder, stretching her jaw, doing everything she could to make the tape lose its stickiness.

Finally, it peeled from one side of her mouth, and she spat and shook her head, trying to get it off further. It clung to the other side, but it didn't matter. She could speak.

"Chris! Chris is that you?"

Her voice sounded hollow and desperate.

Another moan came as a reply.

Is it him?

Could she really tell just from a moan?

Movement came beside her, a scrape and shuffle, the sound of something heavy being moved. The warm weight of the form beside her vanished, leaving her exposed, bereft.

Had the person stood by themselves and moved away, or had someone else moved them?

"Hey!" she shouted. "What the fuck is going on?"

She wanted to tell whoever was doing this that she was a detective and that he'd messed with the wrong person, but her words would be pointless. The man who'd taken them knew exactly who she was. He even knew where she lived.

A male voice came back, cold and emotionless. "Don't worry, DI Swift, your husband is right here."

"Don't you hurt him! This has nothing to do with him."

A laugh. "Of course it does. He's married to you."

Slow, deliberate footsteps approached, and she sensed the form of someone leaning over her. Fingers touched her cheek, and she yelped and jerked away. But they found her again and caught the corner of the tape around her eyes, tearing it from her face.

Erica gasped. The tape felt as though it had taken her eyebrows and eyelashes with it, pain burning her skin. But she blinked open her eyes, terrified she'd been wrong and he'd taken her sight after all.

The light was dim, but she could see.

Thank God.

As though he'd read her thoughts, he said, "I wanted this to be the last thing you ever see. Your final memory to take into the dark with you."

"What are you doing to us?" She squinted around, her eyes getting used to the poor light.

In front of her, Nicholas stood with his fingers fisted in the collar of Chris's shirt, holding him upright.

Erica tried to piece together their location. The wall had been bricked up, blocking them off from something. She threw a glance behind her, taking in the curved roof. Ancient posters were faded and peeling from the walls. Graffitied tags in red and blue spray paint had been scrawled across everything.

Behind where Nicholas held Chris was a door-sized gap in the red-brick wall.

In the distance came the rumble of another approaching train.

Her head pounded, and the world spun around her. Her throat felt dry, so it was hard to swallow. Yes, he'd drugged her, and from the look of Chris, the effects of the Midazolam were still working on him. Why had Bailey allowed her to come around but not Chris?

Chris was on his feet, but he swayed from side to side and made no effort to fight back.

Nicholas hadn't hurt her husband, not yet. But she'd seen the other victims and had no doubt that the same fate awaited them.

"Please, let my husband go. This has nothing to do with him. Let's sit down and talk about it."

"You don't even know why you're here, do you?" he snarled. "You're the guilty one. You took something from me, and so I'm going to take something from you."

Ice settled in her veins, chilling her from the inside out. "What are you talking about?"

"What kind of man lets his wife control everything, anyway? I watched him. He sat at home all day, while you earned the money. What a fucking pussy. That's not how it's supposed to work."

She did her best to keep her voice calm, though she wanted to scream at him. "A marriage can work in any way. We're happy, and that's all that matters."

Nicholas stepped back, dragging Chris with him. The movement took them both closer to the gap in the brick wall.

The wind. She'd been feeling the wind each time a train went by, which meant where they were must open onto the tunnel at some point.

Their location suddenly hit her. They must be in an abandoned Underground station. The brick had walled off the platform from the trainline on the other side, so the people on the train wouldn't even know it was here.

Only there was a gap in the wall now—big enough for a person to step through.

Or be pushed.

"Happy?" Nicholas continued. "I don't even know what that feels like anymore. I haven't since my mum died, and me and my brother had to cover it up. Do you know why we did that, DI Swift?"

She remembered reading how the boys had been brought in and questioned about it, though neither of them had been charged.

Frantic, she shook her head.

"Because we wanted to stay together. We were brothers. We hid her death so the social wouldn't come along and separate us. Only it didn't work, because the cops figured out what we did, and they did separate us, for a while, at least. But when we got old enough, we found each other again. We'd have stayed together if you hadn't failed him."

"Daniel wasn't well, Nicholas. It was no one's fault."

"Lies!" he yelled.

She jumped in response.

"You didn't do your job!" he continued. "You didn't take him seriously. You could have saved him."

She shook her head. "No, I tried, I really did."

"You took something from me, DI Swift. The most important person in the world."

What was about to happen suddenly hit her.

"No, Nicholas, please. Don't do this."

He took another step to the gap in the wall. The train track lay beyond.

"You should be grateful that I chose your husband and not your daughter."

The mention of Poppy stabbed terror through her heart. "Leave her out of this!"

He shook his head. "The children are always the ones who end up punished."

"And if you hurt us, you'll hurt her as well." She couldn't bring herself to say her daughter's name in this man's presence.

"She'll be better off without you in her life. You'll only let her down."

A train burst past the gap, racing through the tunnel. A blur of lights and windows, a snapshot of the shapes of people within the carriages.

And then it was gone. In a rush of hot air and noise and a blast of movement.

Erica exhaled a long breath.

Three minutes. She had around three minutes until the next one.

Chapter Thirty-One

Shawn pulled up at the front of Erica's house. He'd been expecting to find her outside, waiting for him, but there was no sign of her. Maybe she hadn't been able to wait and had already gone knocking on the neighbours' doors to find out if they'd seen anything. It wouldn't surprise him. Erica had never been someone to wait around for help when she was more than capable of doing something herself.

He turned off the engine, opened the door, and climbed out.

An item was sitting in the driveway.

He frowned. Hadn't Erica said that Chris's car was still here? He was sure that was part of the reason she'd been so worried—that the door was unlocked, and his car was still in the drive. Of course, the car having still been outside the house didn't necessarily mean anything. Chris might have decided to walk somewhere or had taken the Tube or a bus, but from Erica's reaction, he thought that probably wasn't something Chris would do. It no longer being here, though, was strange.

He stepped closer, moving onto the drive, towards the item on the ground. He recognised it—a small, brown leather square with a long strap that could be worn across the body.

Erica's handbag.

Had she dropped it in her panic?

Shawn reached into his pocket for his phone. Something about this scenario didn't sit right with him. Erica wasn't the sort of woman who'd be careless enough to leave her handbag in the middle of her drive. He swiped the screen and pulled up her number. Hers was the last one he'd called—as often was the case—and he hit the small green phone symbol to call.

On the ground, the handbag started to ring.

Fuck.

He didn't bend down to pick up the bag or the phone, knowing this could potentially be a crime scene. Instead, he hung up.

"Erica?" he called, heading towards the house. What if she was hurt inside, and he was standing out on the driveway like an idiot? He remembered the front door had been locked so quickly hurried around the side of the building to the back door. Keeping in mind that this could be a potential crime scene, he used the sleeves of his jacket to open the door and stepped into the kitchen.

"Erica?" he called again. "It's Shawn. Can you hear me?"

At a brisk pace, he moved through the house. In the corner of the room currently being used as a living room-slash-study, a chair had been knocked over, and a cup of tea had been spilt across the desk.

"Erica?"

He left the downstairs to check the other rooms, making sure not to touch anything. One room clearly belonged to Erica and Chris, the other a little girl's room—Poppy's, he guessed by all the pink—and the third was the room Erica's dad had been using before he'd gone to the care home. It was such a sad situation, for a man who'd had such a great career to end up like that. Shawn had never met him personally—he'd retired due to ill health long before Shawn had joined the Met—but almost anyone in the force who he mentioned Erica Swift to immediately knew who her father was.

She wasn't here.

His phone had been in his hand the whole time. He swiped open the screen again and called a different number.

It answered within two rings.

"DCI Gibbs."

"Sir, it's Turner. I think something has happened to Swift. I've come to meet her at her house, and she's not here, but her handbag and phone are sitting in the middle of her driveway."

He sensed him sitting up.

"What makes you think something bad has happened to her?"

"She asked me to come here because she thought her husband might be missing. He didn't show up to pick their daughter up from school and wasn't answering his phone. Now I've come here, and Swift is the one who's missing."

"So, her husband is there?"

"No, sorry." He rubbed his fingers to his temple. "I mean they're both missing now. The car isn't here either. Erica's car is, but not her husband's, and she said it was in the driveway when she called me."

"Couldn't they be together, and they've taken her husband's car?"

"What, and she's left her handbag in the middle of the drive, with her phone in it?"

"Maybe she put it on the roof of the car, and it fell off when they drove away?" Gibbs suggested.

Shawn understood why he was trying to explain everything away—the most obvious answers were normally the right ones—but none of that rang true to him.

"She knew I was coming here to meet her. Why would she get in Chris's car and leave, and then not notice that her handbag was missing? That isn't like Swift, sir, you know that. She's not flaky. If she was going somewhere else, she'd have called me first."

Gibb's cleared his throat. "What are you suggesting, Turner?"

"Something bad has happened to her. She's in trouble."

"You think the husband has done something to her?"

Shawn had met Chris a couple of times. He seemed like a nice enough bloke. Maybe he was a bit dull for someone like Erica. She was small but fierce. She'd always seemed to him like someone whose husband would be some tough bloke, maybe with a motorbike and tattoos, and he'd been surprised to discover she was married to softly spoken Chris, with his computer skills and easy-going nature. But then he guessed people did say that opposites attracted.

Could someone like Chris really do something bad to Erica? It didn't ring true to Shawn. But often it was the ones they suspected the least who proved to be the most dangerous. Men—and women, too—were capable of living lives completely separate from the ones they displayed on the outside. He'd known that himself from his own experiences growing up. His dad had had a whole other family, and Shawn and his mum had lived for years without having any clue. His dad had always been working away, and if either he or his mum tried to question him about where he'd been, he'd get angry, throwing things around to shut them up. His father had never gone as far as beating either of them up, though he'd got physical often enough, but the moment Shawn's mother had learned of his other family and given him an ultimatum, they'd never seen him again.

He remembered his DCI was still waiting for an answer. "Honestly, I don't know. Either that, or the reason her husband is missing is the same reason Swift is missing now."

"You think someone took them? Why?"

"Maybe she was getting too close on the eye thief case?"

"You don't even have anyone pinned down for that yet."

"There was something—someone. A case from years ago. She knew the name, she said..." He wracked his brains, trying to remember. "Bailey. Daniel Bailey, and his brother, Nicholas. Maybe she found out something and then got distracted by her husband going missing, so she wasn't able to feed it back to me."

"Shit. Stay where you are and protect the scene. I'm sending DI Johnson over to you, together with SOCO to check over the house for any signs of violence. I'll get someone to look into this Bailey connection. See if we can figure out whatever she had."

"Yes, sir."

He ended the call and rubbed his hand across his mouth. He couldn't just stand here and wait for the team to arrive. He had to do something. Houses were both opposite and beside Erica's. Someone must have seen something.

Shawn marched across the street to the property directly opposite. It was an almost identical building to Erica and Chris's house, the living room windows practically looking into each other's. He spotted movement at the window as he approached, and reached into his pocket for ID. Even in this day and age, he was aware that people would see a young black man coming to the door and instantly put up their defences.

He knocked, firm and authoritative.

The door opened a crack, the security chain still on. He caught a glimpse of a woman in her early thirties, her straight brown hair tied back, her eyes wary, with shadows beneath them.

"Yes?"

"My name is DS Shawn Turner." He showed the woman his identification through the crack. "One of your neighbours is missing, and I wondered if I could ask you a couple of questions."

She closed the door again, and there was the clink of the chain being removed, and then she opened it fully. A chubby baby of about eight months old was balanced on her hip.

"Sorry," she said. "Got to be careful now I've got this one to take care of."

"Not at all," he replied. "It's important to be cautious."

She peered out, as though expecting to see more police cars. "So, who's gone missing?"

"Your neighbour across the street. Erica Swift, and possibly her husband, Chris, too. Is there any chance you've seen either of them in the last couple of hours?"

To his surprise, she nodded. "Yes, I did see the car pull out of the drive not long ago. Erica wasn't driving, though."

"Who was?"

"I didn't see their face, 'cause they had one of those hoodies pulled right up." Her cheeks grew pink. "You must think I'm a terrible nosy parker. I'm not normally, honest, but this one"—she jerked her chin at the baby—"hates being put down, and so we just watch the world go by together."

"It's good you keep an eye on things." He hazarded a guess. "Could the person in the hoody have been her husband, Chris?"

She wrinkled her nose and jiggled the baby on her hip. "I don't think so."

"And how long ago would you say that was?"

"Not long. Maybe an hour ago. Possibly a little less."

"Have you noticed anything unusual in the neighbourhood lately? Anyone hanging around who shouldn't be here?"

"No, sorry. I don't think so. But it's a busy road."

Shawn glanced up at the front of her house. "What about security cameras? Do you have any that face in the direction of the house?"

She shook her head. "I've been nagging my husband to get some installed. They're pretty cheap to get now, and you can link them to your mobile phone, but we still haven't got around to doing it." A worried expression crossed her face. "I guess if there's dangerous people around, I should get onto it."

Behind Shawn on the street, a couple of marked vans pulled up. SOCO had arrived. That was fast. Everyone always dropped things quicker when it was one of their own involved.

"Thank you for your help. We may need to ask you a few more questions shortly, if that's all right?"

"Of course. I'll be right here. Don't exactly have much of a social life since this one arrived." She jiggled the baby again, who cooed and lifted a chubby hand to reach for his mother's face.

He took her full name, date of birth, and phone number and then nodded his thanks and backed away, jogging across the road. People were emerging from the vehicles, and Shawn spotted the familiar charcoal-grey suit, dark hair, and lanky figure of Lee Mattocks.

"I hear Swift is in trouble," Mattocks said as Shawn approached.

"Yes. She and her husband are both missing. This is her last known location. A neighbour across the street says she saw Swift being driven away in her husband's car about an hour ago, but there are signs of a disturbance inside the house."

Mattocks nodded at the bag in the driveway. "And that's her handbag?"

"Yes, it is."

"Have you touched it?"

"No, it's exactly as I found it."

Mattocks nodded approvingly. "Good. Leave this with us. If there's anything here that can tell us where she is or who took her, we'll find it."

"Thanks."

More police cars turned into the street and pulled up near the house.

DI Johnson climbed out of one, his sergeant with him, and two uniformed officers appeared from the second vehicle.

Shawn gave Johnson the same rundown he'd just given to Mattocks.

Johnson gave a curt nod. "We'll conduct a neighbourhood canvass immediately. Hopefully, we'll be able to find any evidence that may have been discarded or potential witnesses."

"I've already spoken to the woman who lives directly opposite," Shawn said, "but you'll want to speak to her in more detail. She saw the car containing Swift leaving, with a man in a hoody, who may or may not be Swift's husband in the driver's seat."

"Got it."

Shawn was happy to leave this area in their hands. He already knew Erica wasn't here. The last place she'd been seen was inside her husband's car. He needed to get the registration of Christopher Swift's car and send out an alert, ASAP.

He had to find her.

Chapter Thirty-Two

In the abandoned station, teetering at the gap in the wall, Nicholas Bailey held Christopher Swift like a bad father holding an errant child by the scruff.

She had to stop him.

Three minutes...that was nothing. Already, much of that time had slipped away, sand through an hourglass.

Could she figure out a way to make him let Chris go, or else keep him talking long enough that he'd forget about the trains? There was no point in begging for her husband's life. She already knew what Nicholas Bailey was capable of, had witnessed the aftermath for herself. Her biggest fear when she'd woken up and found herself down here had been that Bailey had already taken her eyes, but now she would have happily swapped her sight if it meant Chris getting out of here alive.

"Why are you doing this, Nicholas?" she asked. "How did you get to this point? Did it start with that first man? The one your brother was questioned about?"

He scoffed. "Your people brought Danny in for it, but they couldn't pin it on him. He was always smarter than everyone else."

"You must have loved your brother very much."

"He took care of me. He knew what to do when we found our mum dead because of the booze. He was younger, but he was the one who buried her in the back garden."

Her mind blurred. Jesus Christ. She was starting to put a picture together in her mind of these two boys and why

Nicholas became who he was today. Two brothers with an alcoholic mother, fending for themselves. It was hard to concentrate on Nicholas's plight, or feel much sympathy for him when he dangled her drugged husband beside the electrified train rails.

"That must have been really hard for you," she said, never taking her eyes off Chris as he swayed from side to side. His head was hanging, shoulders slumped.

She was running out of time.

Come on, Chris. Wake up.

"It was harder on Danny, and you let him die."

How did Nicholas know she was the one who'd been trying to stop Daniel Bailey from jumping?

The answer dawned on her. "You were there that day, weren't you? You saw it happen."

"Yeah, I did. Six years ago today. I bet you were happy he went through with it—just one more troubled kid off the streets."

"No, that's not true, Nicholas. I would have saved him if I could. I tried, I really did. I almost quit the force because I failed your brother so badly. Every night for months afterwards, I went over in my head what I'd said and done, questioning myself constantly to try to figure out what I could have done differently. I promise you that I never wanted him to die."

The roar of an approaching train filtered through to her, and her stomach dropped. Was that why he'd brought her here? Why he'd brought the others here, too? This was his way of connecting with his dead brother.

She had to keep his mind away from hurting Chris.

"Why did you hurt those two men?"

His lips tightened. "The first one hurt me before I hurt him. He called me a freak. I wanted to teach him a lesson."

"What about the second man? He was only a shopkeeper. What could he possibly have done to you to deserve that kind of fate?"

"That guy was a fucking arsehole. He accused me of being a shoplifter, just 'cause I wear a hoody. He banned me from his shithole of a shop, and I hadn't even done anything."

"So, you kidnapped him and cut out his eyes?"

"He thought he saw me, but he didn't. He judged me by what I looked like. People have done that to me my whole life. I couldn't help the way I was born. I thought if these people no longer were able to see, they could stop judging people by how they looked and start seeing people—really seeing people for who they were—for the first time in their lives."

"They can't do anything, Nicholas. Not now. They're dead. Both of them. Lewis Jacobs killed himself. You didn't teach them a thing."

Pale-white electrical lights were dotted along the walls at regular intervals, and Nicholas's face glowed eerily in the illumination.

"I did, though, for a short while. They were sorry. They said so."

Erica shook her head. "Only because they were afraid."

Her gaze darted back to her husband. Nicholas was taller than Chris by a couple of inches, and even without Chris being drugged, he had youth and physical strength on his side.

"Please, come back over here," she begged, desperate to get them both away from the gap in the wall. "We can talk about this."

She'd have given anything to feel the solid shape of Chris's body against her hip and shoulder again. The way he swayed, leaning dangerously out into the tunnel, before Nicholas yanked him back in again, as though her husband was a second thought, made her sick with fear.

The face she loved, the father of their daughter. Maybe they'd even have more children one day, a brother or sister for Poppy. It wasn't easy being pregnant in her job, but she'd have been back at work soon enough, and Chris would have been happy to take care of a baby again.

But Nicholas shook his head. "No."

Erica's self-control snapped. "Chris! Can you hear me? You need to wake up! Open your eyes."

Nicholas laughed and gave him another shake. "He's not going to do any of those things. I made sure the amount of sedative I gave him would be in his system for another few hours yet. I'm being kind, really. He won't know what's happening."

From down the tunnel came the rumble of a distant train.

Oh, God. Was it coming? Or was it a train on a different line, heading in the other direction?

"You know the saying, Erica, an eye for an eye? I think I take that literally."

Erica understood exactly what he was saying. He believed she'd taken his brother from him, so now he was taking her husband from her.

She kicked and thrashed, attempted to yank her hands apart, but it was hopeless. She'd been reduced to a writhing worm on the ground. Without the use of her hands, she couldn't even get to her feet.

"No, please."

The train drew closer, the ground vibrating, the eerie hum of the tracks filling her ears.

"It's coming!" A wild grin stretched across Nicholas's face, his eyes lighting with madness.

"No," she sobbed.

She'd never felt more helpless. She tried to squirm across the ground, desperate to cover the short distance, though she had no idea what she could do when she got there.

Chris let out a moan, his eyes rolling. He swayed again, teetering out into the tunnel, only Nicholas's grip on his shirt preventing him from falling.

Erica stared in horror.

"One," Nicholas counted, "two—"

It all happened so fast. One second, Chris was held in the gap in the bricked-up platform wall, the next, Nicholas let him go. A split second later, the train rushed into view.

The sound of his body hitting the front of the train was barely muffled by the shriek of emergency brakes being slammed on.

Erica screamed.

Chapter Thirty-Three

Shawn was on his way back to the office when the call came in.

"We've located the car," Gibbs said. "It's been abandoned on Whitechapel Road. Traffic police picked up on it. They've already checked it for any sign of Swift or her husband, but there's nothing."

Maybe that was a small blessing. At least her body hadn't been found in the boot. He noted the location, though. They were back in that same area again—near to where the two victims had been found.

"I'm on my way," Shawn said.

"I'll meet you there."

Shawn ended the call then lifted the hand that wasn't on the steering wheel and slammed it in a fist against his thigh.

"Fuck! What is it about that place? What are we missing?"

He put his foot down and used the emergency dash lights to get through traffic. He was horribly conscious of time ticking by and the possibility of someone hurting Erica. He'd only worked with her for the past eighteen months, but he considered them to be close. She was a good DI, considerate and fair, and she didn't throw her weight around like some higher-ranking officers he'd worked with. She genuinely cared about people.

By the time he reached the location, Erica's husband's car had been cordoned off as evidence. Gibbs already stood beside it, his hands on his hips, surveying the area. Close by, Turner noted the other part of their team—Rudd and Howard. Everyone had turned out to help find their DI.

He pulled the unmarked Mondeo over and climbed out. Gibbs spotted him and lifted a hand to motion him over. Gibbs could be a dickhead at times, but even he seemed genuinely concerned about the missing member of their team.

"Nothing in the car," Gibbs said as he approached. "Though there might be a few spots of blood. We'll have to get SOCO to see if they can match it."

A few spots meant she might be injured, but it didn't mean she was dead.

Gibbs frowned. "This has to be linked to the case. The location is too close to where the two victims were found."

Shawn subconsciously copied Gibbs's pose, his hands on his hips as he looked around. "I agree. What are we missing? There's something about this place..."

It was just a normal East London high street with a Citroen garage, an Asian food store, a small, independent cinema. Nothing out of the ordinary. But why had the suspect stopped the car here, clearly in a hurry?

"We can get CCTV footage," DC Rudd suggested. "I'm sure the garage will have it."

"Yes, do it." But he was distracted, something nagging at his mind, telling him he was missing something. There wasn't time to sit around going through CCTV footage. Erica's life was in danger. What if that son of a bitch planned on doing the same thing to her as he'd done to the other victims? The thought of Erica being forced to go through life without her eyes was too horrifying for him to think about.

DC Howard hurried toward them, his face taut with worry. "We're getting calls coming in about an incident on the District line near Whitechapel Station. There's been reports of someone going under."

His stomach sank. "Going under? You mean they've jumped in front of the train?"

"Normally, yes, but this is a bit different. They didn't jump from a platform. The driver's saying it was like they appeared from mid-air."

That didn't sound right. "What the fuck? How the hell does someone jump under a train if it isn't from one of the platforms? Was it one of the Underground workers? Do we have an ID on the jumper yet?"

Howard shook his head. "No, it's too soon. I mean, he'd still be under the train."

Shawn's heart was hammering, a certainty sinking into his bones. "So, we don't even know it was a 'he' for sure?"

"No, we don't. Engineers are shutting electricity off the tracks so they can get down there."

He looked to Gibbs. "This has to have something to do with Swift. It's too much of a coincidence."

Gibbs's nostrils flared. "You don't think it's her, do you?"

"Jesus Christ, I hope not." He thought for a moment. "The incident with the train? Where was it in relation to where we are now?"

Howard frowned. "I'm not sure, exactly. It didn't happen in one of the stations. It was in the tunnels between Whitechapel and Aldgate East."

"So, the train is basically underneath our feet, right now?"

They all stared down at the ground.

"Well, no, not exactly. The train line doesn't run right under here." Howard lifted his hand and pointed to the other side of the street. "It's more beneath where those buildings are."

They turned towards the Citroen garage.

Realisation hit Shawn like a bucket of cold water.

"There used to be an old station here, didn't there? One that was demolished in the war?"

Howard pulled out his phone and quickly checked. "Yes, St Mary's was a station located between Whitechapel and Aldgate East station before it was shut down over seventy years ago."

Shawn was already crossing the road, the others following. "That has to be where he's been taking them. There must still be a way in—maybe even a couple of ways in. If the disused tracks that once led to the station are still in place, he could move along the tracks and find exits to shove his victims out of."

Gibbs spoke up. "Hang on. How does this have anything to do with the person who's under the train?"

"St Mary's Curve is a part of the track that is no longer used, but the tunnel still remains," Shawn said. "That's how he's moving his victims around this part of East London and why we couldn't pinpoint where they were coming from. But the other part of the track is still being used, though the disused station is bricked up between the live track and what would have been the platforms. I'll put money on it that the person went under the train at exactly the point where the train goes past that platform." He paused and exhaled a breath. "Shit. We need to get down there."

"I'm already on it, boss," Rudd said, her mobile phone pressed to her ear. "I'm speaking with someone who knows the London Underground now."

Shawn shook his head in frustration. "There has to be access here. Why else would Bailey have left the car here? It has to be right here!"

Rudd spoke up. "You can get to the bricked-up platforms via an anonymous door off Whitechapel Road."

"Shit." It must be right where they were standing.

He broke into a run, moving between the buildings, desperately hunting for the door. It had to be here.

"Over here!" Gibbs called out. "I found a door!"

Shawn ran over to his DCI. Sure enough, a metal door was built into a wall. Nothing about it said what it led to.

Shawn tried the door. It was unlocked, something he assumed shouldn't be the case. Whoever had left it unlocked would probably lose their jobs over this.

He ran through and raced down the concrete stairs, heading into the darkness. Gibbs and the two DCs followed close behind.

He prayed he wasn't too late.

Chapter Thirty-Four

Erica was reeling from what had happened.
No, not Chris. There has to be some kind of mistake. He can't be dead. Oh God, how is Poppy going to cope?

She didn't want to believe what she'd witnessed with her own eyes. Deep down, she knew she had the drugs he'd injected her with to thank for her not completely losing it. Though they'd worn off to some extent, she knew she wasn't experiencing the full horror of what had happened. Perhaps it was the Midazolam, or maybe it was simply shock, but she knew she'd relive that moment of Nicholas throwing Chris through the gap in the wall and into the path of the oncoming train for the rest of her life, however long that might be.

How was she going to have that conversation with her daughter, telling her Daddy was never coming home again?

Nicholas stepped forward, approaching her. "We're equal now, DI Swift."

"No, we're not, you fucking bastard. Your screwed-up brother chose to take his own life. You just murdered my husband. That is not equal. I'll fucking kill you myself!"

The train had stopped in the tunnel. There were people only a matter of feet away. But they were in near darkness compared with the bright lights inside the carriages, and Nicholas blocked the way. If she could get past him, she could throw herself against the window of one of the train carriages and try to get someone's attention. But then she remembered the electrical current that would still be going through the rails. If she tried that, she would end up dead as well.

Besides, both her hands and feet were still bound. If she'd been capable of doing anything physically, she'd have stopped Nicholas from throwing Chris in front of that train.

The transport police would be here soon. They'd lay down a short-circuiting device to cut off the electricity to the tracks, and then it would be safe for her to try to get help.

Nicholas clearly had the same idea.

"We can't stay here. Your friends will be here soon, and I'm not done with you."

He stalked over to her and leaned down and grabbed her by the arm.

Erica bucked and thrashed. "Let go of me!"

He barked laughter. "Not happening."

He dragged her down the platform until they came to the end, and then he hauled her off and onto a piece of track that was no longer in use. Every movement bumped and cracked her bones, but the pain was nothing compared to what was in her heart.

Chris is dead.

But she couldn't let herself give in to her grief. Poppy still had one parent who was alive, and Erica would fight for her daughter with every last breath she had.

Her hands and feet still bound, he dragged her through the tunnel.

The Underground staff had switched the electricity off to the track, inadvertently allowing their escape.

Erica couldn't drag her thoughts away from the thought of Chris, what the velocity and weight of the train would have done to his body. Bright, fierce hatred burned inside her. This man had robbed her daughter of her father and stolen her husband from her.

When they'd made it a safe enough distance away from the train and the abandoned station, Nicholas drew to a halt and released his hold on her.

"There. That should give us enough time to do what is needed."

She didn't even want to ask, but she couldn't help it. "Are you going to blind me, like you did the others."

"Yes, and if you're lucky, I might even let you live."

"You're crazy," she blurted. "You need help."

"I've still got them, you know?"

Her skin crawled, unsure if she even wanted to know the answer. She'd spent years in the force and had witnessed some of the most horrific things—including her own husband's murder—but she had the feeling worse was to come. "What?"

"Do you want to see?"

"I don't want to see anything you've got to show me." She was terrified of his way of making people see, nauseated with fear at the thought of him coming at her with that blade, of the lethally sharp tip penetrating her eyeball.

Her emotions were torn two ways. A part of her wanted to crumple with grief, to beat the ground with her bare hands and rail against the world. But the other part—the part that had made her choose this profession in the first place and the mothering side of her who wanted more than anything to be around to take care of her baby-girl—knew she had to take this bastard down.

"I wanted to keep them," Nicholas said. "They're not as perfect as I'd hoped, but you can still tell what they are."

He reached towards the wall of the tunnel, his fingers vanishing into a nook. When he pulled his hand back out, he brought with it a large jar filled with clear liquid. The liquid wasn't the only thing inside the jar. For a second, she took them to be two pickled onions perhaps, her mind swimming with confusion, but then their true identity dawned on her.

Their eyes.

Oh, God. He'd kept their eyes as trophies.

"These belonged to Patrick Ronson. Don't worry, I've got Lewis Jacobs's in here as well." He reached back into the wall and produced a second jar.

She couldn't bring herself to look, but he was showing her evidence—literally handing her things that could be used to send him to jail for a very long time.

"You didn't see me either, did you, DI Swift? You or your husband. I should have taken his eyes for my collection before I pushed him in front of that train, but yours will do. You didn't see me that day when my brother jumped, and you didn't really see me when we were at your father's care home, either.

"I see you now, Nicholas. I see exactly who you are."

"No, you don't. You're just like everyone else. I'm sick of everyone staring at me like I'm a monster. Like I can help how I was born."

Confusion rippled through her. "What are you talking about?"

"Don't pretend like you don't see it, too. I know how horrifying this is." He pointed at his face. "I know what I look like."

Her mind whirred. They'd believed their suspect to be someone with a facial deformity of some kind, but from what she'd seen of him, Nicholas Bailey was a normal guy. He had a little scarring across his cheeks from where he must have had either acne or chicken pox when he'd been younger, but that was all. In any other circumstances, she'd have thought him to be reasonably attractive.

"I don't know what you mean, Nicholas. You look like everyone else to me."

"You have to say that these days, don't you? It's all about political correctness and acceptance of other people's differences. Well, where was all of that when I was growing up? Eh? Even my own mother couldn't hide her disgust in me."

"There's nothing wrong with your face, Nicholas, you know that, don't you? You look the same as everyone else."

"Stop it. Why are you saying that?"

"We were searching for someone with a deformity, someone who might not like people looking at him because of it, but that's not you, is it?"

"What are you talking about?" His features flashed with anger. "Are you laughing at me?"

"No, I'd never laugh. I'm telling you the truth."

"I've seen this face in the mirror every day for twenty-six years. Do you think I don't see how everything sags? My lower eyelids hang too far down, the corners of my mouth are dragged down. I'm like that old fucking cartoon character, Droopy Dog. My brother, Danny, he was the handsome one. Our mother always told us that."

"I don't know why she told you that, but you don't, Nicholas. You're a perfectly normal twenty-six-year-old man."

He shook his head, a little at first, then the movements became more violent. "No, stop it. Stop it! They stare at me. They all stare at me. And I made them stop."

"No one was staring at you, not like that. Maybe they wondered why you had your hood up all the time, keeping yourself covered when there was no need. Perhaps that did make you appear suspicious, and that's why Patrick Ronson banned you from his shop. But you don't look how you think you do."

"You're lying! Danny would have told me."

"Maybe Danny liked being the stronger brother."

"Shut up, shut up!"

He swiped his arm, and the jar containing Lewis Jacobs's eyes was knocked from the nook in the wall and crashed to the floor. The jar shattered into pieces, and two partially deflated eyeballs, the irises foggy, rolled out onto the tracks.

"Now look what you made me do!" He reached into his back pocket and pulled out a small but lethally sharp blade. "That was my collection. I hope you're planning on replacing them."

Jesus Christ. He was going to cut out her eyes. She'd pushed him too far.

"The police are coming, Nicholas. Pushing Chris in front of that train was a mistake. It's bringing a lot of people down here, and they're going to find you. I have people who'll be searching for me as well. They'll have found Chris's car by now. They'll know what you've done."

He chuckled. "You keep telling yourself that, DI Swift. Or maybe I should call you Erica, since we've become so close. Who's to say that your husband didn't drive himself here and then throw himself in front of that train? No one has any reason to think I'm involved."

Maybe she should let him believe that. If he thought he was safe, he might feel less pressured into acting quickly.

How could this be happening with so many people this close by? Of course, all of the passengers had been told to stay on board the train, and any transport police would be focused on the front of the train and poor Chris's body beneath it. They wouldn't have a clue that there was a killer skulking in the tunnels, with her as his prisoner.

Erica caught sight of the broken glass from the jar. A piece had landed nearby. If she got her wrists over it, she could cut the tape.

She wriggled backwards, using her feet to push herself along the tunnel floor. Near her head, a startled mouse darted away, but she had far bigger things to worry about than a rodent.

A smaller piece of glass cut into her shoulder blade, stabbing her with bright, white pain. Erica gritted her teeth and kept going. A tiny piece like that wasn't going to be enough. She'd already set her sights on the sliver she needed, but it was going to mean dragging her upper torso over the top of it and hoping her weight didn't break it further.

"Danny would have been proud of me," Nicholas said, stepping forward, shadowing her progress. "I wish he'd lived to see what I'd become. Sometimes I imagine what it would be like if he was still alive and we were doing this together. We'd have been a force to deal with, wouldn't we, the two of us? Only *you* had to come along and take that from us."

It seemed pointless trying to reason with him—he was too far gone—but she was trying to buy herself time. "Danny chose to jump. I didn't push him. I tried to stop him."

"But you could have tried *harder!*" He shouted the final word, slamming his fists into his sides, the knife still clutched between his fingers, but pointed outwards so he didn't impale himself in the thigh.

"I did, Nicholas. I did, I swear it. Did you know that the day your brother killed himself was my birthday? *Today* is my birthday. I wish I'd booked that day off and spent it with my family instead, but I was new to the job role, and I didn't want to give the impression that I wasn't committed. Every birthday now, I torture myself, going over every little thing I did and said, wishing I'd done something differently. I had counselling for months afterwards. I couldn't catch the Tube without my heart racing every time I stood on a platform and someone ran for a train or seemed as though they were leaning a little too close to the edge. If there had been any way I could have stopped him dying, I would have done it."

With every word, she wiggled and squirmed, trying not to think about the liquid soaking through her clothes and what it had contained. The eyes still lay close by as well, but she ignored them. They were only flesh, and the person they belonged to no longer had use of them. She needed to focus on keeping her own.

Her fingers scrambled for the piece of glass. A sharp edge sliced into her flesh, cutting her palm, but she only felt the hot gush of blood and not the pain. She didn't care if she was bleeding, but the fluid was making it harder for her to grip the piece of glass.

From farther down the tunnel, in the direction they'd come from and the direction of the train, came a commotion. Her heart contracted, and she squeezed her eyes shut. Had they reached Chris's body? She couldn't let herself think about him now. There would be plenty of time for grieving later. Days and weeks and months and years, she was sure, but she needed to be there for Poppy, so they could grieve together, and their darling daughter didn't need to try to make her way through life without both of her parents.

She was over the largest piece of glass now, pressing down hard. She needed to move her wrists back and forth, creating a sawing action, but at the same time she didn't want Nicholas realising what she was up to. She had one chance at this, and if she blew it, it was all over.

But Nicholas was caught up in a world of his own, and the shadows cast by the intermittent lighting helped to hide her movements. She sawed her wrists over the glass, and for a horrifying moment, she didn't think it was going to work, but then the tape loosened at the part closest to her hands and then split apart.

He towered over her, his feet planted either side of her legs. The sharp filleting blade glinted in the artificial light. He leaned down, the knife in his hand, aimed at her face.

Erica tightened her fingers around the piece of glass. It was glass against a knife, but she had the element of surprise on her side.

"Erica?" From down the tunnel, someone shouted her name. Shawn? Had that been Shawn?

Her heart swelled with hope.

There was a glint of understanding in Nicholas's eyes, and he let out of roar of fury. He knew he'd run out of time.

He dropped to his knees, the knife raised above his head, ready to bring down on her, but she moved fast. Rolling to one side, she yanked her arms out from behind her body. As the knife arced down, she blocked it with her left arm, and with her right, she swung the hand containing the piece of glass.

The knife flew out of his grip, clinking somewhere to the tunnel floor. The glass found its mark, slicing deep into Nicholas's face.

He let out a yell of pain and anger and fell to one side. She still had her ankles bound, so she couldn't get up and run, but she remembered hearing Shawn shout her name.

She opened her mouth and yelled, "Down here! Shawn, he's here!

Nicholas was preoccupied with trying to hold his face together. Blood poured in a torrent, a flap of skin opening right across his cheek.

Footsteps pounded towards her.

She found the knife he'd dropped and used it to cut the tape between her ankles. At least with the knife in her hand, she knew Nicholas wasn't going to be able to pick it up again. From down the tunnel, torches cut swathes through the dark.

"Erica?" Shawn's shout echoed towards her.

She bit back a sob but managed to call back, "I'm over here!"

He found her, dropping to his knees beside her. "Jesus Christ. Thank God you're okay. I thought it might have been—" His voice broke, and he didn't finish his sentence. Instead, he lifted his head and shouted, "We need a medic down here."

"I'm fine," she told him. "Arrest that son of a bitch."

Shawn gave a curt nod and rose to his feet. He wrenched Nicholas's hands behind his back and snapped on a pair of cuffs.

"Nicholas Bailey, you're under arrest for abduction, grievous bodily harm with intent, and the murder of Patrick Ronson."

"And for the murder of Christopher Swift," Erica said before clamping her hand to her mouth, trying to press back her grief. She didn't know how she managed to remain even the slightest bit professional in these circumstances, but she couldn't let the entire team see her at her most vulnerable.

Shawn stared at her. "Fucking hell, Erica."

"He pushed Chris beneath that train. It was revenge for me not stopping his brother from killing himself six years ago."

Shawn tried to reach out to her, to pull her into a hug, but she couldn't let him do it. She would crumble, and she couldn't do that, not yet.

There was still work to do.

Chapter Thirty-Five

The weeks that followed were impossibly hard.

Though she wanted to be around to process the rest of the case, she was too closely linked to it now that her husband had been one of the victims, and she herself had almost joined him. She was now also the key witness in the case that was being brought against Nicholas Bailey, and she was determined to stand up in court and do everything she could to make sure he was sent down for the rest of his life.

But that wasn't the only reason. She was needed at home, too, perhaps even more than she was needed at work.

Telling Poppy that her dad wasn't coming home had been the hardest thing she'd ever done in her life.

She'd brought her daughter into the bed she'd once shared with Chris, and there, cushioned in duvets and pillows that still contained his scent, they'd held each other tight and cried in each other's arms. They'd barely moved for the next few days, wrapped up in each other, mindlessly watching cartoons on the small television positioned on the chest of drawers—a television Chris had insisted on getting—and ordering takeaway food, which they then picked at before eventually throwing away.

Natasha had stepped up, visiting Frank when Erica couldn't bring herself to go, and tidying up the house around them. Eventually, her sister had forced her out of bed, telling her Poppy needed a bath and Erica desperately needed to brush her teeth before she knocked out her own daughter with her breath.

Chris's body wasn't released right away. His body was evidence in part of a murder investigation, and while Erica understood, it made it hard not to be able to say goodbye yet. While she dreaded the thought of a funeral, she knew it was the only way they'd be able to let go properly and start their new lives in this foreign existence they'd discovered themselves in. Right now, they were in limbo.

When she was feeling up to it, she let her sergeant come and visit.

Erica opened her front door to Shawn Turner, self-consciously pulling her cardigan tighter around her body. She looked a mess, but she couldn't bring herself to care.

She showed him into the kitchen. "Thanks for coming, Shawn. Can I get you something? Coffee?"

Shawn shook his head. "Don't worry about that. How are you? How's Poppy?"

"Not great. We've done a lot of crying."

He smiled sympathetically. "I bet you have. Poor kid. Poor you."

Erica's eyes welled up again, and she blinked hard and stared at the floor. "Yeah, poor us. And poor Chris, too. It breaks my heart that he's not going to get to see Poppy grow up."

"We're going to make sure Bailey goes down for this."

Erica nodded. "Tell me."

"Bailey has confessed to everything, even his part in the murder of nineteen-year-old Bobby Finn all those years ago. He'll be going to jail for a very long time. I doubt he'll ever know freedom again."

"Thank you, Shawn."

He glanced up at her. "What for?"

"Finding me. Poppy might be without a mother as well if you hadn't."

He gave a lopsided grin, flashing white teeth. "You looked like you were taking care of things pretty well on your own when we got there."

She clenched her jaw and then forced herself to loosen it. The stress she'd been under lately had hurt her teeth from the pressure "I wish I'd killed the bastard."

"No, you don't. You don't want another death on your conscience."

He was right, but a part of her still wished that Nicholas Bailey was dead.

"His psychiatric evaluation concluded that he suffers from an extreme case of body dysmorphia," Shawn continued. "Seems his mother did a right number on him. She told him how hideous he was from the moment he was born, and he believed it. He thought himself to be disfigured all his life, when he wasn't. The irony is that he will be now. The cut you gave him is going to leave a scar running from beside his left eye, down his cheek, to the corner of his mouth."

"He was lucky he didn't lose his eye," she said bitterly. "Perhaps it would have been justice if he had."

Shawn nodded and glanced down at his hands. "So, when do you think you're coming back to work? Gibbs is driving us all nuts."

"Soon," she said. "But I need to make sure Poppy is all right first. She's got to be my number one priority."

"You are coming back?" he asked tentatively.

"Yes, I am. Natasha has already offered to have Poppy while I'm working." She gave a small laugh. "I'm not sure how she's going to cope with having four children to take care of, but Poppy is keen. Apparently, they get a lot more access to the internet than I allow."

"Bribed with YouTube." He smiled.

She smiled back, and it felt like the first time she had since Chris had died. "Yeah, she's easily bought."

She hadn't been sure about letting Shawn come over at first, but she felt strong after the conversation. She *did* need to get back to work. It wasn't going to be easy, but it was where she was needed, and it was the place where she thrived.

Before he'd died, Chris had told her to go and get the bad guys.

That was exactly what she planned to do.

Acknowledgements

Every book I write takes an entire team of people to lovingly shape it into its final form, but in the case of 'The Eye Thief', I had even more people onboard than usual.

First of all, I want to say a massive thank you to Patrick O'Donnell who heads up the brilliant and extremely helpful 'Cops and Writers' facebook group. I honestly don't know where I'd be without that group! He is also the author of 'Cops and Writers: From the Academy to the Street', so, if you're a civilian crime author who would like to give an authentic edge to your writing, go and check him out.

Patrick very kindly agreed to work on 'The Eye Thief' with me, and I owe him massively for all his excellent points and insight. Any mistakes that were made were mine alone!

I had two editors working on this book, both of whom I consider to be friends as well as colleagues. So thank you Emmy Ellis from Studioenp, and Lori Whitwam, who is my long time editor! You both did a wonderful job and I'm very grateful to you for being able to squeeze me in when my deadlines suddenly change!

Many thanks to Jacqueline Beard, who was lovely enough to volunteer her keen eye to proofread 'The Eye Thief' for me, together with my long time proof-reader Tammy Payne from Book Nook Nuts.

A big thank you and *I miss you*, to my mum, Glynis Elliott, who is my first reader—the one I want to impress the most when I'm writing my book—and also another of my proofreaders. She said 'The Eye Thief' was my 'best yet', so now, of course, I want to beat that with book two! Thank you for inspiring me.

This book was dedicated to Mel Comley, for giving me a kick up the butt to jump into crime and thriller writing, and so thank you to her, and also to all the readers in her ARC group, who've also been super supportive of my new venture.

If you've managed to get through all of that, well done, so one final huge word of thanks to you, the reader. I hope you've enjoyed the book and are looking forward to the next in DI Erica Swift's series!

Until next time!

M K Farrar

About the Author

MK Farrar is the pen name for a USA Today Bestselling author of more than thirty novels. Though 'Some They Lie' was her first psychological thriller, it wasn't her last. When she's not writing, M.K. is rescuing animals from far off places, binge watching shows on Netflix, or reading. She lives in the English countryside with her husband, three daughters, and menagerie of pets.

You can sign up to MK's newsletter over on her website at mkfarrar.com. She can be also be emailed at mkfarrar@hotmail.com. She loves to hear from readers!

Also by the Author

Crime after Crime series, written with M A Comley
Watching Over Me: Crime after Crime, Book One
Down to Sleep: Crime after Crime, Book Two
If I Should Die: Crime after Crime, Book Three
Standalone Psychological Thrillers
Some They Lie
On His Grave
In the Woods